Saragossa

Saragossa

A Story of Spanish Valor

Benito Pérez Galdós

MINT EDITIONS

Saragossa: A Story of Spanish Valor was first published in 1899.

This edition published by Mint Editions 2021.

ISBN 9781513215440 | E-ISBN 9781513213446

Published by Mint Editions®

 MINT
EDITIONS

minteditionbooks.com

Publishing Director: Jennifer Newens
Design & Production: Rachel Lopez Metzger
Project Manager: Micaela Clark
Translated by: Minna Caroline Smith
Typesetting: Westchester Publishing Services

Contents

I

It was, I believe, the evening of the eighteenth when we saw Saragossa in the distance. As we entered by the Puerta de Sancho we heard the clock in the Torre Nueva strike ten. We were in an extremely pitiful condition as to food and clothing. The long journey we had made from Lerma through Salas de los Infantes, Cervera, Agreda, Tarazona, and Borja, climbing mountains, fording rivers, making short cuts until we arrived at the high road of Gallur and Alagon, had left us quite used up, worn out, and ill with fatigue. In spite of all, the joy of being free sweetened our pain.

We were four who had succeeded in escaping between Lerma and Cogollos by freeing our innocent hands from the rope that bound together so many patriots. On the day of the escape, we could count among the four of us a total capital of eleven reales; but after three days of marching, when we entered the metropolis of Aragon and balanced our mutual cash, our common wealth was found to be a sum total of thirty-one cuartos. We bought some bread at a little place next the Orphanage, and divided it among us.

Don Roque, who was one of the members of our expedition, had good connections in Saragossa, but this was not an hour to present ourselves to anyone. We postponed until the next day this matter of looking up friends; and as we could not go to an inn, we wandered about the city, looking for a shelter where we could pass the night. The market scarcely seemed to offer exactly the comfort and quiet which our tired bodies needed. We visited the leaning tower, and although one of my companions suggested that we should take refuge in the plaza, I thought that we should be quite the same as if altogether in the open country. The place served us, none the less, for temporary refuge and rest, and also as a refectory, where we despatched happily our supper of dry bread, glancing now and then at the great upright mass of the tower, whose inclination made it seem like a giant leaning to see who was running about his feet. By the light of the moon that brick sentinel projected against the sky its huddled and shapeless form, unable to hold itself erect. The clouds were drifting across its top, and the spectator looking from below trembled with dread, imagining that the clouds were quiet and that the tower was moving down upon him. This grotesque structure, under whose feet the overburdened soil has settled, seems to be forever falling, yet never falls.

We passed through the avenue of the Coso again from this house of giants as far as the Seminary. We went through two streets, the Calle Quemada and the Calle del Rincon, both in ruins, as far as the little plaza of San Miguel. From here, passing from alley to alley, and blindly crossing narrow and irregular streets, we found ourselves beside the ruins of the monastery of Santa Engracia, which was blown up by the French at the raising of the first siege. The four of us exclaimed at once in a way to show that we all thought the same thing. Here we had found a shelter, and in some cosy corner under this roof we would pass the night!

The front wall was still standing with its arch of marble, decorated with innumerable figures of saints which seemed undisturbed and tranquil as if they knew nothing of the catastrophe. In the interior we saw broken arches and enormous columns struggling erect from the debris, presenting themselves, darkling and deformed, against the clear light flooding the enclosure, looking like fantastic creatures generated by a delirious imagination. We could see decorations, cornices, spaces, labyrinths, caverns, and a thousand other fanciful architectural designs produced by the ruins in their falling. There were even small rooms opened in the spaces of the walls with an art like that of Nature in forming grottos. The fragments of the altar-piece that had rotted because of the humidity showed through the remains of the vaulting where still hung the chains which had suspended the lamps. Early grasses grew between the cracks of the wood and stone. Among all this destruction there were certain things wholly intact, as some of the pipes of the organ and the grating of the confessional. The roof was one with the floor, and the tower mingled its fragments with those of the tombs below. When we looked upon such a conglomeration of tombs, such a myriad of fragments that had fallen without losing entirely their original form, and such masses of bricks and plaster crumbled like things made of sugar, we could almost believe that the ruins of the building had not yet settled into their final position. The shapeless structure appeared to be palpitating yet from the shock of the explosion.

Don Roque told us that beneath this church there was another one where they worshipped the relics of the holy martyrs of Saragossa; but the entrance to this subterranean sanctuary was closed up. Profound silence reigned, but, penetrating further, we heard human voices proceeding from those mysterious deeps. The first impression produced upon us by hearing these voices was as if the spirits of the famous chroniclers who wrote of the Christian martyrs, and of the patriots

BENITO PÉREZ GALDÓS

sleeping in dust below, were crying out upon us for disturbing their slumbers.

On the instant, in the glare of a flame which illuminated part of the scene, we distinguished a group of persons sheltering themselves, huddling together in a space between two of the fallen columns. They were Saragossa beggars, who had made a palatial shelter for themselves in that place, seeking protection from the rain with beams of wood and with their rags. We also made ourselves as comfortable as might be in another place, and covering ourselves with a blanket and a half, prepared to go to sleep.

Don Roque said to me, "I know Don José de Montoria, one of the richest citizens of Saragossa. We were both born in Mequinenza. We went to school together, and we played our games together on the hills of Corregidor. It is thirty years since I have seen him, but I believe that he will receive us well. Like every good Aragonese, he is all heart. We will find him, fellows; we will see Don José de Montoria. I am of his blood on the maternal side. We will present ourselves to him. We will say—"

But Don Roque was asleep, and I also slept.

II

The place where we lay down did not by any blandishments invite us to sleep luxuriously until morning, and certainly a mattress of broken stones is conducive to early rising. We wakened with the dawn; and as we had to spend no time in making a toilet before a dressing-table, we were soon ready to go out and pay our visits.

The idea came to all four of us at once that it would be a good thing to have some breakfast, but at the same time we agreed unanimously that it was impossible, as we had not the wherewithal to carry out such a high purpose.

"Don't be discouraged, boys," said Don Roque; "because very soon I will take you all to the house of my friend, who will take good care of us."

While he was saying this, we saw emerging from our inn two men and a woman, of those who had been our companions there. They looked as if they were accustomed to sleep in the place. One of them was a cripple, a poor unfortunate who ended at his knees, and put himself in motion by the aid of crutches, swinging himself forward on them as if by oars. He was an old man, with a jovial face well burned by the sun. As he saluted us very pleasantly in passing, wishing us a good-morning, Don Roque asked him in what part of the city was the house of Don José de Montoria. The cripple replied:—

"Don José de Montoria? I know him as if he were the apple of my eye. It is twenty years since he used to live in the Calle de la Albarderia. Afterwards he moved to another street, the Calle de la Parra, then,—but you are strangers, I see."

"Yes, my good friend, we are strangers; and we have come to enlist with the troops of this brave city."

"Then you were not here on the fourth of August?"

"No, my friend," I answered him; "we were not present at that great feat of arms."

"You did not see the battle of Eras?" asked the beggar, sitting down in front of us.

"We did not have that felicity either."

"Well, Don José Montoria was there. He was one of those who pulled the cannon into place for firing. Well, well, I see that you haven't seen a thing. From what part of the world do you come?"

"From Madrid," said Don Roque. "So you are not able to tell me where my dear friend Don José lives?"

"Well, I should think I can, man, well, I should think I can!" answered the cripple, taking from his pocket a crust of dry bread for his breakfast. "From the Calle de la Parra he moved to the Calle de Enmedio. You know that all those houses were blown up. There was Stephen Lopez, a soldier of the Tenth Company of the First Regiment of Aragon Volunteers, and he alone, with forty men, himself forced the French to retire."

"That must have been a fine thing to see!" said Don Roque.

"Oh, if you did not see the fourth of August you have seen nothing," continued the beggar. "I myself also saw the fourth of June, because I was crawling along the Calle de la Paja, and I saw the woman who fired off the big cannon."

"We have already heard of the heroism of that noble woman," said Don Roque; "but if you could make up your mind to tell us—"

"Oh, of course. Don José de Montoria is a great friend of the merchant Don Andrés Guspide, who on the fourth of August was firing from near the narrow street of the Torre del Pino. Hand-grenades and bullets were raining all about him, and my Don Andrés stood like a rock. More than a hundred dead lay about him, and he alone killed fifty of the French."

"Great man, this one! And he is a friend of my friend?"

"Yes, señor," replied the cripple; "and they are two of the best gentlemen in all Saragossa, and they give me a little something every Saturday. For you must know that I am Pepe Pallejas, and they call me Sursum Corda, as twenty-four years ago I was sacristan of the Church of Jesus, and I used to sing—But this is not coming to the point, and I was going on to say I am Sursum Corda, and perhaps you have heard about me in Madrid?"

"Yes," said Don Roque, yielding to his generous impulses; "it seems to me that I have heard the Señor Sursum Corda mentioned there, haven't we, boys?"

"Well, it's likely, and you must know that before the siege I used to beg at the door of this monastery of Santa Engracia, which was blown up by the bandits on the thirteenth of August. I beg now at the Puerta de Jerusalem, at the Jerusalem Gate—where you will be able to find me whenever you like. Well, as I was saying, on the fourth of August I was here, and I saw Francisco Quilez come out of the church, first sergeant of the First Company of fusileers, who, you must already know, with thirty-five men, cast out the bandits from the Convent of the Incarnation. I see that you look surprised—yes! Well, in the orchard of the convent at the back is where the Lieutenant Don Miguel Gila died. There are at the least two hundred bodies in that orchard; and there Don Felipe San Clement, a merchant of Saragossa, broke both his legs. Indeed, if Don Miguel Salamero had not been present—don't you know anything about that?"

"No, sir, my friend," said Don Roque; "we don't know anything about it, and although we have the greatest pleasure in your telling us of so many wonders, what most concerns us now is to find out where we are going to find my old friend Don José. We four are suffering from a disease called hunger, which cannot be cured by listening to the recounting of sublimities."

"Well, now, in a minute I will take you where you want to go," replied Sursum Corda, offering us a part of his crust; "but first I will tell you something, and that is that if Don Mariano Cereso had not defended the Castle Aljaferia as he did defend it, nothing would have been done in the Portillo quarter. And this man, by the grace of God, this man was Don Mariano Cereso! During the attack of the fourth of August, he used to walk in the streets with his sword in its antique sheath. It would terrify you to see him! This Santa Engracia quarter seemed like a furnace, señors. The bombs and the hand-grenades rained down; but the patriots did not mind them anymore than so many drops of water. A good part of the convent fell down; the houses trembled, and all this that we see seemed no more than a barrier of playing cards, by the way it caught fire and crumbled away. Fire in the windows, fire at the top, fire at the base! The French fell like flies, fell like flies, gentlemen. And as for the Saragossans, life and death were all the same to them. Don Antonio Quadros went through there, and when he looked at the French batteries, he was in a state to swallow them whole. The bandits had sixty cannon vomiting fire against the walls. You did not see it? Well, I saw it, and the pieces of brick of the wall and the earth of the parapets scattered like crumbs of a loaf. But the dead served as a barricade,—the dead on top, the dead below, a perfect mountain of the dead. Don Antonio's eyes shot flame. The boys fired without stopping. Their souls were all made of bullets! Didn't you see it? Well, I did, and the French batteries were all cleaned out of gunners. When he saw one of the enemy's cannon was without men, the commander shouted, 'An epaulet to the man who spikes that cannon!' Pepillo Ruiz started and walked up to it as if he was promenading in a garden among butterflies and may flowers, only here the butterflies were bullets, and the flowers were bombs. Pepillo Ruiz spiked the cannon, and came back laughing. And now another part of the convent was falling down. Whoever was smashed by it, remained smashed! Don Antonio Quadros said that that did not bother him any, and seeing that the enemy's batteries had opened a large hole in the wall, went to stuff it full of bags of wool. Then a bullet struck him in the head. They brought him here; he said that was nothing either, and died."

"Oh," said Don Roque, impatiently, "we are sufficiently astonished, Señor Sursum Corda, and the most pure patriotism inflames us to hear you relate such great deeds; but if you could only make up your mind to tell us where—"

"Good Lord!" exclaimed the beggar, "who said I wouldn't tell you? If there is anyone thing I know better than another, and have seen most of anything in my life, it is the house of Don José de Montoria. It is near the San Pablo. Oh, you did not see the hospital? Well, I saw it. There the bombs fell like hail; the sick, seeing that the roofs were falling down, threw themselves from the windows into the street. Others crawled or rolled down the stairs. The partitions burned, and you could hear wailings. The lunatics bellowed in their cages like mad beasts. Many of them escaped and went through the cloisters, laughing and dancing with a thousand fantastic gestures that were frightful to see. They came out into the street as on carnival day; and one climbed the cross in the Coso, where he began a harangue, saying that he was the River Ebro, and he would run over the city and put out the fire. The women ran to care for the sick, who were all carried off to Del Pilar and to La Seo. You could not get through the streets. Signals were given from the Torre Nueva whenever a bomb was coming, but the uproar of the people prevented their hearing the bells. The French advanced by this street of Santa Engracia. They took possession of the hospital and of the Convent of San Francisco. The fighting began in the quarter of the Coso, and in the streets thereabouts. Don Santiago Sas, Don Mariano Cereso, Don Lorenzo Calvo, Don Marcos Simono, Renovales, Martin Albantos, Vicente Codé, Don Vicente Marraco, and others fearlessly attacked the French. And behind a barricade made by herself, awaited them, furious, gun in hand, the Countess de Bureta."

"What a woman, a countess, making barricades and firing guns!" cried Don Roque, enthusiastically.

"You did not know it?" he returned. "Well, where do you live? The Señora Maria Consolacion Azlor y Villavicencio, who lives near the Ecce Homo, also walked through the streets, saying words of good cheer to those who were discouraged. Afterwards she made them close the entrance to the street, and herself took the lead of a party of peasants, crying, 'Here we will all die before we will let them pass!'"

"Oh, what sublime heroism!" exclaimed Don Roque, yawning with hunger. "How much I should enjoy hearing those tales of heroism told on a full stomach! So you say that the house of Don José is to be found—"

"It is just around there," said the cripple. "You know already that the French had entangled themselves and stuck fast near the Arch of Cineja. Holy Virgin del Pilar, but that was where they killed off the French! The rest of the day was nothing beside it. In the Calle de la Parra and the Square of Estrevedes, in the Calles de los Urreas, Santa Fe, and Del Azoque, the peasants cut the French to pieces. The cannonading and the roar of that day still ring in my ears. The French burned down the houses that they could not defend, and the Saragossans did the same. There was firing on every side. Men, women, and children,—it was enough to have two hands to fight against the enemy. And you did not see it? You really have seen nothing at all! Well, as I was saying, Palafox came out of Saragossa towards—"

"That's enough, my friend," said Don Roque, losing patience. "We are charmed with your conversation; but if you can take us this instant to the house of my friend, or direct us so that we can find it, we will go along."

"In a minute, gentlemen. Don't hurry," replied Sursum Corda, starting off in advance with all the agility of which his crutches were capable. "Let us go there. Let us go, with all my heart. Do you see this house? Well, here lives Antonio Laste, first sergeant of the Fourth Company of Regulars, and you must know he saved from the treasury sixteen thousand, four hundred pesos, and took from the French the candles that they stole from the church."

"Go on ahead, go on, friend," I said, seeing that this indefatigable talker intended stopping to give all the details of the heroism of Antonio Laste.

"We shall arrive soon," replied Sursum; "on the morning of the first of July I was going past here, when I encountered Hilario Lafuente, first corporal of fusileers of the Parish of Sas, and he said to me, 'Today

BENITO PÉREZ GALDÓS

they are going to attack the Portillo;' then I went to see what there was to see and—"

"We know all about this, already," said Don Roque. "Let us go on fast. We can talk afterwards."

"This house which you see here burned down and in ruins," continued the cripple, going around a corner, "is the one that burned on the fourth, when Don Francisco Ipas, sub-lieutenant of the Second Company of fusileers of the parish of San Pablo, stood here with a cannon, and these—"

"We know the rest, my good man," said Don Roque. "Forward, march! and the faster the better."

"But much better was what Codé did, the farmer of the parish of La Magdalena, with the cannon of the Calle de la Parra," persisted the beggar, stopping once more. "When he was going to fire the gun, the French surrounded him, everybody ran away; but Codé got under the cannon, and the French passed by without seeing him. Afterwards, helped by an old woman who brought him some rope, he pulled that big piece of artillery as far as the entrance of the street. Come, I will show you!"

"No, no, we don't want to see a thing. Go along ahead."

We kept at him, and closed our ears to his tales with so much obstinacy, that at last, although very slowly, he took us through the Coso and the Market to the Calle de la Hilarza, the street wherein stood the house of the person whom we were seeking.

III

But, alas! Don José de Montoria was not in his house, and we found it necessary to go a little way out of the city to look for him. Two of my companions, tired of so much going and coming, left us with the idea of trying on their own account for some military or civil situation. Don Roque and myself therefore started with less embarrassment on our trip to the country house, the "torre," of our friend. (They call country houses torres at Saragossa.) This was situated to the westward of the town; the place bordered on the Muela road, and was at a short distance from the Bernardona road. Such a long tramp was not at all the right thing for our tired bodies, but necessity obliged us to take this inopportune exercise. We were very well treated when we at last met the longed-for Saragossan and became the objects of his cordial hospitality.

Montoria was occupied, when we arrived, in cutting down olive-trees on his place, a proceeding demanded by the military exigencies of the plan of defence established by the officers in the field, because of the possibility of a second siege. And it was not our friend alone who destroyed with his own hands this heritage of his hacienda. All the proprietors of the surrounding places occupied themselves with the same task, and they directed the work of devastation with as much coolness as if they were watering or replanting, or busy with the grape harvest.

Montoria said to us, "In the first siege I cut down my trees on my property on the other side of the Huerva; but this second siege that is being prepared for us is going to be much more terrible, to judge by the great number of troops that the French are sending."

We told him the story of the surrender of Madrid, and as this seemed to depress him very much, we praised the deeds done at Saragossa between the fifteenth of June and the fourteenth of August with all sorts of grandiloquent phrases. Shrugging his shoulders, Don José said, "All that was possible to be done was done."

At this point Don Roque began to make personal eulogies of me, both military and civil, and he overdrew the picture so much that he made me blush, particularly as some of his announcements were stupendous lies. He said, first, that I belonged to one of the highest families of lower Andalusia, and that I was present as one of the marine guards at the glorious battle of Trafalgar. He said that the junta had made me a great offer of a concession in Peru, and that during the siege of Madrid I had performed prodigies of valor at the Puerta de los Pozos, my courage being so great that the French found it convenient after the capitulation to rid themselves of such a fearful foe, sending me with other Spanish patriots to France. He added that my ingenuity had made possible the escape of us four companions who had taken refuge in Saragossa, and ended his panegyric by assuring Don José that for my personal qualities also I deserved distinguished consideration.

Meantime Montoria surveyed me from head to foot, and if he observed the bad cut of my clothes and their many rents, he must also have seen that they were of the kind used by a man of quality, revealing his fine, courtly, and aristocratic origin by the multiplicity of their imperfections. After he had looked me over, he said to me, "Porra! I shall not be able to enlist you in the third rank of the company of fusileers of Don Santiago Sas, of which I am captain, but you can enter the corps where my son is; and if you don't wish to, you must leave Saragossa, because here we have no use for lazy men. And as for you, Don Roque, my friend, since you are not able to carry a gun, porra! we will make you one of the attendants in the army hospital."

When Don Roque had heard all this, he managed to express, by means of rhetorical circumlocution and graceful ellipses, the great necessity of a piece of meat for each one of us, and a couple of loaves of bread apiece. Then we saw the great Montoria scowl, looking at us so severely that he made us tremble, fearing that we were to be sent away for daring to ask for something to eat. We murmured timid excuses, and then our protector, very red in the face, spoke as follows,—

"Is it possible that you are hungry? Porra! Go to the devil with a hundred thousand porras! Why haven't you said so before? Do I look like a man capable of letting my friends go hungry? porra! You must know that I always have a dozen hams hanging from the beams of my storeroom, and I have twenty casks of Rioja, yes, sir. And you are hungry, and you did not tell me so to my face without any round about fuss? That is an offence to a man like me. There, boys, go in and order them to cook four pounds of beef and six dozen eggs, and to kill six pullets, and bring from the wine-cellar seven jugs of wine. I want my breakfast, too. Let the neighbors come, the workmen, and my sons too, if they are anywhere about. And you, gentlemen, be prepared to punish it all with my compliments, porra! You will eat what there is without thanking me. We do not use compliments here. You, Señor Don Roque, and you,

Señor Don Araceli, are in your own house today, porra! tomorrow and always, porra! Don José de Montoria is a true friend to his friends. All that he has, all that he owns, belongs to his friends."

The brusque hospitality of the worthy man astonished us. As he did not receive our compliments with good grace, we decided to leave aside the artificial formalities of the court, and, assuredly, the most primitive fashions reigned during the breakfast.

"Why don't you eat more?" Don José asked me. "It seems to me that you are one of these compliment-makers who expect to live on compliments. I don't like that sort of thing, my young gentleman. I find it very trying, and I am going to beat you with a stick to make you eat. There, despatch this glass of wine! Did you find any better at court? Not by a long way. Come now, drink, porra! or we shall come to blows." All this made me eat and drink more than was good for me; but it was necessary to respond to the generous cordiality of Montoria, and too it was not worth while to lose his good will for one indigestion more or less.

After the breakfast, the work of cutting down trees was continued, and the rich farmer directed it as if it were a festival performance.

"We will see," he said, "if this time they will dare to attack the Castle. Have you not seen the works that we have built? They will find it a very complicated task to take them. I have just given two hundred bales of wool, a mere nothing, and I would give my last crust."

When we returned to the town, Montoria took us to look over the defensive works that were built in the western part of the city. There was in the Portillo gate a large semi-circular battery that joined the walls of the Convent de los Fecetas with those of the Augustine friars' convent. From this building to the Convent of the Trinitarios extended a straight wall, with battlements along all its length and with a good pathway in the centre. This was protected by a deep moat that reached to the famous field of Las Eras, scene of the heroic deeds of the fifteenth of June. Further north, towards the Puerta Sancho, which protected the breastworks of the Ebro, the fortifications continued, terminated by a tower. All these works, constructed in haste, though intelligently, were not distinguished by their solidity. Anyone of the enemy's generals, ignorant of the events of the first siege, and of the immense moral force of the Saragossans, would have laughed at those piles of earth as fortifications offering material for an easy siege. But God ordains that somebody must escape once in a while the physical laws that rule war. Saragossa, compared with Amberes, Dantzig, Metz, Sebastopol, Cartagena, Gibraltar, and other famous strongholds, was like a fortress made of cardboard.

And yet—!

IV

Before we left his house, Montoria became vexed at Don Roque and me because we would not take the money that he offered us for our first expenses in the city; then were repeated the blows on the table, and the rains of "porras" and other words that I will not repeat. But at last we arrived at an arrangement honorable for both parties.

And now I begin to think I am saying too much about this singular man before I describe his personality. Don José was a man of about sixty years of age, strong, high-colored, of over-flowing health, well placed in the world, contented with himself, fulfilling his destiny with a quiet conscience. His was an excess of patriotic virtues and of exemplary customs, if there can be an excess of such things. He was lacking in education, that is to say, in the finer and more distinguished training which in that time some of the sons of such families as his were beginning to receive. Don José was not acquainted with the superficialities of etiquette, and by character and custom was opposed to the amenities and the white lies which are a part of the foundations of courtesy. As he always wore his heart upon his sleeve, he wished everybody to do the same, and his savage goodness tolerated none of the frequent evasions of polite conversation. In angry moments he was impetuous, and let himself be carried to violent extremes, of which he always repented later. He never dissimulated, and had the great Christian virtues in a crude form and without polish, like a massive piece of the most beautiful marble where the chisel has traced no lines. It was necessary to know him to understand him, making allowances for his eccentricities, although to be sure he should scarcely be called eccentric, when he was so much like the majority of the men of his province.

His aim was never to hide what he felt; and if this occasionally caused him some trouble in the course of life in regard to questions of little moment, it was a quality which always proved an inestimable treasure in any grave matter, because, with his soul wholly on view, it was impossible to suspect any malice or any double dealing whatever. He readily pardoned offenders, obliged those who sought favors, and gave a large part of his numerous goods to those in need. He dressed neatly, ate abundantly, fasted with much scrupulousness during Lent, and loved the Virgin del Pilar with a fanatical sort of family affection.

His language was not, as we have shown, a model of elegance, and he himself confessed, as the greatest of his defects, the habit of saying porra every minute, and again, porra! without the slightest necessity. But more than once I heard him say, knowing his fault, he had not been able to correct it, for the porras came out of his mouth without his knowing it.

Don José had a wife and three children. She was Doña Leocadia Sarriera, by birth a Navarraise. The eldest son and the daughter were married, and had given grandchildren to the old man. The younger son was called Augustine, and was destined for the church, like his uncle of the same name, the Archdeacon of La Seo. I made the acquaintance of all these on the same day, and found them the best people in the world. I was treated with so much kindness that I was overwhelmed by their generosity. If they had known me since my birth, they could not have been more cordial. Their kindness, springing spontaneously from their generous hearts, touched my very soul; and as I have always had a faculty for letting people love me, I responded from the first with a very sincere affection.

"Señor Don Roque," I said that night to my friend as we were going to bed in the room which was given us, "I have never seen people like these. Is everybody in Aragon like this?"

"There are all kinds," he answered; "but men made of stuff like Don José and his family are plentiful in this land of Aragon."

Next day we occupied ourselves with my enlistment. The spirit of the men who were enlisting filled me with such enthusiasm that nothing seemed to me so noble as to follow glory, even afar off. Everybody knows that in those days Saragossa and the Saragossans had obtained a fabulous renown, that their heroism stimulated the imagination. Everything referring to the famous siege of the immortal city partook on the lips of narrators of the proportions and colors of the heroic age. With distance, the actions of the Saragossans acquired great dimensions. In England and Germany, where they were considered the Numantines of modern times, those half-naked peasants, with rope sandals on their feet and the bright Saragossan kerchief on their heads, became like figures of mythology.

"Surrender, and we will give you clothes," said the French in the first siege, admiring the constancy of a few poor countrymen dressed in rags.

"*We do not know how to surrender*," they made answer; "*and our bodies shall be clothed with glory*."

The fame of this and other phrases has gone round the world.

But let us go back to my enlistment. There was an obstacle in the way, Palafox's manifesto of the thirteenth of December, in which he ordered the expulsion of all strangers within a period of twenty-four hours. This measure was taken on account of the numbers of people who made trouble, and stirred up discord and disorder; but just at the time of my arrival another order was given out, calling for all the scattered soldiers of the Army of the Centre which had been dispersed at Tudela, and so I found a chance to enlist. Although I did not belong to that army, I had taken a place in the defence of Madrid and the battle of Bailen. These were reasons which, with the help of my protector Montoria, served me in entering the Saragossan forces. They gave me a place in the battalion of volunteers of the Peñas of San Pedro, which had been badly weakened in the first siege, and I received a uniform and a gun. I did not enter the lines, as my protector had said, in the company of the clergyman of Santiago Sas, because this valiant company was composed exclusively of residents of the parish of San Pablo. They did not want any young men in their battalion; for this reason Augustine Montoria himself, Don José's son, could not serve under the Sas banner, and enlisted like myself in the battalion of Las Peñas de San Pedro. Good luck bestowed upon me a good companion and an excellent friend.

From the day of my arrival I had heard talk of the approach of the French army; but it was not an incontrovertible fact until the twentieth. In the afternoon a division arrived at Zuera, on the left bank of the river, to threaten the suburb; another, commanded by Suchet, encamped on the right above San Lamberto. Marshal Moncey, who was the general in command, placed himself, with three divisions, near the canal, and on both sides of the Huerva. Forty thousand men besieged us.

It is known that the French, impatient to defeat us, began operations early on the twenty-first, attacking simultaneously and with great vigor Monte Torrero, and the Arrabal, the suburb on the left of the Ebro, points without whose possession it was impossible to dream of conquering the valiant city. But if we were obliged to abandon Torrero on account of the danger of its defence, Saragossa displayed in the suburb such audacious courage that that day is known as one of the most brilliant of all her brilliant history.

From four o'clock, from day-dawn, the battalion of Las Peñas de San Pedro guarded the front of the fortifications, from Santa Engracia to the Convent of Trinitarios, a line which seemed the least exposed in all the circuit of the city. Behind Santa Engracia was established the battery of Los Martires; from there ran the battlements of the wall as far as the Huerva bridge, defended by a barricade; it deflected afterwards towards the west, making an obtuse angle, and joining another redoubt built in the Torre del Pino; it continued in a straight line as far as the Convent of Trinitarios, and enclosed the Puerta del Carmen.

Whoever has seen Saragossa can well understand my imperfect description, for the ruins of Santa Engracia still remain, and in the Puerta del Carmen may still be seen, not far from the Glorieta, its ruined architrave and worm-eaten stones.

We were, as I have said, occupying the position described, and part of the soldiers had a bivouac in a neighboring orchard, next to the Carmen college.

Augustine Montoria and I were inseparable. His serene character, the affection he showed me from the moment we met, and the inexplicable concord in our thoughts, made his company very agreeable. He was a young man of beautiful figure, with large brilliant eyes and open brow, and an expression marked by a melancholy gravity. His heart, like that of his father, was filled by generosity which overflowed at the least impulse; but he was not likely to wound the feelings of a friend, because education had taken from him a great deal of the national brusqueness. Augustine entered manhood's estate with the security of a kind heart, firm and uncorrupted judgment, with a vigorous and healthy soul; the wide world only was the limit of his boundless goodness. These qualities were enriched by a brilliant imagination of sure and direct action, not like that of our modern geniuses, who most of the time do not know what they are about. Augustine's imagination was lofty and serene, worthy of his education in the great classics. Although with a lively inclination to poetry,—for Augustine was a poet,—he had learned theology, showing ability in this as in everything. The fathers at the Seminary, who were fond of the youth, looked upon him as a prodigy in the sciences, human and divine, and they congratulated themselves on seeing him with one foot at least over the threshold of the Church.

The Montoria family had many a pleasant anticipation of the day when Augustine would say his first mass, as a holy event that was fast approaching. Yet,—I am obliged to say it,—Augustine had no vocation for the Church. Neither his family nor the good fathers of the Seminary understood this, nor would they have understood it, even if the Holy Spirit had come down in person to tell them. This precocious theologian, this humanist who had Horace at the ends of his fingers, this dialectician who in the weekly discussions astonished the fathers with intellectual gymnastics of scholastic science, had no more vocation for the Church than Mozart for war, Raphael for mathematics, or Napoleon for dancing!

V

G abriel," he said to me one morning, "dost thou not feel like smashing something?"

"Augustine, dost thou not feel like smashing something?" I responded. It will be seen that we were "thee-ing" and "thou-ing" each other after three days' acquaintance.

"Not very much," he said, "suppose the first ball strikes us dead!"

"We shall die for our country, for Saragossa; and although posterity will not remember us, it is always an honor to fall on the field of battle for a cause like this."

"You are right," he answered sadly; "but it is a pity to die. We are young. Who knows for what we are destined in life?"

"Life is a trifle, and its importance is not worth thinking of."

"That is for the aged to say, but not us who are just beginning to live. Frankly, I do not wish to die in this terrible circle which the French have drawn about us. In the other siege, however, all the students of the Seminary took arms, and I confess that I was more valiant then than now. A peculiar zeal filled my blood, and I threw myself into places of greatest danger without fear of death. Today does not find me the same. I am timid and afraid, and when a gun goes off, it makes me tremble."

"That is natural. Fear does not exist when one does not realize the danger. As far as that is concerned, they say the most valiant soldiers are the raw recruits."

"There is nothing in that. Indeed, Gabriel, I confess that the mere question of dying does not strike me as the greatest evil. But if I die, I am going to entrust you with a commission which I hope you will fulfil carefully like a good friend. Listen well to what I tell you. You see that tower that leans this way, as if to see what is passing here, or hear what we are saying?"

"The Torre Nueva? I see it. What charge are you going to give me for that lady?"

Day was breaking, and between the irregular-tiled roofs of the city, between the spires and minarets, the balconies and the cupolas of the churches, the Torre Nueva, old and unfinished, stood out distinctly.

"Listen well!" said Augustine. "If I am killed with the first shot on this day which is now dawning, when the battle is ended, and they break ranks, you must go there."

"To the Torre Nueva? Behold me! I arrive. I enter!"

"No, man, not enter. Listen, I will tell you. You arrive at the Plaza de San Felipe where the tower is. Look yonder! Do you see there near the great pile there is another tower, a little belfry? It seems like an acolyte before his lord the canon, which is the great tower."

"Yes, now I see the altar-boy. And if I am not mistaken, it is the belfry of San Felipe. And the damned thing is ringing this minute!"

"For mass, it is ringing for mass," said Augustine, with great emotion. "Do you not hear the cracked bell?"

"Very plainly. Let us know what I have to say to this Mr. Altar-boy who is ringing the cracked bell."

"No, no, it is nothing about him. You arrive at the Plaza of San Felipe. If you look at the belfry, you will see it is on a corner, and from this corner runs a narrow street. You enter there, and at the left you will find at a little distance another street, narrow and retired, called Anton Trillo. You follow this until you reach the back of the church. There you will see a house. You stop there—"

"And then I come back again?"

"No; close to the house there is a garden, with a little gateway painted the color of chocolate. You stop there."

"There I stop, and there I am!"

"No, old man. You will see—"

"You're whiter than your shirt, my Augustine. What do all these towers and stoppages signify?"

"They mean," continued my friend, with increasing embarrassment, "that in a little while you will be there. I desire you to go by night. All right, you arrive there. You stop. You wait a little, then you pass to the opposite sidewalk. You stretch your neck, and you will see a window over the wall of a garden. You pick up a pebble and throw it against the panes of glass lightly, to do little damage."

"And in a second she will come!"

"No; have patience. How do you know whether she will come or not come?"

"Well, let us suppose that she comes."

"Before I tell you another thing, you must understand that it is there the goodman Candiola lives. Do you know who Candiola is? Well, he is a citizen of Saragossa, a man who, as they say, has in his house a cellar full of money. He is avaricious and a usurer, and when he lends he guts his customers. He knows more about debtors, laws, and foreclosures than the whole court and council of Castile. Whoever goes to law with him is lost."

"From all this, the house with a gate painted chocolate color should be a magnificent palace."

"Nothing of the sort. You will see a wretched-looking house that seems about to fall down. I tell you that that goodman Candiola is a miser. He does not waste a real that he can help. And if you should see him about here you would give him alms. I will tell you another thing; he is never seen in Saragossa, and they call him goodman Candiola in mockery and contempt. His name is Don Jeronimo de Candiola; he is a native of Mallorca, if I am not mistaken."

"And this Candiola has a daughter?"

"Wait, man, how impatient you are! How do you know whether or not he has a daughter?" he answered, hiding his agitation by these evasions. "Well, as I was just going to tell you, Candiola is detested in the city for his great avarice and wicked heart. Many poor men has he put in prison after ruining them. Worse still, during the other siege he did not give a farthing for the war, nor take up arms, nor receive the wounded into his house, nor could they wring a peseta from him; and, as he said one day it was all one to him whether he gave to John or to Peter, he was on the point of being arrested."

"Well, he is a pretty piece, this man of the house of the garden of the chocolate-colored gate! And what if when the pebble strikes the window, goodman Candiola comes out with a cudgel and gives me a good beating for flirting with his daughter?"

"Don't be an idiot! Hush! You must know that as soon as it gets dark, Candiola shuts himself in an underground room, and there he stays counting his money until after midnight. Bah! He is well occupied now. The neighbors say they hear a muffled sound as if bags of coins were being tumbled out."

"Very well. I arrive there. I throw the stone. She comes, and I tell her—"

"You tell her that I am dead. No, don't be cruel; give her this amulet. No, tell her—no, it will be better to tell her nothing."

"Then I will give her the amulet?"

"By no means. Do not take the amulet to her."

"Now, now I understand. As soon as she comes I am to say goodnight and march myself away singing, 'The Virgin del Pilar says—'"

"No, it is enough that she learns of my death. You must do as I tell you."

"But if you don't tell me anything."

"How hasty you are! Wait. Perhaps they'll not kill me today."

"True. And what a bother about nothing!"

"There is one thing which I have left out, Gabriel, and I shall tell it to you frankly. I have had many, very many great desires to confide to you this secret which weighs upon my breast. To whom could I tell it but to you, my friend? If I did not tell you, my heart would break like a pomegranate. I have been greatly afraid of telling it at night in my dreams. Because of this fear I cannot sleep. If my father, my mother, my brother, suspected it, they would kill me."

"And the fathers at the Seminary?"

"Don't name the fathers. You shall see. I will tell you what has befallen me. Do you know Father Rincon? Well, Father Rincon loves me very much, and every evening he used to make me come out for a walk by the river or towards Torrero or the Juslibol road. We would talk of theology and literature. Rincon is so enthusiastic about the great poet Horace that he used to say, 'It is a pity that that man wasn't a Christian so that he could be canonized.' He always carries with him a little Elzevir, which he loves more than the apple of his eye. When we were tired walking, he would sit down and read, and between the two of us we would make whatever comments occurred to us. Well, now I will tell you that Father Rincon was a kinsman of Doña Maria Rincon, the deceased wife of Candiola, who has a little property in the Monzalbarba road, with a wretched little country house, more like a hut than a house, but embowered in leafy trees, and with delightful views of the Ebro. One afternoon, after we had been reading the *Quis multa gracilis te puer in rosa*, my teacher desired to visit his relative. We went there; we entered the garden, and Candiola was not there; but his daughter came to meet us, and Rincon said to her, 'Mariquilla, get some peaches for this young man, and get me a glass of you know what.'"

"And is Mariquilla nice?"

"Don't ask that. What if she is nice? You shall see. Father Rincon stroked his beard, and turning towards me said, 'Augustine, confess that in your lifetime you have never seen a more perfect face than this one. Look at those eyes of fire, that angel's mouth, and that bit of heaven for a brow.' I was trembling, and Mariquilla laughed, her face all rosy red. Then Rincon continued, saying, 'To you, who are a future father of the church, an example, a young pattern, without other passion than that for books, this divinity may show herself. Jove! admire here the admirable work of the Supreme Creator. Observe the expression of that face, the sweetness of those glances, the grace of that smile, the freshness, the delicacy of that complexion, the fineness of that skin, and confess that if heaven is beautiful, flowers, mountains, light, all the creations of God are nothing beside woman, the most perfect and finished work of the immortal hand.' Thus spoke my teacher, and I, mute and astonished, did not cease to contemplate that master work which was certainly better than the Æneid. I cannot tell you what I felt. Imagine the Ebro, that great river, which descends from its springs to give itself to the sea, all at once changing its channel and trying to run upward, returning to the Asturias. The same thing took place in my spirit. I myself was astonished that all my ideas had been changed from their wonted course and turned backward, cutting I know not what new channels. I assure you I was astonished, and I am yet. Looking at her without satisfying the longing of my soul or of my eyes, I said to myself, 'I love her in a wonderful way! How is it that until now I have never fallen in love?' I had never seen Mariquilla until that moment."

"And the peaches?"

"Mariquilla was as much disturbed before me as I before her. Father Rincon went to talk with the gardener about the encroachments that the French had made upon the property (that was soon after the first of September, a month after the raising of the first siege), and Mariquilla and I remained alone. Alone! My first impulse was to cut and run; and she, as she has told me, also felt the same. Neither she nor I ran. We stayed there. All at once I felt an extraordinary movement of my intellect. Breaking the silence, I began to talk with her. We talked about all sorts of indifferent things at first, but to me came thoughts beyond my usual understanding, surpassing the ordinary, and all, all, all, I uttered. Mariquilla answered me little, but her eyes were only more eloquent than when I was talking to her. At last Father Rincon called, and we marched away. I took leave of her, and in a low voice said that we would soon meet again. We returned to Saragossa. Yes, the street, the trees, the Ebro, the cupola of the Pilar, the belfries of Saragossa, the passersby, the houses, the walls of the garden, the pavements, the sound of the wind, the dogs of the street, all seemed different to me, all, heaven and earth had been changed. My good teacher began to read again in Horace, and I said that Horace wasn't worth anything. He wished me to dine with him, and threatened me with the loss of his friendship. I praised Virgil with enthusiasm, and repeated the celebrated lines—

"This was about the first of September," said I, "and since then?"

"From that day a new life began for me. It commenced with a burning disquiet that robbed me of sleep, making distasteful to me all that was not Mariquilla. My own father's house was hateful to me; and wandering about the environs of Saragossa without any companion, I sought peace for my spirit in solitude. I hated the college, all books and theology, and when October came, and they wished me to bind myself to live shut up in the holy house, I feigned illness in order to remain in my own. Thanks to the war that has made us all soldiers, I have been able to live free, to go at all hours, day and night, and see and talk with her frequently. I go to her house, make the signal agreed upon; she descends, opens her grated window; we talk long hours. People pass by, but I am muffled in my cloak even up to the eyes. With this and the darkness of night, no one recognizes me. As far as that is concerned, the boys in the street ask one another, 'Who is this admirer of the Candiola?' The other night, fearing discovery, we stopped our talks at the grating. Mariquilla came down, opened the garden gate, and I entered. No one could discover us, because Don Jeronimo, believing her to be in bed, retired to his room to count his money, and the old servant, the only one in the house, took us under her wing. Alone in the garden we sat down upon some stone steps and watched the brightness of the moonlight through the boughs of a great black poplar. In that majestic silence our souls contemplated the divine, and we experienced a deep sentiment, beyond words to express. Our felicity is so great that at times it is a living torment. If there are moments in which one might desire to be a hundred beings, there are also moments in which one might desire not to exist. We pass long hours there. The night before last we were there until daybreak. My teacher believed me to be with the guards, so I was not obliged to hasten. When morning first began to dawn, we separated. Over the top of the wall of the garden appeared the roofs of the neighboring houses and the top of the Torre Nueva. Pointing it out to me, Mariquilla said, 'When that tower stands straight, then only shall I cease to love you.'"

Augustine said no more. A cannon-shot sounded from the side of Mount Torrero, and we both turned in that direction.

VI

The French had assaulted with great vigor the fortified positions of the Torrero. Ten thousand men defended them, commanded by Don Philip Saint March and by O'Neill, both generals of great merit. The volunteers of Bourbon, Castile, Campo Segorbino, of Alicante, and of Soria, the sharp-shooters of Fernando VII, the Murcia regiment, and other bodies that I do not remember, answered the fire. From the redoubt of Los Martires we saw the beginning of the action, and the French columns which extended the length of the canal and flanked the Torrero. The fire of the fusileers continued for sometime, but the struggle could not be prolonged very long, for that point could not be held without the occupation and fortification of others close by, like Buena Vista, Casa Blanca, and the reservoir of the canal. But none the less our troops did not retire except slowly and in the best order, retreating by the Puente de America, and carrying with them all the pieces of artillery except one, which had been dismantled by the enemy's fire. Amidst it all we heard a great noise which resounded at a great distance, and as the fire had almost ceased, we supposed that there was another battle outside the town.

"There is the Brigadier Don José Manso," said Augustine to me, "with the Swiss regiment of Aragon, which Don Mariano Walker commands, the volunteers of Huesca, of whom Don Pedro Villacampa is leader, the volunteers of Catalonia, and other valiant corps. And here are we, hand in hand! Along this side it appears to be about finished. The French will content themselves today with the conquest of Torrero."

"Either I am greatly deceived," I replied, "or they are now going to attack San José."

We all looked at the spot indicated, an edifice of huge dimensions which arose at our left, separated from the Puerta Quemada by the valley of the Huerva.

"There is Renovales," said Augustine,—"the brave Don Mariano Renovales, who distinguished himself so highly in the other siege, who now commands the troops of Orihuela and of Valencia."

In our position we were all prepared for an energetic defence. In the redoubt del Pilar, in the battery of Los Martires, in the tower of Del Pino, the same as in the Trinitarios, the artillery stood guard with burning matches, and the infantry waited behind the parapets in positions that seemed to us quite secure, ready to fire if any columns should attempt to assault us. It was cold, and most of us were shivering. One might almost have believed that it was from fear; but no, it was cold, and anybody who had said the contrary would have lied.

The movement which I had foreseen was not slow in taking place, and the convent of San José was attacked by a strong column of French infantry. It was an attempt at an attack, or, rather, a surprise. To all appearances, the enemy had a poor memory, and in three months they had forgotten that surprises were impossible in Saragossa. None the less they arrived within gunshot, and doubtless the graceless whelps believed that merely at sight of them our warriors would fall dead with fear. The poor men had just arrived from Silesia, and did not know what manner of warfare there was in Spain. And, furthermore, as they had gained the Torrero with so little difficulty, they believed themselves in train to swallow the world. They were advancing thus, as I have said, and San José was not making any demonstration. When they were nearly within gunshot of the loopholes and embrasures of that edifice, all at once these began vomiting such a terrible fire that my brave Frenchmen took to their heels with the utmost precipitation. Having had enough doubtless, they remained stretched out at full length; and upon seeing the outcome of their valor, those of us who were watching the onset from the battery of Los Martires broke out into exclamations, applause, cries, and huzzas. In this ferocious manner the soldier celebrates in battle the death of his fellow-creatures. He who instinctively feels compassion at the slaying of a rabbit on a hunt jumps for joy on seeing hundreds of robust men fall,—young, happy men who have never done harm to anybody.

Such was the attack upon San José, a futile attempt quickly punished. By that time, the French should have understood that if Torrero was abandoned, it was by calculation and not on account of weakness. Alone, embarrassed, deserted, without external defences, without forces or forts, Saragossa renewed again her earthworks, her defences of bricks, her bastions of mud heaped up the evening before to be again defended against the first soldiers, the first artillery, and the first engineers of the world. Pomp and show of a nation, formidable machines, enormous quantities of power, scientific preparation of materials, force, and intelligence in their greatest splendor, the invaders bring to attack the fortified place which appears to be guarded by boys. It is indeed almost like this: all succumb, all is reduced to powder in front of those walls which might be kicked over. But behind this movable defensive material is the well-tempered steel of Aragon souls, which cannot be broken or bent, nor cast into moulds, nor crushed, nor robbed of breath, and which surrounds the whole region like a barrier, indestructible by human means.

The whole district about the Torre Nueva was resounding with clamors and alarms. When to this district comes such mournful sounds, the city is in danger and needs all her sons. What is it? What is passing? What will happen?

"Matters must be going badly back of the town," said Augustine.

Meanwhile they attacked us yonder to occupy the attention of the crowd on this side of the river. The same thing was done in the first siege.

"Al arrabal, al arrabal!" was our cry. "To the suburb!"

And while we were saying this, the French sent us some balls to show us that we must stay where we were. Fortunately Saragossa had enough people within her walls, and could readily assist and support all parts.

My battalion abandoned the wall near Santa Engracia, and began to march towards the Coso. We did not know where we were being conducted, but it is probable that they were taking us to the suburb. The streets were full of people. Old men and women came out, impelled by curiosity, wishing to see at close quarters and near at hand the points of danger, since it was impossible for them to be placed in the same peril. The streets of San Gil, San Pedro, and La Cuchilleria, which lead to the bridge, were almost impassable. A great multitude of women were passing through them, all walking in the direction of the Pilar and La Seo.

The booming of the cannon excited rather than saddened the fervent people, and all were jostling one another to get nearest the front. In the Plaza de la Seo, I saw the cavalry which, with all these people, obstructed the bridge and obliged my battalion to look for an easier way to the other side. While we were passing before the porch of this sanctuary, we heard the sound of the prayers wherewith all the women of the city were imploring their holy patroness. The few men who wished to come into the temple were expelled by them.

We went to the bank of the river near San Juan de los Panetas, and took up our place on a mound, awaiting orders. In front and on the other side of the river, the field of battle was divided. We saw at the end nearest us the grove of Macanaz, over there and close to the bridge the little monastery of Altabas, yonder that of San Lazarus, and further on the Monastery of Jesus. Behind this scene, reflected in the waters of the great river, could be seen a horrible fire. There was an interminable turmoil, a hoarse clamor of the voices of cannon and of human yells. Dense clouds of smoke, renewed unceasingly, mounted confusedly to the heavens. All the breastworks of this position, which were constructed with bricks from neighboring brickyards, formed with the earth of the kilns a reddish mass. One might have believed that the ground had been mixed together with blood.

The French held their front towards the Barcelona road and the Juslibol, where more kilns and gardens lie at the left of the second of those two ways. Thence the Twelfth had furiously attacked our intrenchments, making their way by the Barcelona road, and challenging with impetuous intrepidity the cross-fires of San Lazarus and that of the place called El Marcelo. Their courage lay in striking audacious blows upon the batteries, and their tenacity produced a veritable hecatomb. They fell in great numbers; the ranks were broken, and, being instantly filled by others, they repeated the attack. At times they almost reached the parapets, and a thousand individual contests increased the horror of the scene. They went in advance of their leaders, brandishing their cutlasses, like desperate men who had made it a question of honor to die before a heap of bricks, and in that frightful destruction which wrenched the life from hundreds of men every minute, they disappeared, flung down upon mother earth, soldiers and sergeants, ensigns, captains, and colonels. It was a veritable struggle between two peoples; and while the fires of the first siege were burning in our hearts, the French came on thirsting for vengeance with all the passion of offended manhood, worse even than the passion of the warrior.

It was this untimely bloodthirstiness that lost them the day. They should have begun by demolishing our works with their artillery, observing the serenity which a siege demands, and not have engaged in those hand to hand combats before positions defended by a people like the one that they had met on the fifteenth of July, and the fourth of August. They ought to have repressed their feeling of contempt or scorn of the forces of the enemy,—a feeling that has always been the bad star of the French. It was the same in the war with Spain, as in the recent conflict with Prussia. They ought to have put into execution a calmly considered plan which would have produced in the besieged less of disgust than exaltation.

It is certain that if they carried with them the thought of their immortal general who always conquered as much by his admirable logic as by his cannons, they would have employed in the siege of Saragossa a little of the knowledge of the human heart, without which the pursuit of war, brutal war—it seems a lie!—is no more than cruel carnage.

Napoleon, with his extraordinary penetration, would have comprehended the Saragossan character, and would have abstained from attacking the unprotected columns, whose boast was of individual personal valor. This is a quality at all times difficult and dangerous to encounter, but above all in the presence of nations who fight for an ideal and not for an idol.

I will not go into further details of the dreadful battle of the twenty-first of December, the most glorious of the second siege of Aragon. As I did not see it at close quarters, and can only give the story of what was told me, I am moved not to be prolix, because there are so many and such interesting adventures which I must narrate. This makes a certain restraint necessary in the description of these sanguinary encounters. It is enough now to know that the French believed when night came that it was time to desist from their purpose, and they retired, leaving the plain covered with bodies of the dead. It was a good moment to follow them with cavalry; but after a short discussion the generals, I am told, decided not to put themselves in peril in a sally which could only be dangerous.

VII

Night came, and when a part of our troops fell back upon the city, all of the people hastened to the suburb to look at the field of battle from near at hand, and to gladden their imaginations by going over, one by one, the scenes of heroism. The animation, the movement, the clatter of noise in that part of the city were immense. At one side were groups of soldiers singing with feverish joy, on the other bands of merciful people carrying the wounded into their houses. Everywhere was hearty satisfaction, which showed itself in lively dialogues, question, joyous exclamations,—tears and laughter mingling with the rejoicings and enthusiasm.

It was, possibly, about nine o'clock before my battalion broke ranks; because, lacking quarters, we did not permit ourselves to leave the position, although there was no danger.

Augustine and I ran to Del Pilar, where a great crowd was rushing. We entered with difficulty. I was surprised to see how some persons jostled and pushed others in order to approach the chapel of the Virgin del Pilar. The prayers, the entreaties, and the demonstrations of rejoicing, taken all together, did not seem like the prayers of any class of the faithful. The prayers were like talks mingled with tears, groans, the most tender words, and other phrases of intimate and ingenuous affection, such as the Spanish people are wont to use with their saints that are most beloved. They fell upon their knees; they kissed the pavement; they grasped the iron gratings of the chapel; they addressed the holy image, calling it by names the most familiar and the most pathetic of the language. Those who could not—because of the crowd of people—come near her were talking to her from afar off, waving their arms wildly about. There were no sacristans to stop these wild ways and seemingly irreverent noises, because they were themselves children of this overflowing delirious devotion. The solemn silence of sacred places was not observed. All there were as if in their own house, as if the house of their cherished Virgin, their mother, their beloved, the queen of Saragossans, were also the house of her children, her servants and subjects.

Astonished at such fervor which the familiarity made more interesting, I fought my way to the grating, and saw the celebrated image. Who has not seen her, who does not know her, at least by the innumerable sculptures and portraits which have reproduced her endlessly from one end of the peninsula to the other?

She was at the left of the little altar which is in the depth of the chapel in a niche adorned with oriental luxury, a little statue, then as now. A great profusion of wax candles illuminated her, and precious stones covered her clothing and crown, darting dazzling reflections. Gold and diamonds gleamed in the circlet about her face, in the votive bracelets hung upon her breast, and in the rings on her hands. A living creature would have given way under so great a weight of treasure. Her garments, falling without folds, stretched straight from head to feet, and left visible only her hands. The child Jesus, sustained on her left side, revealed a bit of his brown little face between the brocade and the jewels. The face of the Virgin, burnished by time, is also brown. A gentle serenity possesses her, symbol of her eternal blessedness. She looks outward, her sweet gaze scanning constantly the devoted concourse. There shines in her eyes a ray of the clearest light, and this artificial gleam seems like the intensity and fixedness of the human gaze. It was difficult when I saw her for the first time to remain indifferent in the midst of that religious demonstration, and not to add a word to the concert of enthusiastic tongues talking with distinct voices to the Señora.

I was watching the statue, when Augustine pressed my arm, saying,—
"Look, there she is!"
"Who, the Virgin? I am looking at her now."
"No, man, Mariquilla! There, in front, close to the column."

I looked, but I saw only a great many people. We immediately quitted our place, looking about for a way to get through the multitude to the other side.

"She is not with Candiola," said Augustine, joyously. "She has come with the servant." And, saying this, he elbowed his way to one side and the other to make a road, punching backs and breasts, stepping on feet, matting down hats, and rumpling clothing. I followed behind him, causing equal destruction right and left. At last we came to the beautiful young girl, and it was really she, as I could see at once with my own eyes.

The enthusiastic passion of my good friend did not deceive me. Mariquilla was worth the trouble of being extravagantly, madly loved. Her pale brunette skin, her deeply black eyes, her perfect nose, her incomparable mouth, and her beautiful low forehead attracted attention to her at once. There was in her face as in her body a certain light and delicate voluptuousness. When she lowered her eyes, it seemed to me as if a sweet and lovely mist surrounded her. She smiled gravely; and when she approached us, her looks revealed timidity. Everything about her showed the reserved and circumspect passion of a woman of character, and she seemed to me little given to talking, lacking in coquetry, and poor in artifices. I afterwards had reason to confirm this, my early judgment. There shone in the face of Mariquilla a heavenly calm, and a certain security in herself. Different from most women, like few among them, that soul would not readily change, except for just and righteous reasons.

Other women of quick sensibility pour themselves out like wax before a small fire; but Mariquilla was made of the best metal, yielding only to a great fire, and when that came she was of necessity like molten metal that burns when it touches.

Besides her beauty, the elegance and even luxury of her dress attracted my attention. Having heard much of the avarice of Candiola, I supposed that he would have reduced his daughter to the utmost extremes of wretchedness in matters of dress. It was not so. As Montoria told me afterwards, the stingiest of the stingy not only permitted his daughter some expenses, but now and then made her some little present which he looked upon as the *ne plus ultra* of mundane splendor.

If Candiola was capable of letting some of his relations die of hunger, to his daughter he gave a phenomenal, a scandalous amount of pocket-money. Although he was a miser, he was a father; he loved his girl very much, finding in his generosity to her perhaps the only pleasure of his arid existence.

Somewhat more must be said in regard to this, but it will appear little by little in the course of the story. And now I must say that my friend had not yet spoken ten words to his adored Mariquilla, when a man approached us abruptly, and after having looked at the two for an instant with flashing eyes, spoke to the young girl, taking her by the arm, and saying, with a show of anger,—

"What is going on here? And you, good Guedita, what brought you to the Pilar at such an hour? Go to the house, go to the house immediately!"

And pushing before him mistress and maid, he carried them both off towards the door and the street, and the three disappeared from our sight.

It was Candiola. I remember him well, and the remembrance makes me tremble with horror. Further on you will know why. Since the brief scene in the church del Pilar, the image of that man has been engraven on my memory, and certainly his face was not one which would let itself be quickly forgotten. Old, bent, of miserable and sickly aspect, crooked and disagreeable, lean of face, with sunken cheeks, Candiola roused antipathy from the first moment. His nose, sharp and hooked like the beak of a bird, his chin, peaked also, the coarse hair of his grizzled eyebrows, the greenish eyes, the forehead furrowed as if by a ruler with deep parallel wrinkles, the cartilaginous ears, the yellowish skin, the metallic quality of the voice, the slovenly clothes, the insulting grimaces,—all his personality from head to foot, from his bag wig to the sole of his coarse shoe, produced at sight an unconquerable repulsion. It can readily be understood that he had not a single friend.

Candiola had no beard; his face, according to the fashion, was quite clean shaven, although the razor did not enter the field more than once a week. If Don Jeronimo had had a beard, it would have made him seem very much like a certain Venetian shop-keeper whom I afterwards came to know very well, travelling in the great world of books, and in whom I find certain traits of physiognomy that recalled the man who had so brusquely presented himself to us in the temple del Pilar.

"Did you see that miserable and ridiculous old man?" Augustine asked me when we were alone, looking towards the door where the three people had disappeared.

"He evidently doesn't like his daughter to have admirers."

"But I am sure that he did not see me talking with her. He has suspicions, nothing more. If he should pass from suspicion to certitude, Mariquilla and I would be lost. Did you see that look he threw us, the damned miser?—he is black from his soul to his Satanic hide."

"Bad sort of father-in-law to have."

"Bad enough," said Montoria, sadly. "He would be dear in exchange for a spoonful of verdigris! I am sure he will abuse her tonight; but fortunately he is not in the habit of ill-treating her."

"And would not the Señor Candiola be pleased to see her married to the son of Don José de Montoria?" I asked.

"Are you mad? I see you talking to him of that! The wretched miser not only watches his daughter as if she were a bag of gold, and is not disposed to give her to anybody; but he has also an ancient and profound resentment against my father, because he freed some unhappy debtors from his fangs. I tell you, that if he discovers that his daughter loves me, he will keep her locked up in an iron chest in that cellar of his where he keeps his hard cash. I don't know what would happen if my father came to know of it. My flesh creeps just to think of it. The worst nightmare which disturbs my slumbers is that which shows me the moment when señor my father and señora my mother learn of my great love for Mariquilla. A son of Don José de Montoria enamoured of a daughter of Candiola, a young man who is formally destined to be a bishop,—a bishop, Gabriel! I am going to be a bishop, in the minds of my parents!"

Saying this, Augustine dashed his head against the sacred wall on which we were leaning.

"And do you think you will go on loving Mariquilla?"

"Don't ask me that!" he replied with energy. "Did you see her? If you saw her, how can you ask me if I will go on loving her? Her father and mine would rather see me dead than married to her. A bishop, Gabriel, they wish me to be a bishop! Think of being a bishop and loving Mariquilla for all of my life, here and hereafter, think of that and pity me!"

"But God opens unknown ways," I said.

"It is true, and sometimes my faith is boundless. Who knows what tomorrow will bring forth? God and the Virgin shall guide me henceforth."

"Are you devoted to this Virgin?"

"Yes. My mother places candles before the one we have in our house, that I may not fall in battle; and I say to her 'Sovereign Lady, may this offering also serve to remind you that I cannot cease from loving the daughter of Candiola.'"

We were in the nave upon which opened the chapel del Pilar. There is here an aperture in the wall, by which the devout, descending two or three steps, approach to kiss the pedestal which sustains the revered image. Augustine kissed the red marble. I kissed it also; then we left the church to go to our abode.

VIII

The following day, the twenty-second, Palafox said to the messenger who came under a flag of truce from Moncey to propose terms of surrender.

"*I do not know how to surrender. After death, we will talk about that.*"

He followed this with a long and eloquent article which was published in the "Gazette;" but, according to general opinion, neither that document nor any of the proclamations which appeared with the signature of the commanding general were his own composition, but that of his friend, Basilio Boggiero, a man of great judgment, who was often seen in situations of danger, in the company of patriots and military leaders.

It is excusable to say that the army of the defence was very much inspired by the glorious action of the twenty-first. It was necessary to give expression to this ardor, to arrange a sortie, and so in effect it was done; but it happened that all wished to take part in this at the same time, and it was necessary to bury the dead. The sorties, arranged with prudence, were expedient; because the French, extending their lines around the city, were preparing for a regular siege, and had begun upon their outer works.

The district of Saragossa contained many people, which seemed to the common mind a great advantage, but which seemed to the intelligent a great danger, because of the immense destruction of human life which hunger would quickly bring,—hunger, that terrible general who is always the conqueror of overcrowded besieged cities. Because of this excess of people, the sorties were timely.

Renovales made one on the twenty-fourth with the troops of the fortress of San José, and cut down an olive grove which hid the works of the enemy.

Don John O'Neill made a sally from the suburb on the twenty-fifth with the volunteers of Aragon and Huesca, taking the chance of advantage from the enemy's lack of preparation, and killing many of the enemy's men.

On the thirty-first was made the most telling sally of all, striking in two distinct places and with considerable forces. During the early part of the day we had divided to perfection the works of the first French parallel, thrown up about three hundred and twenty yards from the walls. They were working actively, not resting by night, and we could see that they had signals of colored lanterns along the whole line. From time to time we discharged our guns, but we caused very little destruction. If troops were especially needed for a reconnoissance, they were despatched in less than no time.

The morning of the thirty-first arrived, and my battalion was charged to be ready to march upon orders from Renovales to attack the enemy in their centre, from the Torrero to the Muela road, while General Butron did the same by the Bernardona, that is to say, by the French left, sallying with sufficient forces of infantry and cavalry by the gates of Sancho and Portillo.

In order to distract the attention of the French, the general commanded that a battalion should be divided into skirmishing parties by the Tenerias, calling the attention of the enemy in that direction. In the mean time, with some of the soldiers of Olivenza and part of those of Valencia, we advanced by the Madrid road straight towards the French lines. The skirmishing parties were on both sides of the road when the enemy became aware of our presence, and now we were quicker than deer in doing up the first troop of French infantry which came to meet us. Behind a half-ruined country house some fortifications had been thrown up, and they began firing with good aim and much slaughter. For an instant we remained undecided, then some twenty men of us flanked the country house, while the rest followed the high road, pursuing the fugitives; but Renovales dashed forward and led us on, cutting down and bayoneting those who were defending the house. At the moment when we set foot within the first defence I noticed that my rank was thinned out. I saw some of my companions fall, breathing their last sighs. I looked to my right, fearing not to find my beloved friend among the living; but God had preserved him. Montoria and I were unharmed.

We could not spend much time in communicating to each other the satisfaction that we felt at finding ourselves still alive, because Renovales gave orders to follow on, in the direction of the line of intrenchments that the French were raising. We abandoned the high road and made a deflection, turning to the right with the intention of joining the volunteers of Huesca, who were attacking by the Muela road.

It may be understood by what I have related that the French did not expect that sortie, and that, taken completely unawares, they were holding there, besides the scanty force that kept the works, the engineers occupied in digging the trenches of the first parallel. We attacked them vigorously, turning upon them a murderous fire, improving the minutes well before the dreaded reinforcements should arrive. We took prisoners those whom we met without arms; we shot those who had them. We took the picks and spades,—all this with unequalled energy, animating one another with fiery words, exalted above all by the thought that they were watching us from the city.

In this attack we were fortunate, for while we were destroying those at work on the intrenchments, the troops who had made the sortie on the left were carrying on a successful struggle with the detachments which the enemy had in the Bernardona. While the volunteers of Huesca, the grenadiers of Palafox, and the Walloon guards defeated the French infantry, the squadron of Numancia and Olivenza cavalry cautiously emerged through the Puerta de Sancho, and making a wide détour occupied the Alagon road on one side, and the Muela on the other, exactly when the French drew back from the left to the centre, in need of greater auxiliary forces. Finding themselves in their element, our fiery cavalry sprang forward, destroying whatever was encountered in the way, and then the disgraced infantry, who were fleeing towards Torrero, fell, and were trampled underfoot.

In their dispersion, many fell beneath our bayonets, and if their desire to flee from the horses was great, great also was our anxiety to receive them in manner worthy of our swords. Some ran, throwing themselves into the trenches, not being able to jump over them; others surrendered at discretion, throwing down their arms; some defended themselves with heroism, permitting themselves to be slain before giving up; and at the last there failed not a few who, shutting themselves up in the brick kiln filled up with boughs and timber, set fire to it, preferring to die by roasting, rather than be taken prisoners.

All this which I have related in detail passed in a very short time, while the French commander, having seen enough in this hour, detached sufficient forces to hold back and punish our too audacious expedition. They beat the drum in Monte Torrero, and we saw a great force of cavalry coming against us; but we who were with Renovales had had our desire, the same as those with Butron, and were not obliged to wait for those horsemen who arrived at the end of the action; so we retired, giving them from a distance a "Good-day" of the most sharp and pointed phrases in our vocabulary. We still had time to make useless some pieces placed ready for employment on the following day.

We took a multitude of tools and spades, and we destroyed in all haste whatever we could of their intrenchments without losing hold upon the dozens of prisoners, of which we had taken up a collection.

Juan Pirli, one of our companions in the battalion, was carrying home to Saragossa the steel helmet of an engineer for the admiration of the public, and also a frying-pan in which were still the remnants of a breakfast begun in camp before Saragossa and ended in the other world.

We had had nine killed and eight wounded in our battalion. When Augustine rejoined me near the Carmen gate, I noticed that one of his hands was stained with blood.

"Are you wounded?" I asked, examining the hand. "It is nothing more than a scratch."

"It is a scratch," he replied; "but it was not made by ball, lance, nor sabre, but by teeth, because when I gripped that Frenchman who lifted up his pick to brain me, the damned fellow set his teeth into my hand like a dog at bay."

When we entered the city, some by the Puerta del Carmen, some by the Portillo, all the pieces of the redoubts and forts of Mediodia poured a fire against the columns which were coming after us. The two sorties combined had done damage enough to the French. In addition to losing many men, a small part of their intrenchments had been made useless to them, and we had possessed ourselves of a considerable number of their tools. Besides this, the official engineers that Butron took with him on that daring venture had had time to examine the works of the besiegers, and measure them, and could give descriptions of them to the commanding general.

The rampart wall was invaded by the people. They had heard within the city the shooting of the skirmishes, and men and women, old people and children had run out to see what glorious action was bulletined on the plaza. We were received with exclamations of rejoicing, and from San José all the way to the Trinitarios, the long line of men and women, looking towards the battlefield, climbed upon the walls, and clapping their hands at our arrival, waving their handkerchiefs, presented a magnificent sight. After the cannon sounded, the redoubts together poured a fire upon the field that we had just abandoned, and their voices seemed a triumphal salvo, as it mingled with the huzzas and shouts of joy.

In the surrounding houses, the windows and balconies were filled with women, and the interest or curiosity of some of those in the streets was such that they went into the hurrying crowd in numbers, and up to the cannons, to congratulate the brave souls and soothe with kind words their nerves, high strung with the noise of artillery, which is unlike anything else in the world. It was necessary to command the multitude to depart from the fortress at the Portillo. The crowd in the Santa Engracia gave that place the aspect of a theatre, of a public festival. The fire of the cannon ceased at last, having no more need to protect our retreat, and the Castle Aljaferia alone sent an occasional shot against the works of the enemy.

In reward for our action on that day it was granted us on the next to wear a red ribbon on the breast by way of decoration; in justice to the hazards of that sortie, Father Boggiero told us, among other things uttered by the mouth of our general, "Yesterday you marked the last day of the year with an action worthy of yourselves. At the sound of the bugle your swords leaped from their scabbards and struck to the ground haughty heads humbled by your valor and patriotism. Numantia! Olivenza! I have now seen that your light horse will know how to preserve the honor of this army and the enthusiasm of these sacred walls! Wear these blood-stained swords that are the sign of your glory and the protection of your country."

IX

From that day, as memorable in the second siege as Eras in the first siege, began the great work in whose frenzy and exaltation both besiegers and besieged lived for the next month and a half. The sorties made during the first days of January were not of much importance. The French, having finished their first parallel, advanced in a zig-zag towards opening their second, and worked on it with so much activity that very soon we saw our two best positions in the Mediodia, San José and the redoubt del Pilar, threatened by siege batteries, everyone with a dozen cannon. I must be excused for saying that we did not cease to make trouble for them, keeping up an incessant fire, and surprising them with sudden skirmishes, but this was all. Junot, who now took the place of Moncey, carried forward the work with great diligence.

Our battalion remained in the redoubt raised at the outer end of the Huerva bridge. The radius of our fire was considerable, crossing that of San José. The batteries of Los Martires, of the Botanical Garden, and of the Torre del Pino further within the city were less important than the two bodies holding the advanced positions, and served as auxiliaries.

Numbers of Saragossan volunteers were with us in the garrison, some of the soldiers of the guard, and various armed peasants who rather elected themselves to our corps than came into it by our choice. Eight cannons held the redoubt. Don Domingo Larripa was our leader. The artillery was commanded by Don Francisco Betbezé. As chief of engineers, we had the great Simono, high official of that distinguished service, and a man of such quality that he was able to quote himself as a model of all good military men, both in valor and in knowledge.

The redoubt was a work sufficiently strong for the purpose, and not lacking in any material requisite for defending itself. Over the entrance gate at the extremity of the bridge its constructors had placed a tablet with this inscription,—

The indestructible redoubt of our Lady of the Pillar. Saragossans! Die for the Virgin del Pilar or conquer!

We had our lodging within the redoubt, and though the place was not altogether bad, we went on poorly enough. The rations were provided by a committee recommended by the military administration; but this committee, to our sorrow, was not able to attend to us properly. By good fortune, and to the honor of that generous people, food was sent to us from the neighboring houses, the best of their provisions; and we were frequently visited by the charitable women, who since the battle of the thirty-first had taken it upon themselves to nurse and care for our poor wounded heroes.

I have not spoken of Pirli. Pirli was a boy from outside the city, a rustic about twenty years of age, and in such jolly condition that the most dangerous situations only moved him to a nervous and feverish joy. I never saw him sad. He met the French singing; and when the bullets whistled past his head, he capered about, making a thousand grotesque gestures, throwing up his hands and fairly dancing. When the fire was thick as hail, he called the bullets "hailstones." He called the cannon-balls "hot cakes;" he called the hand-grenades, "señoras;" and the powder he called "black flour," using other queer terms which I do not now remember. Pirli, although not at all a serious person, was a charming companion.

I do not know whether I have spoken of Tio Garces. He was a man of forty-five years, a native of Garrapinillos, very brave, bronzed, sawed-off looking, with limbs of steel; there was no one so active or so imperturbable under fire. He was somewhat talkative, and was a little inclined to be imprudent in his conversation, but with a certain wit in his garrulity. He had a small estate in the environs, and a very modest house; but he had levelled it with his own hands, and cut down his pear-trees, so that the enemy could not use them. I heard of a thousand of his valorous deeds in the first siege, and he wore a decoration on his right sleeve, the embroidered shield of distinction of the sixteenth of August. He dressed badly, and went almost half-naked, not because he lacked clothing, but because he had not time to put it on. He and others like him were without doubt those who inspired the celebrated phrase of which I have already made mention: "Their bodies were clothed only in glory." He slept without shelter, and ate less than an anchorite; indeed with two pieces of bread and a couple of bites of dried beef hard as hide, he had rations for the day.

He was a man somewhat given to meditation. When he saw the works of the second parallel, he said, looking at the French: "Thanks be to God, they are drawing near. Cuerno! Cuerno! these people are a trial to one's patience!"

"What a hurry you are in, uncle Garces," we said to him.

"I should say so. I want to plant my trees again before winter is over. And next month I want to build my little house again."

Truly Tio Garces should have worn a tablet on his brow like that on the bridge, reading, "An unconquerable man."

But who comes there, advancing slowly along the valley of the Huerva, leaning upon a thick stick and followed by a lively little dog which barked at all the passersby, merely for mischief, without any intention of biting? It is the friar, Father Mateo del Busto, reader and qualifier of the order of Saint Francis de Paula, chaplain of the second company of Saragossa volunteers, an important man, who, in spite of his age, was seen during the first siege in all places of danger, succoring the wounded, helping the dying, carrying ammunition to the well, and cheering all by his gentle accents. Entering the redoubt, he showed us a large and heavy basket which he had toiled to bring here, and in which was food better than that of our ordinary table.

"These cakes," said he, placing it on the ground, and taking out one by one things which he named as he produced them, "have been given me in the house of that most excellent lady, the Countess de Bureta, and this in the house of Don Pedro Ric. Here you have a couple of slices of ham from my convent, which was for Father Loshollos, whose stomach is not strong, but he renounced this luxury and gave it to me to take to you. See, how does this bottle of wine look to you? How much would those foreign fellows yonder give for it?"

We all looked towards the plain. The little dog, leaping impudently upon the wall, began to bark at the French lines.

"I have also brought you a couple of pounds of dried fruit which has been kept in the dispensary at our house. We were going to preserve them in liquor, but you taste them first of anyone, my brave boys. I have not forgotten thee at all, my beloved Pirli," he continued, turning to the boy of that name; "and as you are half naked, and without a cloak, I have brought you a magnificent covering. Do you see this bundle? Well, here is an old gown that I have kept to give to a poor man. Now, I present it to you as a covering for your body. It is unsuitable clothing for a soldier; but if the gown does not make the monk, neither does the uniform make the soldier. Put it on, and you will be very comfortable in it."

The friar gave our friend his parcel, and Pirli put on the garment, laughing and dancing about; and as he was still carrying on his head the engineer's helmet which he had taken in the enemy's camp on the thirty-first, he presented a figure stranger than can readily be imagined.

A little later, several women also arrived with baskets of provisions. The arrival of femininity swiftly transformed the aspect of the redoubt. I do not know from where they produced a guitar; it is certain that they produced one from somewhere. One of those present graciously began to play the measures of that incomparable, divine, immortal dance, the *jota*, and in a moment a great revelry of dancing was going on.

Pirli, whose grotesque figure began in a French engineer and ended in a Spanish friar, was the most carried away of any of the dancers, and could not keep tune with his partner, a most graceful girl in Spanish highland dress, who was called Manuela, whom I noticed the first moment that I saw her. She was about twenty-two years of age, and was slender, of a pure pale complexion. The excitement of the dance quickly flushed her cheeks, and by degrees her movements grew more lively, unmindful of fatigue. With her eyes half shut, her cheeks rosy, her arms moving to the music of the sweet strains, she shook her skirts with lively grace; taking her steps lightly, and presenting to us now her brow, and now her shoulders, Manuela held us enchanted.

The ardor of the dancing crowd, the lively music, and the enthusiasm of the rest of the dancers augmented her own, until at last, breathless with fatigue, she dropped her arms and fell to earth like a stone or a pomegranate.

Pirli stood over her, and surrounded her by a sort of corral formed of himself and the basket of provisions.

"Let us see what you have brought us, Manuelilla," said Pirli. "If twere not for thee and Father Busto, we should die of hunger. And if it were not for this little dance with which we get rid of the bad taste of the 'hot cakes' and the 'señoras,' what would become of us poor soldiers?"

"I bring you whatever there is," replied Manuela, opening the basket of provisions. "Wait a little. If the siege lasts, you will be eating bricks."

"We shall have bullets mixed with black flour," said Pirli. "Manuelilla, have you got over being afraid of the bullets yet?" Saying this, he seized his gun, and shot it off into the air. The girl gave a sharp scream, and, startled, sprang up as if to escape.

"It is nothing, daughter," said the friar; "brave women are not afraid of powder. On the contrary, they should take as much pleasure in it as in the sound of castanets and mandolins."

"When I hear a ball," said Manuela, coming slowly and timidly back, "there is not a drop of blood left in my veins."

At this moment the French, wishing to try the artillery of their second parallel, shot off a cannon, and the ball came against the wall of the redoubt, shattering the loose bricks into a thousand pieces.

Everybody rose to look at the enemy. The highland girl cried out in terror; and Tio Garces was moved to scream through a loop-hole at the French, heaping upon them the most insolent words, accompanied by many exclamations. The little dog, running from one end of the place to the other, barked furiously.

"Manuela, let us dance another jota to the sound of this music, and viva the Virgin del Pilar," cried Pirli, jumping about like one out of his senses.

Manuela rose on tiptoe, impelled by curiosity, and slowly stretched up her head to look at the camp from the wall. Then, casting her glance over the level plain, she seemed to dissipate, little by little, the terrors of her fainting spirit; and at last we saw her surveying the enemy's lines with a certain serenity, and even with a little complacency.

"One, two, three cannon!" she said, counting the fiery mouths which were discernible at that distance. "Come, little boys, don't be afraid. This is nothing to you!"

Over near San José was heard the booming of guns, and on our redoubt sounded the drum calling to arms. From the neighboring stronghold had sallied forth a little column that exchanged distant shots with the French workmen. Some of these, running to their left, placed themselves within arm's length of our fire. We all ran to the walls, disposed to send them a few hailstones, and without waiting orders, some of us discharged our guns with loud huzzas.

All the women fled by the bridge towards the city except Manuela. Did fear prevent her from moving? No. Her fear was great; she trembled, and her teeth chattered; her face grew pale; but an irresistible curiosity kept her in the redoubt. She fastened her gaze on the sharp-shooters, and on the cannon that was about to be discharged.

"Manuela, are you not going?" said Augustine. "Doesn't it frighten you to look at all that?"

The girl, with her attention fixed on the spectacle, terrified, trembling, with white lips and palpitating bosom, neither moved nor spoke.

"Manuelilla," said Pirli, running up to her, "take my gun and shoot it off."

Contrary to what we expected, Manuelilla did not show any sign of terror.

"Take it, please," cried Pirli, making her take the gun. "Put your thumb here. Aim over yonder. Fire! Viva the second artillery woman! Viva Manuela Sancho and the Virgin del Pilar!"

The girl took the gun, and, to judge by her actions, and the stupor of her looks, it seemed as if she did not know what she was doing. But, raising the gun with a trembling hand, she aimed at the field, pulled the trigger, and fired.

A thousand fiery shouts of applause greeted the discharge, and the girl left the gun. She was radiant with satisfaction, and her delight deepened the roses in her cheeks.

"Do you see? You have already lost your fear?" said the priest. "There is nothing more in these things than taking hold of them. All the Saragossan women ought to do the same, and then Augustina Casta Alvarez would not be the one glorious exception to her sex."

"Bring another gun," exclaimed the girl; "I wish to fire again."

"They have already marched off, if you please! Aren't you a good one!" said Pirli, preparing to make an onslaught on the provision basket. "Tomorrow, if you like, you shall be invited for a few 'hot cakes.' Well, let us make ourselves comfortable and eat."

The friar, calling his little dog, said to him: "That is enough, my son; don't bark so, nor take it so much to heart that you make yourself hoarse. Keep your boldness until tomorrow. Today, we have no wish to employ it, for if I am not mistaken they are hurrying away to get behind their works."

In fact the skirmish at San José had concluded, and for the moment the French were not in sight. A short time afterwards the sound of the guitar was renewed, and the women returning, the sweet undulations of the jota began again with Manuela Sancho and the great Pirli in the first line.

X

W hen I woke at daybreak the next morning I saw Montoria, who was passing by the wall.

"I believe that the bombardment is going to begin," he said to me; "there is a great activity in the enemy's lines."

"They will try to demolish this redoubt," I said, getting up lazily. "How gloomy the sky is, Augustine! Day dawns very sadly."

"I believe they will attack on all sides at once, until they have made their second parallel. Do you know that Napoleon in Paris, knowing the resistance shown by this city in the first siege, was furious with Lefebre Desnouettes because he assaulted the plaza by the Portillo and the Castle Aljaferia. He called for a plan of Saragossa, and they gave it to him, and he showed that the city should be attacked by Santa Engracia."

"By this place? A black day is indeed dawning for us if the orders of Napoleon are carried out. Tell me, have we anything to eat here?"

"I did not show it to you before because I wished to surprise you," he said to me, showing me a basket which served as the tomb of two cold roast fowls, some comfits and fine preserves.

"You brought these last night? Indeed! How could you go out of the redoubt?"

"I got leave from the general for an hour, and Mariquilla prepared this feast. If Candiola knows that two of the hens from his chicken-corral have been killed and roasted to regale two of the defenders of the city, the devil will be to pay. Let us eat then, Señor Araceli, while we await the bombardment. Here it comes. One bomb! Another, another!"

The right batteries opened fire upon San José and the Pilar, and what a fire! The whole army seemed behind the cannon. Away with breakfasts, away with the morning meal, away with tidbits!—the men of Aragon will have no food but glory!

The unconquerable fortress answered the insolent besieger with a tremendous cannonade, and soon the great soul of our fatherland moved within us. The balls, beating upon the brick walls and the earthworks, beat down the redoubt as if it were a toy pelted with stones by a boy. The grenades, falling among us, burst with a great noise, and the bombs, passing with awful majesty over our heads, went on to fall into the streets and upon the roofs of the houses.

Everybody out! Let there be no idle or cowardly people in the city. The men to the walls, the women to the bloody hospitals, the children and priests to carry ammunition! Let no notice be taken of these dreadful and burning things which bore through roofs, penetrate dwelling-houses, open gates, pierce floors, descend to the cellars, and, bursting, scatter the flames of hell upon the tranquil hearth, surprising with death the aged invalid on his couch and the child in his cradle. Nothing of this sort matters. Everybody out into the street, and thus save honor though the city perish, and the churches and convents and hospitals and the estates which are but earthly things! The Saragossans, despising material good as they despised life, lived by their spirits in the infinite spaces of the ideal.

In the first moments the Captain-General and many other distinguished personages visited us,—such as Don Mariano Cereso the priest of Sas, General O'Neill, San Genis, and Don Pedro Ric. There was also there the brave and generous Don José Montoria, who embraced his son, saying to him: "Today is the day to conquer or to die. We will meet each other in heaven."

Behind Montoria, Don Roque presented himself; he had become a brave fellow, and as he had been employed in the sanitary service, he began to show a feverish activity before there were any wounded, and displayed to us a good sized pile of lint. Various friars mingled among the combatants during the early firing, encouraging us with mystic fervor.

At the same time, and with equal fury, the French attacked the redoubt del Pilar and the fortress of San José. The latter, although more formidable in aspect, had less power of resistance, perhaps because it presented a broader target for the enemy's fires. But Renovales was there with the Huesca and the Valencia volunteers, the Walloon guards, and various members of the militia of Soria. The great lack of the fortress was in its having been constructed for the protection of a vast edifice, which the enemy's artillery converted into ruins in a little while; pieces of the thick wall were forced in from time to time, and many of its defenders were crushed. We were better off. Over our heads we had only the heavens, and if no roof guarded us from the bombs, neither did masses of masonry fall upon us. They demolished the wall by the front and sides, and it was a pity to see how that fragile mass fell away little by little, placing us in an exposed position. Nevertheless, after four hours of incessant fire by powerful artillery, they were not able to open a breach.

Thus passed the day of the tenth with no advantage for the besiegers from us, even if they had succeeded in getting near San José and opening a wide breach, which, together with the ruined condition of the building, forced the unhappy necessity of its surrender. Yet, in the mean time, the fortress had not been reduced to powder, and, dead or alive, its defenders had hope. Fresh troops were sent there, because the battalions working there since morning were decimated; and when night fell, after the opening of the breach and the fruitless attempt at an assault, yet Renovales held the blood-soaked ruins, among the heaps of corpses, with only the third part of his artillery.

When night interrupted the firing, there had been great carnage on both sides. We ourselves had lost many by death, and more were wounded. The wounded were carried at the time into the city by the friars and the women; but the dead still gave their last service with their cold bodies, for they were stoically thrown into the open breach, which was being stopped up with sacks of wool and earth.

During the night we did not rest for one single moment, and the dawn of the eleventh found us inspired by the same frenzy, our pieces already pointed against the enemy's intrenchments, and already piercing with musket shots those who were coming to flank us, without hindering for a moment the work of stopping up the breach, which was widening, hour by hour its dreadful spaces. So we endured all the morning until the moment when they began the assault upon San José, now converted into a heap of ruins, and with most of its garrison dead. Centring the forces upon these two points, they fell upon the convent, and directed an audacious movement upon us; and it was with the object of making our breach practicable that they advanced by the Torrero road with two cannons protected by a column of infantry.

At that moment we thought ourselves lost. The feeble walls trembled, and the bricks were shattered into thousands of pieces. We ran up to the breach, which was widening every instant, where they poured upon us a horrible fire. Seeing that the redoubt was being shattered to pieces, they took courage to come to the very borders of the fosse itself. It was madness to try to fill that terrible space, and to show an uncovered place was to offer victims without number to the fury of the enemy. We protected ourselves as well as we could with sacks of wool and shovels of earth, and many stood as if petrified on the spot. The firing of the cannon ceased because it seemed necessary; there was a moment of indefinable panic; the guns fell from our hands; we saw ourselves routed, destroyed, annihilated by that rain of fire that seemed to fill the air. We forgot honor, the fatherland, the glory of death, the Virgin del Pilar, whose name adorned the bridge and the "unconquerable" defences. The most dreadful confusion reigned in our ranks. Descending suddenly from the high moral level of our souls, all those who had not fallen desired life of one accord, and, leaping over the wounded and trampling the dead under foot, we fled towards the bridge, abandoning that horrible sepulchre before it should shut us in, entombing us all.

On the bridge we were swallowed up by insupportable terror and disorder. There is nothing more frenzied than a coward. His abject meannesses are as great as the sublimities of his valor.

Our leaders kept crying out to us, "Back, you rabble! The redoubt del Pilar has not surrendered!" striking our swords with their sabres. We turned back on the bridge, unable to go further, as reinforcements came, and we stumbled over one another, the fury of our fear mingling with the impetus of their bravery.

"Back, cowards!" cried our officers, striking us in the faces, "and die in the breach!"

The redoubt was vacated. None but the dead and the wounded were there. Suddenly we saw advance amid the dense smoke and the blackness of powder, leaping over the lifeless bodies and the heaps of earth and the ruins, and the guns we had thrown down, and the shattered works, a figure, dauntless, pale, splendid, of tragic calmness. It was a woman who had made her way forward and, penetrating the abandoned place, was marching like a queen towards the horrible breach. Pirli, who was lying on the ground, wounded in the leg, exclaimed in affright,

"Manuela Sancho, where are you going?"

All this passed in much less time than I take to tell it. After Manuela Sancho, first one, then another, then many hurried, then all, urged on by the leaders whose sabre-cuts had prodded us to the point of duty. This portentous transformation came about by the impulse of every man's heart obeying sentiments which all feel without anyone's knowing whence the mysterious force emanates. I do not know why we were cowards, nor why we were brave a few moments later. What I do know is that, moved by an extraordinary power, immense and superhuman, we hurled ourselves into the breach behind the heroic woman, at the point where the French were attempting the assault with ladders. Without in the least knowing how to explain it, we felt our strength increased a hundred-fold, and crushed them back, hurling into the ditch those men of cotton who a little while ago had seemed to us men of steel. With shots and sabre-cuts, with shells, with shovels full of earth, by blows, and bayonet-thrusts, we fought. Many of our number died to defend others with their dead bodies. We defended the breach, indeed, and the French were obliged to retire, leaving many dead and wounded at the bottom of the wall. The cannons again began firing, and the unconquerable redoubt did not fall on the eleventh into the hands of the French.

When the tempest of fire was calmed, we did not know ourselves. We were transfigured, and something new and unknown palpitated in the depths of our souls, giving us an unheard-of fierceness. The following day Palafox said, with much eloquence: "Nor balls, nor bombs, nor shells shall make our faces change color, nor can all France accomplish that!"

XI

The fortress of San José had surrendered, or rather the French had entered it when their artillery had reduced it to powder, and all of its defenders had fallen, one by one, to lie among its fragments. The Imperial soldiers, on entering, found heaps of bodies and stones matted together with blood. They could not establish themselves there because they were flanked by the batteries of Los Martires and the Botanical Garden, so they continued operations by mining, in order to possess themselves of those two points. The fortifications which we held were so nearly destroyed that a general agreement was urgent, and the terrible orders, calling upon all the inhabitants of Saragossa to work in renewing them. The proclamation said that every citizen should carry a gun in one hand and spade in the other.

The twelfth and thirteenth were without rest, the fire diminishing a little because the besiegers, warned by sad experience, did not wish to risk anymore hand-to-hand conflicts. Understanding that theirs was a work of patience and skill, rather than of boldness and bravery, they opened slowly, and with security, roads and mines which should lead to the possession of the redoubt without loss of men. It was almost necessary to build our walls anew, or rather to substitute sacks of earth for them, an operation in which many friars, canons, civil officials, children, and women were occupied. The artillery was almost useless, the fosse about filled up, and it was necessary to continue the defence at short range. And so we wore through the thirteenth, protecting the works as we rebuilt them, suffering much, and seeing ourselves constantly decreasing in numbers, although new men came to take the places of the many that we lost. On the fourteenth the enemy's artillery tried to demolish our new walls, opening breaches for us on the front and at the sides. They did not dare to try a new assault, contenting themselves with opening a mine in such a direction that we could not in anyway cover it with our fire, nor with that of any battery near by.

Our valorous tantalizing earthworks would soon be covered by the fires of the French batteries, which were hurling to the four winds the earth of which they were formed. In this situation, surrender was inevitable sooner or later. Indeed we were at the mercy of the French arms as a ship at the mercy of the waves of the ocean. Flanked by roads and zig-zags, through which a strong and clever enemy might walk without danger, protected by all the resources of science, our bulwarks of defence were like one man surrounded by an army. We had no serviceable cannons, nor could we bring other new ones, because the walls would not have borne them. Our only resource was to keep watch of the redoubt in order to fly from it at the moment when the French should enter and destroy the bridge, in order to prevent them from following us. This was done; and on the night of the fourteenth they worked without rest on the mine, and we placed small mines at the bridge, hoping that the following day the enemy would try to mount by that wall. But this did not happen. Not daring to make another assault without all the precautions and security possible, they continued their work of digging very nearly up to our fosse. In this labor our indefatigable fusileers did them little damage. We were desperate, but without power to do anything. Our desperation was of no avail; it was a useless force, like the rage of a lunatic in his cage.

We drew out the nails from the tablet which proclaimed ours to be the unconquerable redoubt, in order to take away with us that witness of our justifiable arrogance. At nightfall the fortification was abandoned, only forty remaining to keep it until the end, and shoot all they could, as our captain said that no chance might be lost to lose the enemy a couple of men. From the Torre del Pino we saw the retreat of the forty at about eight o'clock in the evening, after they had met the invaders with bayonet-thrusts; they retreated fighting bravely.

The interior mine of the redoubt had had little effect, but the small mines of the bridge acquitted themselves so well that the passage was destroyed and the redoubt isolated from the other bank of the Huerva. Gaining this position and San José, the French would have enough protection to open their third parallel and to demolish at their leisure the whole circuit of the city. We were saddened and just a little discouraged; but of what importance is a little depression when on the day following one has a diversion and a feast? After being madly discouraged, a little jollity does not come amiss, especially when time is wanting to bury the dead; nor was there room in the houses for the many who were wounded. It is true that there were hands for all that had to be done, thanks be to God.

The reason for the general rejoicing was that glorious rumors were in circulation of Spanish armies that were coming to succor us, on the heels of the French, in many parts of the Peninsula. The people crowded into the Plaza de la Seo, and in front of the Magdalene arch, waiting until the

BENITO PÉREZ GALDÓS

"Gazette" should appear; and at last it came out, cheering everybody's spirits, and making all hearts palpitate with hope. I do not know if such rumors had really reached Saragossa, or if they originated in the wits of the chief editor, Don Ignacio Assor. It is certain that they told us in print that Reading was coming to succor us with an army of sixty thousand men, that the Marquis of Lazan, after routing the mob in the north of Catalonia, had entered France, spreading terror in every direction, and that also the Duke del Infantado was coming to our aid, who with Blake and la Romana had routed Napoleon, slaying twenty thousand men, including Berthier, Ney, and Savary, and that at Cadiz had arrived several millions in hard cash sent by the English for the expense of war. What did it all mean? Could the "Gazette" explain all this?

In spite of the size of these mouthfuls of rumor, we swallowed them; and there were demonstrations of joy, ringing of church bells, running through the streets, and singing the music of the jota, with many other patriotic excesses, which at least had the advantage of affording us a little of that cooling off of our mental temperature which was necessary. Do not believe that in consideration of our joy the rain of bombs had ceased! Very far from that! They seemed to jeer at the news of our "Gazette," as they repeated their dose. Feeling a lively desire to laugh at them to their faces, we went to the walls. The musicians of the regiments played in a tantalizing fashion, and we all sang in an immense chorus the famous words,—

> *"The Virgin del Pilar says*
> *She wouldn't like to be a Frenchwoman!"*

They were in a mood for answering jests, and in less than two hours a greater number of projectiles were sent into the city than during all the rest of the day. There was now no longer a secure refuge; there was not a hand's breadth of ground or of roof free from that Satanic fire. Families fled from their homes, or took refuge in the cellars. The wounded, who were numerous in the principal houses, were carried to the churches, seeking shelter in their strong vaults. Others went dragging themselves along. Some more active ones carried their bedding upon their shoulders. Most of them were accommodated in the Pilar; and after the floor was all filled, they were stretched out upon the altars and crowded into the chapels. In spite of their misfortunes, they were consoled by looking at the Virgin, who seemed to say to them unceasingly with her brilliant eyes that she would not care to be a Frenchwoman!

XII

My battalion did not take part in the sorties of the days of the twenty-second and twenty-fourth, nor in the defence of the Molino and the positions situated at the back of San José, made glorious by the destruction of many of our troops, where they had made the French feel the strength of their hand. It was not because they had not been careful to take precautions, for indeed from the mouth of Huerva to the Carmen gate they stationed fifty cannon, most of them of heavy calibre, directing them with great skill against our weakest points. In spite of all this, we laughed, or pretended to laugh, at them, as in the vain-glorious response of Palafox to Marshal Lannes (who had placed himself since the twenty-second at the head of the besieging army), in which he said to him, "The conquest of this city will be a great honor to Monsieur the Marshal if he gains it in open fight, and not with bombs and grenades, which only terrify cowards."

Of course, after a few days had passed, it was known that the hoped-for forces and the powerful armies that were coming to free us were all mists of our imaginations, and especially of that of the journalist who invented them. There were no such armies of any sort roaming about to help us.

I understood very soon that all that which was published in the "Gazette" of the sixteenth was a canard, and so I said to Don José de Montoria and his wife, who in their optimism attributed my incredulity to a lack of public spirit. I had gone with Augustine and others of my friends to the Montoria house to help them at a task that was wearying them greatly. A part of their roof had been destroyed by the bombs, and this threatened the walls with destruction also. They were trying to remedy this with all possible speed. The eldest son of Montoria, wounded in battle at the Molino, had been lodged with his wife and son in the cellar of a house close by, and Doña Leocadia gave her hands and feet no rest, going and coming between the two houses, carrying things which were necessary.

"I can't let anything be done by others," she said to me; "that is my nature. Although I have servants, I am not content unless I do everything myself. How has my son Augustine borne himself?"

"Like what he is, señora, a brave boy," I answered; "and his talent for war is so great that I should not be surprised to see him a general in a couple of years."

"A general!" she exclaimed in surprise. "My son is going to chant masses as soon as the siege is ended. Indeed you know we have educated him for that. God and the Virgin del Pilar bring him in safety through battle, that the rest of his days may go on in appointed ways! The fathers at the Seminary have assured me that I shall see my son with his mitre on his head and his crosier in his hand."

"It will be so, señora, I do not doubt it. But seeing how he manages arms, I cannot bring myself to the thought that with the same hand with which he pulls the trigger, he will also scatter benedictions."

"It is true, Señor de Araceli; and I have always said that the trigger is not becoming to churchmen. But you see how it is. Here we have great warriors,—Don Santiago Sas, Don Manuel Lasartesa; the incumbent of San Pablo, Don Antonio La Casa; the parish priest of San Miguel, Don José Martinez; and also Don Vicente Casanova, who is famous as the first theologian of Saragossa. Indeed they all fight, my son also, though I suppose he will be eager to return to the Seminary and plunge into his studies. Would you believe it? Lately he was studying books so large that they weighed two quintals. God's blessing be on the boy! I am quite foolish over him when he recites some grand things all in Latin. I suppose they are all about our Lord, and his love for his church, because there is a great deal about *amorem* and *formosa* and *pulcherrima*, *inflamavit*, and other words like those."

"Exactly," I replied, imagining that his recitations were from the fourth book of a certain ecclesiastical work called the Æneid, written by a certain Friar Virgil of the order of Predicadores.

"It must be as I say," said Doña Leocadia. "And now, Señor de Araceli, let us see if you can help me move this table."

"With the greatest pleasure, dear lady. I will move it for you myself," I replied, taking charge of it at the moment that Don José de Montoria entered, pouring out "porras" and "cuernos" from his blessed mouth.

"How is this, porra!" he cried; "men occupied in women's business? It is not for moving tables and chairs that a gun has been placed in your hands! And you, wife? How can you distract in this manner a man needed on the other side? You and the children, porra! can you not move the furniture? Are you made of paste or cheese? Look! In the street below is the Countess de Bureta with a bed on her shoulders, and her two maids carrying a wounded soldier on a cot."

"Very well," said Doña Leocadia, "there is no need of making such a noise about it. The men may go. Everybody out into the street, and leave us alone! Away with you, too, Augustine my son, and God preserve you in the midst of this inferno."

"We must carry twenty sacks of flour from the Convent of Trinitarios to the headquarters of supplies," said Montoria. "Come, let us all go."

And when we were in the street, he added, "The numbers of people in Saragossa will soon make half rations necessary. It is true, my friends, that there is much concealed provision, and although it has been ordered that everybody declare what he has, many do not take any notice of the order, and keep what they have to sell at fabulous prices. It's a bad business. If I discover them, and they fall into my hands, I will make them understand that Montoria is president of the junta of supplies."

We had reached the parish church of San Pablo when we were met by a friar, Father Mateo del Busto, who was coming with much fatigue, forcing his feeble steps, and accompanied by another friar whom they called Father Luengo.

"What news do your reverences bring us?" Montoria asked them.

"Don Juan Gallart has twenty pounds of inlaid work which he places at the disposal of the committee."

"And Don Pedro Pizueta, the shop-keeper of the Calle de las Moscas, generously offers sixty sacks of wool, and all the salt and wool of his storehouses," added Luengo.

"But we have just been dealing with the miser Candiola," said the friar; "a battle with which not even the Eras can compare."

"How is that?" asked Don José, with astonishment. "Has not that wretched niggard understood that we will pay him for his flour? He is the only citizen of Saragossa who has not given a penny for the provisioning of the army."

"There is no use in preaching to Candiola," said Luengo. "He has said decisively that we need not return there unless we bring him one hundred and twenty-four reales for each sack of flour, and he has seventy-eight of them in his storehouse."

"Is there any infamy equal to his!" exclaimed Montoria, letting loose a string of porras, which I do not copy for fear of wearying my reader. "What! A hundred and twenty-four reales are necessary to make that stingy piece of flint understand the duties of a son of Saragossa in times like these! The Captain-General has given me authority to take whatever provisions are necessary, paying the fixed price for them."

"Do you hear what I tell you, Señor Don José?" said Busto; "Candiola says that who wants flour must pay for it. He said that if the city is not able to defend itself, it must surrender; that he has no obligation to give anything for the war, because he was not the one who brought it on."

"Let us go there," said Montoria, with anger, which showed itself in his gestures, his altered voice, his darkened visage. "It is not the first time that I have had that dog, that blood-sucker, in my hands."

I came behind with Augustine, who was pale and downcast. I wished to speak with him, but he made signs to keep silence. We followed to see how this would end. We found ourselves quickly in the Calle de Anton Trillo; and Montoria said to us,—

"Boys, go on ahead and knock at the door of this insolent Jew. Force it open, if no one opens it; enter, and tell him to come down to see me. Take him by the ear, but be careful he does not bite you, for he is a mad dog and a venomous serpent."

When we were walking on, I looked again at Augustine, and saw that he was livid and trembling.

"Gabriel," he said, "I wish to run away. I wish that the earth would open and swallow me. My father will kill me, but I cannot do what he has commanded me."

"Come, lean on me; then act as if you had twisted your foot, and cannot go on."

This was done, and our other companions and I began knocking at the door. The old woman showed herself at the window, and greeted us with a thousand insolent words. A few minutes passed, and then we saw a very beautiful hand raise the curtain, permitting us to see for a moment a face changed and pale, whose great dark eyes cast terrified glances towards the street.

At that moment my companions and the boys who were following were crying in hoarse concert,—

"Come down, uncle Candiola. Come down, dog of a Caiaphas!"

Contrary to our expectation, Candiola obeyed; but he did it believing that he had to do with the mob of vagabond boys who were in the habit of giving him such serenades, with no suspicion that the president of the junta of supplies, and two others in authority, were there to talk with him on a matter of importance. He soon had occasion to know that this was a serious matter, for at the opening of the door, as he came running out with a cudgel in his hand, and his ugly eyes glowing with wrath, he came face to face with Montoria, and drew back in alarm.

"Ah, it is you, Señor de Montoria," he said, with very bad grace. "How is it that you, being a member of the committee of public safety, have not been able to disperse this rabble which has come to make this noise before the gate of the house of an honorable citizen?"

"I am not a member of the committee of public safety, but of the junta of supplies, so I come in search of the Señor Candiola, and make him come down; but I will not enter this dark house full of cobwebs and mice."

"The poor cannot live in palaces like Señor José de Montoria, administrator of the goods of the commune, and for a long time tax-collector," replied Candiola.

"I made my fortune by work, not by usury," exclaimed Montoria. "But let us make an end of this. Señor Don Jeronimo, I have come for that flour. These two good fathers have acquainted you with our need of it already."

"Yes, I will sell it, I will sell it," answered Candiola, with a crafty smile; "but I cannot part with it at the price which these señors indicated. It is too little. I do not part with it for less than one hundred and sixty-two reales for a sack of a hundred pounds."

"I do not ask *your* price," said Don José, restraining his indignation.

"The junta may dispose as it likes with its own; but in my house no one sells anything but myself," answered the miser. "And that is all there is to say. Each one may do in his own house as I do in mine."

"Come, look here, you blood-sucker!" exclaimed Montoria, catching him by the arm, making him jump, "look here, Candiola of a thousand devils, I have said that I have come for the flour, and I will not go without it! The army of defence of Saragossa must not die of hunger, porra! and all citizens must contribute to maintain it."

"To maintain it! to maintain the army!" cried the miser, venomously. "Perhaps I am the author of its being?"

"Miserable pig, is there not in your black and empty soul one spark of patriotism?"

"I do not maintain vagabonds. What need was there that the French should bombard us and destroy the city? You want me to feed the soldiers. I will give them poison."

"Wretch, worm, blood-sucker of Saragossa, disgrace of the Spanish people!" exclaimed my protector, threatening with his doubled fist the miser's wrinkled face. "I would rather be damned to hell forever than to be what you are, to be Candiola for one minute. You black conscience, you perverse soul, are you not ashamed of being the only one in this city who has refused all his resources to the patriotic army of his country?

Does not everybody's hatred of you for this vile conduct weigh upon you more heavily than if all the rocks of Moncayo had fallen upon you?"

"Stop your music and leave me in peace," said Don Jeronimo, starting to the door.

"Look here, you unclean reptile," cried Montoria, detaining him, "I have told you that I am not going without the flour. If you do not produce it with good grace, as every good Spaniard does, you shall be made to give it by force. I will pay you forty-eight reales per sack,—its price before the siege."

"Forty-eight reales," exclaimed Candiola, with an expression of rancor, "I will sell my skin at that price before the flour. I would pay more than that for it. The accursed mob! Shall they be supported by me, Señor de Montoria?"

"You may thank them, miserable usurer, because they have not put an end to your useless life. Does not the generosity of this people surprise you? In the other siege, while we were enduring the greatest privations in order to get money together, your heart of stone remained insensible, and they could not pull out of you one old shirt to cover the nakedness of a poor soldier, or one piece of bread to appease his hunger. Saragossa has not forgotten your infamies. Do you not remember that after the battle of the fourth of August, when the wounded were distributed throughout the city, and two were assigned to you, and rang at your door, it was not possible for them to get their shadows into this wretched door? On the night of the fourth they arrived at your door, and with their weak hands they rang for you to open to them; but their moans and suffering did not move your heart of brass. You came to the door, and kicked them into the street, saying that your house was not a hospital. Unworthy son of Saragossa! but you have not the soul of a son of Saragossa. You were born a Mallorcan, of the blood of a Jew!"

The eyes of Candiola shot fire. His jaw quivered, and his fingers closed convulsively upon the cudgel in his right hand.

"Yes, you have the blood of a Mallorcan Jew. You are no son of this noble city. Do not the moans of those poor wounded men sound in your bat's ears? One of them, who was bleeding badly, died on this spot where we are standing. The other managed to creep to the market, where he told of what had happened. Infamous scarecrow! Do you suppose that the people of Saragossa are going to forget the morning of the fifth? Candiola, Candiolilla, give me that flour, and we will close this transaction in peace."

"Montoria, Montorilla," replied the other, "my ground and my work will not go to fatten idle vagabonds. Ya! Talk to me of charity and generosity and the needs of the poor soldiers! I have heard enough talk about those wretched sponges who are fed at the public cost. The committee of supplies will have no chance to laugh at me. As if we did not understand all this music about 'succor of the army.' Montoria, Montorilla, you have a little dough in your own house, isn't that true? Good dough can be found in the ovens of every patriot, made of the flour given by the foolish blockheads that the committee of supplies knows. Forty-eight reales! A pretty price! Then, in the accounts which will go to the Captain-General it will be set down as if bought at sixty reales, with a snapper of 'The Virgin del Pilar would not like to be a Frenchwoman.'"

When he said this, Don José de Montoria, who was already choking with wrath, lost his stirrups, as the saying is, and powerless to contain his indignation, went straight up to Candiola, apparently to slap his face; but the other had with one strategic glance foreseen the movement, and prepared to repel it. Quickly taking the offensive, he threw himself with a catlike spring upon my protector, grasping his neck with both hands and fastening upon him with his strong and bony fingers, at the same time making ready with his teeth, as if he were about to take between them the entire person of his enemy.

There was a brief struggle in which Montoria strove to free himself from those feline claws which had so suddenly made him their captive; but it could be seen in an instant that the nervous strength of the miser could not hold against the muscular strength of the Aragonese patriot. He shook him off violently. Candiola fell to the ground like a dead man.

We heard the cry of a woman from an upper window, and then the snap of a window-shutter closing. In this dramatic moment I wheeled about anxiously towards Augustine, but he had disappeared.

Don José de Montoria, mad with rage, kicked angrily at the prostrate body, stammering thickly in his wrath.

"You dirty pick-pocket, enriched with the blood of the poor, you dare to call me a thief, to call the members of the committee of supplies thieves! By a thousand porras! I will teach you to respect honest people, and you may be thankful that I do not tear out that miserable tongue of yours and throw it to the dogs."

All this struck us fairly dumb; but presently we snatched the unlucky Candiola from under the feet of his enemy. His first movement was made as if to jump upon him again, but Montoria had gone into the house, calling:

"Come, boys, we will go into the storehouse and get the flour. Quickly, let us make haste, quickly!"

The great number of people who had congregated in the street prevented old Candiola from entering his own house. The gamins, who had come running from all over the neighborhood, took charge of him themselves. Some pulled him forward, others pushed him backward, tearing his clothing to shreds. Others, taking the offensive from afar, threw great chunks of street mud at him. In the mean time a woman came to meet those of us who had entered the lower floor where the storerooms were. At the first glance I recognized the beautiful Mariquilla, altered and trembling, wavering at every step, without power to stand erect or speak, paralyzed with terror. Her fear was so great that we all pitied her, even Montoria.

"You are the daughter of Señor Candiola," he said, drawing from his pocket a handful of money, and making a brief reckoning on the wall with a bit of charcoal which he picked up from the floor. "Sixty-eight sacks of flour at forty-eight reales is three thousand two hundred and sixty-four. They are not worth half that, for they seem to me decidedly musty. Take it, child, here is the exact amount."

Mariquilla Candiola made no movement whatever towards taking the money, and Montoria put it down upon a box, saying,—

"There it is!"

Then the girl with a brusque and energetic movement which seemed, as it certainly was, the inspiration of her offended dignity, took the money, gold, silver, and copper, and threw it as if it were so many stones into the face of Montoria. The money was scattered all over the floor, and rolled out of the door without much promise of anyone's finding it all in the future. Immediately afterwards the señorita went without a word into the street. She beheld her father jammed into the crowd; and presently, aided by some young men, unable to see with indifference a woman in distress, she freed him from the infamous captivity in which the boys held him.

The father and daughter entered by the garden gate, as we were beginning to remove the flour.

XIII

When we had finished carrying out the flour, I went and looked for Augustine; but I could find him nowhere, neither in his father's house, nor at the headquarters of supplies, nor in the Coso, nor in Santa Engracia. At nightfall I found him in the powder mill near San Juan de los Panetes. I have forgotten to say that the Saragossans had improvised a work shop where were turned out daily nine or ten quintals of powder. I saw Augustine helping the workmen put into sacks and barrels the powder made during the day. He was working with feverish activity.

"Do you see this enormous heap of powder?" he said to me when I approached him. "Do you see those sacks and those barrels all full of the same material? Well, Gabriel, it seems to me very little."

"I don't know what you are trying to say."

"I say that if this immense quantity of powder were as big as Saragossa I should like it still better. Yes, and in such a case I should like to be the only inhabitant of this great city. What a pleasure! Listen, Gabriel! If it were so, I would myself set fire to it, and fly into the clouds, torn to pieces in the horrible explosion like pieces of rock which a volcano throws to a distance of a hundred leagues. I would be hurled to the fifth heaven, and of my members, scattered everywhere, there would be no memory! Death, Gabriel, death is what I desire! But I desire a death—I do not explain it to you. My desperation is so great that to die of a gunshot or a sabre-thrust would not satisfy me. I long to be rent asunder, and diffused through space in a thousand burning particles. I pant to feel myself in the bosom of a flame-bearing cloud. My spirit yearns, if only for an infinitesimal instant, the delight of seeing this wretched body reduced to powder. Gabriel, I am desperate. Do you see this powder? Imagine within my breast all the flames which this could make. Did you see her when she went out to get her father? Did you see her when she threw the money? I was in a corner where I could see it all. Mariquilla does not know that that man who maltreated her father is my own! Did you see how the boys threw mud at poor Candiola? I realize that Candiola is a wretch. But she, what fault has she? She and I, what fault have we? None, Gabriel. My heart is broken, and thirsts for a thousand deaths. I cannot live. I will run into the place of greatest danger and fling myself into the fire of the French. After what I have seen today, I and the earth on which I dwell may not be together."

BENITO PÉREZ GALDÓS

I drew him away from the place, taking him to the walls; and we went to work on the fortifications which were being made in Las Tenerias, the weakest point in the city since the destruction of San José and Santa Engracia. I have already said that from the mouth of the Huerva to San José stretched a line of fifty mouths of fire. Against this formidable line of attack what avail was our fortified circuit?

The quarter of Las Tenerias extended from the eastern part of the city, between the Huerva and the old part of the town, perfectly outlined yet by the wide road which is called the Coso. It was at the beginning of this century a village of mean houses, almost all inhabited by laborers and artisans, and the religious houses there had none of the splendor of the monuments of Saragossa. The general plan of this district is approximately the segment of a circle whose arc curves out to the open country, and whose chord unites it to the city, from the Puerta Quemada to the rise at the Sepulcro.

From that line to the circumference ran several streets, some of them broken, like the Calles de la Diezma, Barrio Verde, de los Clavos, and de Pabostre. Some of these were marked not by rows of houses, but by walls, and lacking sometimes one thing and sometimes another. The streets spread out into formless little squares or yards or barren gardens. I describe badly because in the days I refer to the heaps of ruins left by the first siege had been used to mount batteries and raise barricades in points where the houses did not offer a natural defence.

Near the fortification of the Ebro were some remnants of an ancient wall, with various little towers of masonry which some persons supposed to be from the hands of the Romans, and others judged to be the work of the Moors. In my time—I do not know how it may be now—these pieces of wall seemed to be mortised into the houses, or rather the houses were mortised into them, appearing like props and corners of that ancient work, blackened but not crumbled by the passing of so many centuries. The new had been built in a confused way upon the ruins of the old, as the Spanish people had developed and grown upon the spoils of other peoples of mixed bloods, until they became as they are today.

The general aspect of the district of Las Tenerias brought to the imagination pleasant fancies of all that had taken place during Moorish rule, the abundance of brick, the long gable ends, the irregular fronts, the window lattices with shutters, the complete architectural anarchy, making it impossible to know where one house ended and another began, or of distinguishing whether this had two floors or three, or if that roof served to support the walls of that one over there. The streets at best ended in yards with no ways out. The archways, which gave entrance to a little square, reminded me that here was a vista upon another Spanish people, very different from those now here.

This amalgamation of houses which I have described to you, this suburb built up by many generations of laborers and peasants and tanners, according to the caprice of each, without order or harmony, had prepared itself for the defence on the twenty-fourth and twenty-fifth days of January, at the time when the French began to display their pomp of attack by placing forces on that side. All the families living in the houses of this suburb proceeded to build works according to their own strategic instincts. There were military engineers in petticoats who demonstrated a profound knowledge of war by walling up certain spaces and opening others to the light, and for purposes of firing. The walls of the eastern side were spiked along their length. The turrets of the wall of Cæsar Augustus, built to resist arrows and sling stones, now upheld cannon.

If anyone of these pieces were turned upon one of the neighboring roofs, the roof or the entire house, whatever was there, would be immediately blown to pieces. Many passages had been obstructed, and two of the religious edifices of the suburb, San Augustine and Las Monicas, were veritable fortresses. The wall had been rebuilt and strengthened; the batteries had been joined together, and our engineers had calculated the positions and the reach of the enemy's guns very well, in order to accommodate our defences to them.

Our line had two advanced points, the mill of Goicoechea and a house which, because it belonged to a certain Don Victoriano Gonzalez, has gone into history by the name of the Casa de Gonzalez. This line, running from the Puerta Quemada, met first the battery of Palafox, then the Molino, the mill, in the city, then the garden of San Augustine; it continued to the mill of Goicoechea, situated a little out of the district, then to the orchard of Las Monicas, and on to those of San Augustine; further up, a great battery and the house of Gonzalez. This is all that I remember of Las Tenerias. There was over there a place called the Sepulcro, because of its nearness to a church of that name. More than one portion of the suburb, indeed, deserved the name of sepulchre. I tell you no more in order not to tire you with these descriptive minutiæ, unnecessary to one who knows those glorious places, and insufficient for one who has been unable to visit them.

XIV

Augustine Montoria and I stood guard with our battalion in the Molino until after nightfall, the hour when we were relieved by the Huesca volunteers; then we permitted ourselves to be all night outside the lines. But it must not be believed that during these hours we strolled about hand in hand; for when our military services were over, there were others no less onerous in the interior of the city, where the wounded had already been carried to La Seo and to the Pilar,—burning houses to carry things out of, or materials to carry to the friars, the canons, and the civil officials, who were making cartridges in San Juan de los Panetes.

Montoria and I went there by way of the Calle de Pabostre. I walked along munching a crust of bread with good appetite. My companion, taciturn and gloomy, amused himself by throwing his to the dogs that we met as we walked along. Although I exerted my imagination in efforts to cheer his sad spirit, he remained dull and insensible to it all, replying but sadly to my merry chatter. As we entered the Coso, he said to me,—

"It is ten by the clock of the Torre Nueva. Do you know—I wish to go there tonight."

"Tonight you will not be able to go. Try to stifle the flame of love in its ashes, while we are threatened by those other burning hearts, the flaming bombs which are coming to break in the houses and among the people."

It was even so. The bombarding, which had not ceased during all the day, was continued during the night, though with a little less vigor; and from time to time projectiles fell, augmenting the already large number of victims within the city.

"I must go there this night," he said. "Did not Mariquilla see me among all those who crowded in front of the door of her house? Will she not think me one of those who abused her father?"

"I don't believe so. That young woman would know how to distinguish between individuals. She has already made inquiries, and now is no time for stolen sweets. Do you see? From that house coming this way are some poor women in need of help. Look, one of them is not able to creep further, and falls to the ground. Is it not possible that the Señorita Doña Mariquilla Candiola has also gone to care for the wounded at San Pablo or the Pilar?"

"I do not believe so."

"Or perhaps where they are making cartridges?"

"I believe that still less. She would be in her house, and there is where I wish to go, Gabriel. You may go and see to the carrying of the wounded, or to the powder, or whatever you please, but I am going there!"

As he said this, Pirli presented himself to us in his friar's habit, already torn and hanging in a thousand fragments, and on his head the French engineer's helmet, badly battered, but plated and plumed, and making our hero look less like a soldier than a carnival figure.

"Are you coming to help carry the wounded?" he asked. "They have just killed two more for us that we are carrying to San Pablo. They need men there to open the ditch where they are burying our dead of yesterday, but I have worked enough. I am going to the house of Manuela Sancho to see if I can get a snatch of sleep. But, first, we are going to dance a little. Don't you want to come along?"

"No, we are going to San Pablo," I replied, "to bury the dead. There is enough to do."

"They say that so many dead make the air bad, and that is why there are so many ill of the fever. That is finishing them faster than their wounds, over by the other barricade. I would rather have some 'hot cakes' than the epidemic. A 'señora' wouldn't scare me, but a chill and a fever would. So then you are going to bury the dead?"

"Yes," said Augustine, "let us bury the dead."

"In San Pablo there are no less than forty wounded," answered Pirli; "and, at the rate we're going there, we'll soon be more dead than living. Don't you want a little diversion? If you are not going to work on the ditch, why not come along to the cartridge factory? All the girls will be there, and from time to time they will give us some singing, or cheer our souls with a little dancing."

"We have no fault to find with all that. Will Manuela Sancho be there too?"

"No, the girls there are the young ladies of Saragossa, the señoritas who have been called into service by the committee of safety. There are a great many of them in the hospitals too. They invite themselves for that service. And it would be a queer one who would use her eyes so little as not to make a match for herself, if not for this year, then for next!"

We heard the rushing sound of many footsteps behind us, and, turning, we saw a great number of people, among whose voices we recognized that of Don José de Montoria. He was very angry at seeing us there, and exclaimed,—

"What are you doing here, idiots? Three strong hearty men standing here with their hands folded, when there is such a lack of men for the work to be done! Go along with you! Clear out of here! March, you little tin soldiers! Do you see those two posts there on the Trenque knoll with beams crossed on top from which six ropes are hanging? Do you see that gallows set up in that place for traitors? Well, it's for loafers, too. Get along to work, or I'll show your carcasses how to move with my fists."

We followed him until we came quite near the gallows, where the six ropes were swaying commandingly in the wind, ready to strangle traitors or cowards. Montoria seized his son by the arm, and pointed to the horrible apparatus with an energetic gesture, saying,—

"Here you can see what we have been getting ready this evening. Look! There's where those who do not do their duty will be entertained. On with you! I who am old never get tired, but you young healthy men act as if you were made of putty. The invincible men of the first siege have almost all worked themselves to death; and we old men, sirs, are obliged to set an example to these dandies who if they miss dining for a week begin to complain and beg for broth. I would give you broth of powder, and soup of cannon balls, you cowards! Go, and see that you help to bury the dead and carry ammunition to the walls."

"And assist at the hell which this damned epidemic is spreading," said one of those who had accompanied Montoria.

"I don't know what to think of this thing which the doctors call the epidemic," answered Don José. "I call it fear, sirs, pure fear. They take a chill; then they have spasms and a fever; then they turn green, and they die. What is all that but the effect of fear? Our strong men all seem to be gone, yes, señors. Ah, what men those were in the first siege! Now when the soldiers have been firing and been fired at for a trifle of ten hours, they begin to fall down with fatigue, and say they can do no more. There's one man who had lost only a leg and a half who began screaming and calling upon all the holy martyrs, begging that they put him to bed. Nothing but cowardice, pure cowardice! Today several soldiers left Palafox's battery who had a good sound arm apiece left to fight with. And they began to beg for broth! They had better drink their own blood, which is the best broth in the world. I say the race of men of courage is finished and done with, porra! a thousand porras!"

"Tomorrow the French will attack Las Tenerias," said the other. "If, as a result, there are many wounded, I don't see where we are going to put them."

"Wounded!" exclaimed Montoria. "We don't wish to see any wounded here. The dead do not hinder us. We can pile them up in a heap; but the wounded—ugh! Our soldiers are no longer fearless, and I'll wager that those who are defending the best positions will not risk seeing themselves decimated; they will abandon them as soon as they see a couple of dozen French heads above each rampart. What feebleness! After all, 'twill be as God wills, and as for the wounded and sick, we will take care of them. Why not? Have you taken many fowls today?"

"Several dozens, of which more than half were given, and for the rest we paid six reales and a half. A few were not willing to give."

"All right. To think that a man like me should occupy himself with fowls in days like these! What's that you say? Some were not willing to give? The Captain-General authorized me to impose fines upon those who do not contribute to the defence. We will just gently get the law on those milksops and traitors. Hark, señors! A bomb fell then in the neighborhood of the Torre Nueva. Did you see it? Did you hear it? What a horrible explosion! I'll wager that it is Divine Providence more than the French batteries that have sent it against the house of that petrified, soulless Jew who looks on with indifference and contempt at his neighbors' distress. People are running that way. It seems that the house is on fire, or falling down. No, don't you run, you miserable fellows. Let it burn, let it fall to the earth in a thousand pieces. It is the house of the miser Candiola, who would not give one peseta to save the whole human race from a new deluge. Eh, where are you going? You are going to run there too? No, come along. Follow me! We can be of more use elsewhere."

We were going in a crowd to the Orphanage. Augustine, impelled no doubt by the beating of his heart, suddenly started as if to direct his steps towards the Plazuela San Felipe, following the great crowd hastening towards that place. But detained forcibly by his father he continued, though with bad grace, in our company. Something was certainly burning near the Torre Nueva, and on the tower the precious arabesques and bricks shone redly, because of the nearness of the fire. That graceful leaning column could be distinguished, crimson in the black night, and at the same time from its huge belfry a great lamentation fell upon the air.

We reached San Pablo.

"Go on, boys, loungers! Help those who are opening the ditch. It must be wide and deep. It is a garment wherein they will enrobe forty bodies."

We began upon the work, digging earth from the ditch which was being opened in the court of the church. Augustine was digging with me, but at every instant he turned his eyes in the direction of the Torre Nueva.

"It is a terrible fire. It seems as if it is going down a little, Gabriel. I long to throw myself into this grave which we are opening."

"Don't be in a hurry," I answered him. "Perhaps tomorrow will throw us into it without our asking. This is no time for foolishness; it is time to work."

"Do you not see? I believe that the fire is extinguished."

"Yes, the whole house has probably burned down. Candiola was sure to be shut up in his cellar with his money, and the fire couldn't reach him. Don't worry."

"Gabriel, I must go there, if only for a moment. I wish to see if the fire was really in his house. If my father returns, tell him that I will be back in a second."

The sudden appearance of Don José de Montoria prevented Augustine making the flight which he had just planned, and we two continued digging in the great sepulchre. They began to bring out bodies; and the sick and wounded, who were constantly being brought from without, saw, as they were taken into the church, the wide bed which we were preparing for them. At last the ditch was sufficiently deep, and we were ordered to cease digging. The work went on, and corpses were brought, one by one, and cast into the great sepulchre, while clergymen and pious women upon their knees repeated the mournful words of the service. There was room enough for all, and nothing remained to be done for them but to cover them with earth. Don José Montoria, with head uncovered, reciting in a low voice a paternoster, threw the first handful. Then our shovels and spades began with all speed to cover them. Our work ended, we all knelt down, and prayed in hushed tones. Augustine Montoria said to me when this was done,—

"We will go now. My father will march himself off. Go and tell him that we are going to relieve two friends on duty who have a sick one in their family and wish us to see him. Tell him, for God's sake! I haven't the courage, then in an instant we can be there."

XV

We deceived the old man and went. The night was now far advanced, as the interment which I have just described had lasted more than three hours. The light of the fire could no longer be seen. The mass of the tower was lost in the darkness of night, and its great bell did not sound except now and then to announce the coming of a bomb. We arrived soon at the Plazuela of San Felipe. Seeing the roof of a house near the church still smoking, we knew that it was this, and not the house of Candiola, which three hours before the flames had attacked.

"God has preserved it!" cried Augustine, joyously. "If the meanness of her father should bring divine anger upon that roof, the virtues and innocence of Mariquilla would preserve it! Let us go there."

In the Plazuela of San Felipe there were a few people, but the Calle de Anton Trillo was deserted. We stopped close to the wall of the garden and listened attentively. All was in such deep silence that the house seemed abandoned. Could it really be abandoned? Although this quarter was one of those least damaged by the bombardment, many families had left it, or were living as refugees in their own cellars.

"If I go in," said Augustine to me, "you must come in with me. After the scene of today, I am afraid that Don Jeronimo, suspicious and cowardly, like a good miser, will be up all night and about his garden, lest they return and carry off his whole place."

"In that case it is better not to go in," I answered, "because besides the danger of falling into the hands of that old scoundrel, there would be a great scandal, and all Saragossa will know that the son of Don José Montoria, the young man destined for a bishop's mitre, goes by night to see the daughter of the goodman Candiola."

But this and all that I could say to him was like preaching in the desert. Without listening to reason, and insisting that I should follow him, he made the signal of love, waiting and watching with great anxiety for the reply. Sometime passed, and at last, after long looking and looking again from the pavement in front, we saw a light in a high window. We heard the fastening of the gate drawn back softly, and it was opened without creaking. Love had taken precautions, and the ancient hinges had been oiled. We two entered meeting, unexpectedly, not a perfumed and fascinating damsel, but a vinegary countenance which I recognized at once as that of Doña Guedita.

"He lets hours pass before he comes, and then he comes with another," she grumbled. "Young men, be so kind as to make no noise. Walk on tip-toe, and be careful not to stumble over even a dried leaf, because Señor Candiola seems to me to be very wide awake."

This she said to us in a voice so low that we heard with difficulty; then she went on before, making signs that we should follow her, putting her finger to her lips to enjoin absolute silence. The garden was small. We soon crossed it, and came to the stone staircase which led up to the doorway of the house. Here there came to meet us a shapely figure wrapped in a mantle, or cloak. It was Mariquilla! Her first gesture was to impose silence, indicating with anxiety, as I saw, a window which opened upon the garden. She then showed surprise that Augustine had not come unaccompanied. But he knew how to soothe her, saying, "It is Gabriel, my best, my only friend, of whom I have spoken so many times."

"Speak lower," whispered Mariquilla; "my father went out of his room a little while ago with a lantern, and made the rounds of the house and the garden. I doubt if he is asleep yet. The night is dark. Let us hide in the shadow of the cypress, and talk in a very low voice."

The stone stairway led up to a kind of balcony with a wooden railing. The great cypress in the garden cast a deep shadow at the end of the balcony, forming there a refuge against the clear light of the moon. The bare boughs of an elm spread above the other end of the balcony, casting a thousand fantastic shadows upon the floor, upon the walls of the house, and upon ourselves. In the protection of the cypress, Mariquilla seated herself upon the only seat that was there, and Montoria threw himself upon the floor beside her, resting his hands upon her knees. I seated myself also upon the floor not far from the pair. It was a January night, still, dry, and cold. Perhaps the two lovers with hearts aflame did not feel the low temperature; but I, a creature stranger to their fires, wrapped myself in my cloak to keep myself from the chill of the tiles. Guedita had disappeared. Mariquilla led the conversation, plunging at once into the difficulty.

"I saw you in the street this morning. When Guedita and I heard the noise of the people crowding about our gate, I went to the window, and I saw you on the sidewalk in front."

"It is true, I was there," replied Montoria, with emotion, "but I was obliged to go at once. I couldn't stand it."

"Didn't you see how those barbarians were trampling my father underfoot? When that cruel man struck him, I looked everywhere, hoping that you would come forward in his defence. But I did not see you anywhere."

"I tell you, Mariquilla of my heart," said Augustine, "that I was obliged to go. After they told me that your father had been so ill-treated, I came as soon as I could get a chance."

"A pretty time to come! Among so many, so many people," said Mariquilla, weeping, "not one lifted a hand to help him. I nearly died of fright, seeing him in such danger. I looked anxiously into the street, and there was no one but enemies, no one; not one kind hand or voice among all those men! One of them, more cruel than all, knocked my father down. Oh, oh, remembering this, I scarcely know what happened next! When I saw it, my fright paralyzed me for a few moments. Until then I never knew what violent anger was, how a sudden impulse, an inward fire, could drive me on. I came to him. My poor father was lying on the ground, and the wretch was trampling upon him as if he were a venomous reptile. When I saw that, I felt my blood boil in my veins. As I have told you, I ran about the house, looking for a weapon, a knife, an axe, anything. When I heard the cries of my father, I flew down. Finding myself among so many men, I felt a strange, uncontrollable timidity, and could not stir a step. The same man who had kicked him handed me a fistful of gold. I did not want to take it, but I did; then I threw all the coins into his face, with all my strength. My hand was as if filled with thunderbolts, and I felt as if I were avenging my father, hurling them at that villain. I went out afterwards, looking everywhere for you; but I could not see you. I found my father alone in that inhuman crowd, down in the mud, begging for mercy."

"Oh, Mariquilla, Mariquilla of my heart!" cried Augustine in anguish, kissing the hands of the unhappy daughter of the miser. "Don't talk anymore about all that. You tear my soul in two! I could not defend him. I—I had to go. I believed the crowd was after something—else. You are right. But let us talk no more of this which grieves me so, and gives me such bitter pain."

"If you had come to the defence of my father, he would have felt gratitude towards you. From gratitude one passes readily to affection. You would have been received openly in the house."

"Your father is incapable of affection for anyone," replied Montoria. "Do not hope that we can accomplish anything in that way. Let us trust that we may arrive at the fulfilment of our desires by hidden ways, perhaps by the help of God when it least seems likely. Let us not depend

BENITO PÉREZ GALDÓS

upon aught else, or think of what is before us. We are surrounded by dangers and obstacles that seem unsurmountable. Let us hope for help from the unseen, and filled by faith in God and the power of our love, let us wait for the miracle which will unite us. For it will be a miracle, Mariquilla, a wonder like those they tell of in olden times, that we refuse to believe."

"A miracle!" exclaimed Mariquilla, sadly. "It is true. You are a young gentleman of position, the son of parents who would never consent to see you married to the daughter of Señor Candiola. My father is abhorred all over the city. Everybody flees from us. No one visits us. If I go out they point at me, and look at me with insolent contempt. Girls of my own age will not associate with me, and the young men of the city who go about singing serenades under the windows of their sweethearts, come to mine to utter insults against my father, calling me also dreadful names to my face. Oh, my God, I understand that it would be indeed a miracle for me to be happy! Augustine, we have known each other now for nearly four months, and you have not yet told me the name of your parents. It certainly cannot be as odious as mine. Why do you hide it? If it were necessary that our love should be made public, you would not dare meet the looks of your friends, you would flee with horror from the daughter of Candiola."

"Oh, no, don't say that!" cried Augustine, pressing against Mariquilla, and hiding his face in her lap. "Don't say that I am ashamed of loving you. In saying that you insult God. It is not true. Today our love remains a secret, because it is necessary that it should be so. But when it is necessary to make it known, I will make it known, and defy the anger of my father face to face. Yes, Mariquilla, my parents will curse me, and turn me out of doors. A few nights ago you said to me, looking at that monument which we can see from here, 'When that tower becomes straight, I will leave off loving you.' I swear to you that the strength of my love is more immovable than the equilibrium of yonder tower; for that could fall to the ground, but could never stand upright. The works of man are variable, those of Nature are unchangeable and rest evermore upon an everlasting base. You have seen the Moncayo, that great rock which is near Poniente in the suburb? Well, when Moncayo gets tired of being in that place, and moves and comes walking towards Saragossa, putting one of its feet upon our city and reducing it to powder, then and then only will I cease to love you."

By this sort of hyperbole and poetic naturalism my friend expressed his great love, flattering the imagination of the beautiful girl, who responded, leaning forward, moved by an impulse like his own. They were both silent for a moment, then the two, or rather the three of us, exclaimed all together, looking at the tower whose belfry had flung to the winds two signals of alarm. At the same moment a globe of fire ploughed the black space, describing rapid circles.

"A bomb! It is a bomb," exclaimed Mariquilla, trembling, and throwing herself into the arms of her lover. The dreadful light passed swiftly over our heads, over the garden and the house, illuminating on its way the tower, the neighboring houses, and the nook where we were hidden. Then the report was heard. The bell began to ring violently, and was joined by others near and far, loud, heavy, sharp, jangled; and we heard the noise of feet and voices of people in the nearest streets.

"That bomb will not kill us," said Augustine, soothing his sweetheart. "Are you afraid?"

"Yes, very, very much afraid," she answered. "I spend the nights praying, asking God to keep the fire away from our house. Until now no misfortune has come near us, either now or in the other siege. But how many unhappy ones have perished, how many houses of good people who never harmed anyone have been destroyed by the flames! I long earnestly to go like other women and take care of the suffering; but my father forbids me, and is angry with me whenever I propose it."

As she said this, we heard within the house a distant sound of talking, in which the harsh tones of Candiola were mingled with the voice of Guedita. We three, obeying one impulse, drew into the shadow and held our breaths, fearing to be surprised. Then we heard the voice of the miser coming nearer, and saying,—

"What are you doing up at this hour, Señora Guedita?"

"Señor," answered the old woman, showing herself at a window which opened upon the balcony, "who can sleep during this dreadful bombardment? Perhaps a bomb may come and meddle with us here. What if the house should take fire, and the neighbors should come to drag out the furniture and put out the fire, and find us in our night-clothes? Oh, what a lack of modesty! I do not intend to undress myself while this devilish bombardment lasts."

"Is my daughter asleep?" asked Candiola, appearing at another garden window.

"She is upstairs sleeping like a kitten," replied the duenna. "They speak truly when they say that there are no dangers for innocence. A bomb does not frighten the child anymore than a sky-rocket."

"I wonder if I can see from here where the projectile has fallen," said Candiola, stretching his body out of the window, in order to be able to extend his range of vision. "I can see the light of a fire, but I cannot say whether it is near or far."

"Oh, I don't know anything about bombs," said Guedita, who had come out on the balcony. "This one has fallen over there by the market."

"So it seems. If only all would fall upon the houses of those who persist in keeping up the defence and causing the destruction! If I am not deceived, Señora Guedita, the fire is near the Calle de la Triperia. Are not the storehouses of the junta of supplies over there? Oh, blessed bomb, why not fall into the Calle de la Hilarza, upon the house of that cursed, most miserable thief! Señora Guedita, I am going to the Calle de la Hilarza, to see if it has fallen on the house of that proud, meddlesome, cowardly thief, Don José de Montoria. I have prayed for it tonight to the Virgin del Pilar with so much fervor, and also at the Santas Masas and at Santo Dominguito del Val, that at last I believe I have been heard."

"Señor Don Jeronimo," said the old woman, "do not go out! The cold of the night is bad for you, and it is not worth risking your lungs to see where the bomb has fallen. It is enough that it has not meddled with this house. If that one which passed did not fall into the house of that barbarian of an official, another will fall tomorrow. The French have a good handful. Now, your honor, go to rest. I will stay up and look after the house."

Candiola changed his mind about going out, it seemed, in accordance with the good counsels of his servant, and, shutting the window, he was heard no more during all the rest of the night. But although he disappeared, the lovers did not break the silence, fearful of being overheard. And not until the old woman came to tell us that the señor was snoring like a peasant was the interrupted dialogue continued.

"My father wished that the bombs would fall upon the house of his enemy," said Mariquilla. "I should not like to see them fall anywhere; but if at anytime one could wish ill-fortune to a neighbor, it would be now, do you not think so?"

Augustine made no answer.

"You went away. You did not see how that man, the most cruel, the most cowardly of all who came, knocked him down in his blind fury, and trampled upon him. The fiends will kick his soul in hell like that, won't they?"

"Yes," replied the young man, laconically.

"Today, after it all, Guedita and I dressed the wounds of my father. He was stretched upon his bed, crazy, desperate. He was twisting about, gnawing his fists and lamenting that he was not stronger than his enemy. We tried to console him, but he told us to be silent. He struck me in the face, he was so angry when he heard that I had thrown away the money for the flour. He was furious with me. He told me that since he could not get anymore, the three thousand reales on account should not be despised. He said that I am a spendthrift, and am ruining him. We could not calm him in anyway. Towards nightfall we heard another noise in the street, and were afraid that the same ones who were here in the middle of the day were returning. My father was raging, and determined to get up. I was greatly frightened; but I took courage, realizing that courage was necessary. Thinking of you, I said, 'If he were in the house, no one would dare insult us.' As the noise in the street increased, I plucked up all my courage. I shut and fastened the doors and gates, and, begging my father to keep quiet in his bed, I waited, resolved. While Guedita was on her knees, praying to all the saints in heaven, I searched the house for a weapon. At last I found a big knife. The sight of it has always frightened me, but today I clutched it fearlessly. Oh, I was beside myself! Now the very thought of it makes me frightened. I am usually unable to look upon a wounded man, and tremble at the sight of a drop of blood. I almost cry if I see anyone beat a dog before me. I have never had the force to kill a mosquito. But this evening, Augustine, this evening, when I heard the noise in the street, when I thought those blows upon the gate had come again, when I expected every moment to see those men before me, I swear to you that if that had happened which I feared, if when I was in my father's room, by his bedside, if that same man had come who abused him a few hours before, I swear to you that there I myself would have struck him through the heart."

"Hush, for God's sake!" cried Montoria, horrified. "You frighten me. Hearing you, you almost make me feel as if your own hands, these divine hands, struck cold steel through my breast. Nobody will maltreat your father again. You see already that your alarm of tonight was nothing but fright. No, you would not have been capable of what you say. You are a woman, and a weak one, sensitive, timid, incapable of killing a man, unless you kill him of love. The knife would have fallen from your hands, and you would not have stained their purity with the blood of a fellow being. These horrible things are only for us men, born for conflict; sometimes we find ourselves in the sad strait of wrenching the life from other men. Mariquilla, do not talk anymore nonsense. Do not think of those who offended you! Forgive them, and do not kill anyone, even in thought."

XVI

While they were talking, I observed the face of Mariquilla, which seemed in the darkness as if modelled of white wax, and of the soft tone and finish of ivory. From her black eyes, whenever she raised them to the heavens, swift lights flashed; her black pupils seemed to reflect the clearness of the sky; in their depths two points of brightness shone or were hidden, according to the changeful mood expressed in her glance. It was curious to observe the passionate creature telling of that stormy crisis which had moved and exalted her sensibilities to the heights of courage. Her languorous attitude, her dove-like cooing, the warm affection which radiated in her atmosphere, did not associate themselves readily with manifestations of heroism in defence of her insulted father. Attentive observation easily discovered that both currents flowed from the same source.

"I admire your noble filial affection," said Augustine. "But you must think of this. I do not exonerate those who maltreated your father. But you must not forget that he is the only one who has not given anything for the war. Don Jeronimo is an excellent person, but he has not an atom of patriotism in his soul. The misfortunes of the city are of no consequence to him, and he even seems to rejoice when we do not come out victorious."

Mariquilla sighed, lifting her eyes to heaven.

"It is true," she said; "everyday and every hour I beseech him to give something for the war. I am able to get nothing; although I exaggerate the necessities of the poor soldiers, and the bad record that he is making in Saragossa. He only gets angry with me, and says that the one who brought on the war is the one to pay for it. In the other siege I was delighted at news of a victory. The fourth of August I went out into the street all alone, unable to resist my curiosity. One night I was at the house of the Urries, and they were celebrating the battle of that day, which had been very brilliant. I also began to rejoice, and show enthusiasm. An old woman who was present said to me in a high voice, and a very unpleasant tone, 'My child, instead of indulging in these emotions, why do you not carry to the hospital an old sheet to stanch blood? In the house of Señor Candiola, whose cellars are full of money, is there not some old rag to give to the wounded? Your miserable papa is the only one, the only one of all the citizens of Saragossa who has not given anything for the war.' Everybody laughed on hearing this; but I was dumb with shame, not daring to speak. I remained in a corner of the room until the end of the party, and nobody spoke another word to me. My few girl friends who used to love me so much did not come near me. I could hear people speak from time to time the name of my father, with harsh comments and ugly nicknames. Oh, it was heartbreaking! When I started to come home, they hardly told me goodbye. The host and hostess dismissed me very abruptly. I came home and went to bed, and cried all night. The shame of it seemed burning in my blood."

"Mariquilla," cried Augustine, lovingly, "your goodness is so great that because of it God will forget the cruelties of your father."

"A few days afterwards," she went on, "on the fourth of August, those two wounded men came that my father's enemy spoke of this morning. When we heard that the committee had assigned two wounded men to our house to be taken care of, Guedita and I were delighted, and, wild with pleasure, began to prepare beds, bandages, and lint. We were waiting for them anxiously, running to the window every minute to see if they were coming. At last they came. My father, who had just come in from the street in a very black mood, complaining that many of his debtors had been killed, losing him all hope of collecting from them, received the wounded soldiers very badly. I embraced him, weeping, and begged him to take them in; but he would not listen to me and in his blind anger, he pushed them down into the gutter, barred the door, and went upstairs, saying, 'Let their own parents take care of them!' It was night. Guedita and I were in perfect despair. We did not know what to do. We could hear the moans of those two poor fellows, dragging themselves along in the street, begging for help. My father shut himself up in his room to make up his accounts, caring nothing for them or for us. We went softly, so that he would not hear us, to the front window, and threw them cloths for bandages; but they could not reach them. We spoke to them, and they held out their hands to us. We fastened a little basket to the end of a cane, and passed them out some food; but one of them was dying, and the other suffering so much that he could not eat. We said what we could to encourage them, and prayed to God for them. At last we resolved to come down and go out to help them, if only for a moment. My father caught us here in the balcony, and was furious. That night, what a night! O Holy Virgin! one of them died in the street, and the other one dragged himself on to find pity elsewhere."

Augustine and I were silent, reflecting upon the monstrous contradictions of that house.

"Mariquilla," my friend said, presently, "how proud I am of loving you! Saragossa does not know your heart of gold, and it must be known. I wish to tell the whole world that I love you, and prove to my parents when they know it that I have made a good choice."

"I am like any other girl," said Mariquilla, with humility; "and your parents will not see in me anything but the daughter of the one whom they call the Mallorcan Jew. Oh, the shame kills me! I wish I could go away from Saragossa, somewhere that I could never again see any of these people. My father came from Palma, it is true; but he is not a Jew. He is descended from the old Christians; and my mother was a woman of Aragon, of the Rincon family. Why are we despised? What have we done?"

Mariquilla's lips quivered in a half disdainful smile. Augustine, tormented doubtless by painful feeling, remained silent, his brow leant upon the hands of his sweetheart. Gruesome shapes of dread raised themselves threateningly between them. With the eyes of the soul he and she beheld them, filled with fear. After a long pause, Augustine lifted his face.

"Mariquilla, why are you silent? Tell me."

"Why are you silent, Augustine?"

"What are you thinking about?"

"What are you thinking about?"

"I am thinking that God will protect us," said the young man. "When the siege is ended, we will marry. If you wish to leave Saragossa, I will go with you wherever you wish to go. Has your father ever spoken to you of marriage?"

"Never."

"He shall not prevent your marrying me. My parents will oppose it; but my mind is made up. I do not understand life except through you, and if I lost you I could not exist. You are the supreme necessity of my soul. Without you I should be like the universe without light. No human power shall separate us as long as you love me. This conviction is so rooted in me that if I should ever think that we must be separated in life, it would be to me as if all nature were overthrown. *I* without *you!* That seems to me the wildest of ideas. I without you! What madness, what absurdity! It is like the sea on the top of the mountains, like the snow in the depths of the ocean. It is like rivers running through the sky, and the stars made into fiery powder in the deserts of the earth. It is as if the trees should talk, and man should live among metals and precious stones in the bowels of the earth. I am a coward at times, and I tremble, thinking of the obstacles that seem overwhelming before us; but the confidence that fills my spirit, like faith in holy things, reanimates me. If sometimes for a moment I fear death, afterwards a secret voice tells me that I shall not die as long as you are alive. Do you see all the destruction made by the siege which we are enduring? Do you see how the bombs and shells shower about us, and how numbers of my companions fall never to rise? Yet, except momentarily, none of this causes me any fear. I believe that the Virgin del Pilar keeps death away from me. Your sensitiveness keeps you in constant communion with the angels of heaven. You are an angel of heaven, and loving you and being loved by you gives me a divine power against which the forces of man avail nothing."

Augustine went on for a long time in this strain, pouring out from his over-flowing fancy the love and the superstitions which held him in thrall.

"Indeed, I too have unchanging confidence, as you say," said Mariquilla. "I am often afraid that you will be killed; but I know not what voices I hear in the depths of my soul telling me that they will not kill you. It may be because I pray so much, pleading with God to preserve your life among all these horrors and in battle. I do not know. At night when I go to rest, thinking of the bombs that have fallen, and those that are falling, and those that will fall, I go to sleep and dream of battle, and never cease hearing the noise of cannon. I am very restless, and Guedita, who sleeps near me, says that I talk in my sleep, saying a thousand mad things. I must certainly say something, for I am always dreaming. I see you on the wall. I talk with you, and you answer me. The balls do not touch you; and it seems to me it is because of the prayers I say for you, waking and sleeping. A few nights ago I dreamed that I went with other girls to take care of the wounded, and that we were taking care of a great many, almost bringing them back to life by what we were doing for them. I dreamed that when I came back to the house I found you here with your father, an old man, who was smiling and talking with mine, both seated upon the sofa in the sala. Then I dreamed that your father smiled at me, and began to ask me questions. Sometimes I dream sad things. When I am awake I listen, and if I do not hear the noise of the bombardment, I ask if it can be that the

French have raised the siege. If I hear a cannonading, I look at the image of the Virgin del Pilar which is in my room, and I question it in thought, and it answers me that you are not dead, without my knowing how the answer is given. I spend the day thinking about the ramparts, and I wait at the window to hear what the soldiers say who pass by in the street. Sometimes I feel tempted to ask them if they have seen you. Night comes; I see you again, and I am, oh, so contented! The next day Guedita and I occupy ourselves in cooking something good, unknown to my father. If it is successful, we save it for you; if it is not quite so nice, that little friar called Father Busto takes it to the wounded and sick. He comes after dark to get it, on the pretext of visiting Doña Guedita, of whom he is a kinsman. We ask him how goes the battle, and he tells us all about it, that the troops are performing deeds of great valor, and the French will be obliged to retire in good time. This news that all goes well makes us wild with joy. The noise of the bombs saddens us afterwards, but praying we recover our tranquillity. Alone in our room at night, we make lint and bandages which Father Busto also takes secretly, as if they were stolen goods. If we hear my father's steps, we hide it all quickly, and put out the light, because if he should find out what we are doing he would be very angry."

Mariquilla smiled almost gayly as she told of her fears and joys with divine simplicity. The peculiar charm of her voice is indescribable. Her words, like the vibration of crystal notes, left a harmonious echo in the soul. As she ceased speaking, the first splendors of dawn illuminated her face.

"The day is breaking, Mariquilla," said Augustine, "and we must go. Today we are going to defend Las Tenerias. This will be a dreadful day, and many will be killed. But the Virgin del Pilar will protect us, and we shall live to rejoice in victory. Mariquilla, the balls will not touch me."

"Do not go yet," replied the daughter of Candiola. "Day is coming, it is true; but they do not need you yet upon the walls."

The bell in the tower sounded.

"Look how those birds cruise about in the heavens, announcing the dawn," said Augustine, with bitter irony.

One, two, three bombs traversed the sky, as yet faintly illumined.

"How frightful!" cried Mariquilla, yielding to the embrace of Montoria. "Will God keep us today as He preserved us yesterday?"

"We must go to the walls," I cried, rising quickly. "Do you not hear all the drums and bells sounding the call to arms?"

Mariquilla, in indescribable panic, was weeping and trying to detain Montoria. I was resolved on going at once, and endeavored to take him away with me. The noise of the drums and the bells in the belfries of the city were sounding the call to arms. And if we did not rush instantly into the lines, we ran the risk of being shot or arrested.

"I must go, I must go, Mariquilla," said my friend, with profound emotion. "Are you afraid? No, this house is sacred because you live in it, and will be respected by the enemy's fire. God will not visit your father's cruelty upon your sacred head."

The Doña Guedita appeared abruptly, saying that her master was up and dressing hastily. Then Mariquilla herself hurried us to the foot of the garden, ordering us to go at once. Augustine was in anguish, and at the gate, hesitated and stepped backward as if to return to the side of the unhappy girl, who, half dead of fright, her hands folded in prayer, was weeping, seeing us go from where she stood in the shade of the cypress which had sheltered us. At the moment when we opened the gate, a cry was heard from the upper part of the house, and we saw Candiola, who, half-dressed, was leaning out in a threatening attitude. Augustine wished to turn back; but I forced him forward, and we went.

"To the lines! To the lines, at once!" I cried. "They will degrade us, Augustine! Leave your future father-in-law to deal with your future wife for the present."

We ran swiftly into the Coso, where we saw that innumerable bombs were being hurled upon the unhappy city. Everybody ran as fast as possible to the various positions of defence,—some to Las Tenerias, some to the Portillo, some to Santa Engracia or to the Trinitarios. As we arrived at the arch of Cineja, we stumbled upon Don José de Montoria, who, followed by some of his friends, was running towards the Almudi. In the same moment a terrible crash behind us proclaimed that one of the enemy's projectiles had fallen upon a neighboring residence. Augustine, hearing this, turned back, longing to return to the place from whence we came.

"Where are you going, porra!" cried his father, detaining him. "To the Tenerias! Make haste! To the Tenerias!"

The people who were coming and going knew the place of the disaster, and we heard them saying,—

"Three bombs have fallen close to the house of Candiola."

"The angels of heaven certainly aimed those guns," laughed Don José de Montoria, noisily. "We shall see how the Mallorcan Jew keeps them off, if he is still alive till he puts his money in a place of safety."

"Let us run and rescue those unfortunate beings!" cried Augustine, with emotion.

"To the lines, cowards!" said his father, holding him with an iron hand. "That is the work of women; men must die in the breach."

It was necessary to make haste to our places, and we went, or rather we were carried by the impetuous surge of the people running to defend the suburb of Las Tenerias.

XVII

While the cannons on the Mediodia were throwing bombs into the centre of the city, the cannon on the east side were discharging solid balls upon the weak walls of Las Monicas, and the fortifications of earth and brick of the oil mill, and the battery of Palafox. Very soon the French opened three great breaches, and an attack was imminent. They defended themselves in the Goicoechea mill, which they had taken the day before, after it had been abandoned and fired by us.

Certain of victory, the French ran forward over the plain, having received orders to attack. Our battalion occupied a house in the Calle de Pabostre, whose walls had been spiked along their whole length. Many peasants and various regiments were keeping watch in the Cortina, fiery of courage and with not the least terror before the almost certain likelihood of death, hopeful of being useful in death also, helping to stay the enemy's advance.

Long hours passed. The French questioned with the artillery to see if they were driving us out of the suburb; the walls were gradually being destroyed; the houses were being shaken down with the dreadful concussion; and the heroic people, few of whom had broken fast even with a bit of bread, were calling from the walls, saying that the enemy was coming. At last, against the right of the breach in the centre advanced strong columns sustained by others in the rear. We saw that the intention of the French was to possess themselves at all hazards of that line of crumbling bricks which some hundreds of madmen were defending, and to take it at any cost. Death-dealing masses were hurled forward, the living columns passing over the dead.

Let it not be said to make our merit less that the French were not fighting under cover. Neither were we, for none of us could show his head above the broken wall and keep it on. Masses of men dashed against one another, and bayonets were fed with brutal anger upon the bodies of enemies. From the houses came incessant fire. We could see the French fall in heaps, pierced by lead and steel, at the very foot of the ruins they were seeking to conquer. New columns took the places of the first, and in those who came after, brutalities of vengeance were added to prodigies of valor.

On our side the number of those who fell was enormous. The dead were left by dozens upon the earth along that line which had been a wall, but was now no more than a shapeless mass of earth, bricks, and corpses. The natural, the human thing would have been to abandon such positions, and not try to hold them against such a combination of force and military skill. But there was nothing of the human or the natural here. Instead, the power of defence was extended infinitely, to limits not recognized by scientific calculation, beyond ordinary valor. The Aragonese nature stood forth, and it is one which does not know how to be conquered. The living took the places of the dead with a sublime aplomb. Death was an accident, a trivial detail, a thing of which no notice should be taken.

While this was going on, other columns equally powerful were trying to take the Casa de Gonzalez, which I have before mentioned. But from the neighboring houses, and the towers of the wall, came such a terrible fire of rifles and cannons that they desisted from their attempt. Other attacks took place, with better results for them, at our right, toward the orchard of Camporeal and the batteries of Los Martires. The immense force displayed by the besiegers along one line of short extent could not fail to produce results. From the house in the Calle de Pabostre, close to the Molino of the city, we were, as I have said, firing upon the besiegers, when behold the batteries of San José, formerly occupied in demolishing the wall, directed their cannons against that ancient edifice. We felt that the walls were trembling; the beams were cracking like the timbers of a ship tossed by a tempest; the wood of the walls was cracking too in a thousand fragments. In short, the place was tumbling down.

"Cuerno, recuerno!" exclaimed Uncle Garces, "what if the house falls down upon us!"

The smoke of the powder prevented us from seeing what was going on without or within.

"To the street! To the street!" cried Pirli, throwing himself out of a window.

"Augustine! Augustine! where art thou?" I called to my friend. But Augustine did not appear. In that moment of alarm, not finding either doorway or ladder to descend, I ran to a window to throw myself out; and the spectacle which met my eyes obliged me to draw back without strength or breath. While the cannons of San José were essaying on the right to bury us in the ruins of the house, and seemed to be accomplishing it without effort, in front of and towards the gardens of San Augustine, the French infantry had succeeded at last in penetrating the breaches, killing those unhappy creatures scarcely to be called men, and finishing those who were already dying, for indeed their desperate agony could not be called life.

From the neighboring alleys came a horrible fire. The cannons of the Calle de Diezma took the place of those of the conquered battery. But the breach taken, the French were securing themselves on the walls. It was impossible for me to feel in my soul a spark of energy on beholding such stupendous disaster.

I fled from the window, terrified,—beside myself. A piece of the wall cracked and fell in enormous fragments, and a square window took the shape of an isosceles triangle; through a corner of the roof I could see the sky. Bits of lime and splinters struck me in the face. I ran further in, following others, who were saying, "This way! this way!"

"Augustine! Augustine!" I called again. At last I saw him among those who were running from one room to another, going up a ladder which led to a garret.

"Are you alive?" I asked him.

"I do not know; it is not important," he answered.

In the garret we broke through a partition wall, and passing into another room, we found an outside staircase. We descended and came to another house. Some soldiers followed, looking for a place to get into the street, and others remained there. The picture of that poor little room is indelibly fixed in my memory, with all its lines and colors, and flooded with plentiful light from a large window, opened upon the street. Portraits of the Virgin and of the saints covered the uneven walls. Two or three old trunks covered with goat-skin stood on one side. On the other side we saw a woman's clothes hanging upon hooks and nails, and a very high but poor-looking bed, although the sheets were fresh. In the window were three large flower-pots with plants in them. Sheltered behind them were two women firing furiously upon the French who occupied the breach. They had two guns. One was charging, the other firing. The one who was firing had been stooping to aim from behind the flower-pots. Resting the trigger a minute, she lifted her head a little to look at the field of battle.

"Manuela Sancho," I exclaimed, placing my hand upon the head of the heroic girl, "resistance is no longer of any use. The next house is already destroyed by the batteries of San José, and the balls are already beginning to fall upon the roof of this. Let us go."

She took no notice, and went on shooting. At last the house, which was even less able than its neighbor to sustain the shock of the projectiles, quivered as if the earth trembled beneath its foundations. Manuela Sancho threw down her gun. She and the woman who was with her ran into an alcove, where I heard them crying bitterly. Entering, we found the two girls embracing an old crippled woman who was trying to get up from her bed.

"Mother, it is nothing," Manuela said soothingly, covering her with whatever came first to her hand; "we are only going into the street because it seems as if the house is going to fall down."

The old woman did not speak. She could not speak. The two girls had taken her in their arms; but we took her in ours, charging them to bring our guns and whatever clothing they could save. We passed out into a court which opened into another street where the fire had not yet reached.

XVIII

The French had taken possession also of the battery of Los Martires. That same afternoon they were masters of the ruins of Santa Engracia and the convent of Trinitarios. Is it conceivable that the defence of one plaza continued after all that surrounded it was taken? No, it is not conceivable; nor in all military prevision has it ever been supposed that after the enemy had gained the walls by irresistible superiority of material strength, the houses would offer new lines of defence improvised on the initiative of every citizen. It is not conceivable that one house taken, a veritable siege must necessarily be organized to take the next one, employing the spade, the mine, the bayonet,—devising an ingenious stratagem against a partition wall. It is not conceivable that one part of a pavement being taken, it would be necessary to pass opposite to it to put into execution the theories of Vauban, and that to cross a gutter it would be necessary to make trenches, zig-zags, and covered ways.

The French generals put their hands to their brows, saying, "This is not like anything that we have ever seen. In the glorious annals of the empire one finds many passages like this: 'We have entered Spandau. Tomorrow we shall be in Berlin.' That which had not yet been written was this: 'After two days and two nights of fighting, we have taken house No. 1 in the Calle de Pabostre. We do not know when we shall be able to take No. 2.'"

We had no time for rest. The two cannons that raked the Calle de Pabostre and the angle of the Puerta Quemada were left entirely without men. Some of us ran to serve them, and the rest occupied houses in the Calle de Palomar. The French stopped firing against the buildings which had been abandoned, repairing them and occupying them as rapidly as they could. They stopped up holes with beams, gravel, and sacks of wool. As they could not traverse without risk the space between their new quarters and the crumbling walls, they commenced to open a ditch and zig-zag from the Molino of the city to the house which we had occupied, and of which now only the lowest story offered any lodgment. We knew that when once masters of that house they would try, by tearing down partition walls, to gain possession of the whole block. In order to prevent this, the troops which we could spare were distributed through all the buildings in danger of such attack. At the same time our troops were raising barricades at the entrances of the streets, availing themselves of the rubbish and fragments in their work. We toiled with frenzied ardor in these various tasks. The fighting was least difficult of all. From inside the houses we threw down over the balconies all the furniture and movables. We carried the wounded outside, leaving the dead to the same fate as the buildings. Indeed, the only funeral honors that we could pay them was to leave them where they would not be disturbed. The French worked also to gain Santa Monica, the convent situated in a line with Las Tenerias, a little to the north of the Calle de Pabostre; but its walls offered a strong resistance, and it was not as easy to take as the fragile houses which the booming of the cannon caused to tremble. The volunteers of Huesca defended it vigorously; and, after repeated attacks, the besiegers left the assault for another day. Having gained possession only of a few houses, they remained in them when night came, like rabbits in a warren. Woe to the head that appeared at a window! The neighboring walls, the roofs, the skylights were filled with attentive eyes that saw the least carelessness of a French soldier, and guns were ready for him.

When night came, we began to make holes in the partition walls in order to open communication between all the houses in the same block. In spite of the incessant noise of the cannon, we could hear within the buildings the picks of the enemy occupied in the same sort of work as ourselves. As the architecture was fragile, and almost all the partition walls were of earth, we had in a short time opened passages between many houses.

About ten o'clock at night, we found ourselves in one which we knew must be very near that of Manuela Sancho, when we heard, through unknown conduits, through cellars and subterranean passages, a sound which we realized must be the voices of the enemy. A terrified woman came up a ladder and told us that the French were opening a gap in the wall of the room below. We descended instantly. We were not yet all in the cold, narrow, dark place, when at its mouth a gun was fired at us, and one of our companions was slightly wounded in the shoulder.

By the dim light we perceived several figures that forced their way into the room, and, advancing, fired, while others came behind. At the noise of gunshots, our friends hurried down to us, and we penetrated boldly into the dark place. The enemy did not remain in it, and as swiftly as possible hurried back through the hole they had opened in the wall, seeking refuge in the place whence they had come. We sent

BENITO PÉREZ GALDÓS

some balls after them. We were not completely in darkness, as they had a lantern some of whose feeble rays came through the aperture diffusing a reddish light over the theatre of the struggle.

I have never seen anything like it, nor did I ever behold a combat between four black walls by the faint light of a lantern that cast flickering shadows like spectres around us. The light was prejudicial to the French; for we were on the safe, dark side of the hole, and they were good targets for us. We shot at them for a short time, and two of our comrades fell, dead or badly wounded, upon the damp earth. In spite of this disaster, others came to push the advantage, assaulting the hole in the wall and penetrating into the enemy's den. But although fire had ceased there, it seemed as if the enemy were preparing for a better attack. Suddenly the lantern went out, and we were left in black darkness. We looked about for the way out, and stumbled against one another. This state of things, together with the fear of being attacked by superior forces, or that they would hurl shells into that sepulchre, made us huddle confusedly into the outer court as soon as we found the way. We took time, nevertheless, to find our two comrades who had fallen during the fray; then we went out and shut up the aperture with stones and rubbish and planks and barrels, whatever came to our hands in the court-yard. On going up, our commander detailed men in different parts of the house, leaving a couple of sentinels in the court to listen to the blows of the hostile pick. He sent me out with others to bring in a little food, of which we were all much in need.

In the street it seemed to us that we had come from a tranquil position into a very hell, for now in the dead of night the firing was continued between the houses and the walls. The clearness of the moonlight made it easy to run from one point to another without stumbling, and the streets were constantly traversed by bodies of troops and peasants who were going where, according to the public voice, there was some real danger. Many, not in the lines, guided by their own instincts, ran here and there, firing whenever opportunity offered. The bells of all the churches sounded a mournful call, and at each step we encountered groups of women carrying the wounded.

In all directions, especially at the extremities of the streets that ended at the walls of Las Tenerias, bodies were seen stacked up in piles, the wounded mingled with those already corpses. It was not possible to tell from which mouths came the pitiful voices that implored aid. I have never seen such horrible suffering. I was impressed more than by the spectacle of the disasters caused by iron and steel, seeing many who were suffering from the epidemic lying on the doorsteps of the houses, or dragging themselves through the throng in search of a safe place. They were dying every moment without having a sign of a wound upon them. Their teeth chattered with the dreadful chill, and they begged for help, holding out their hands because they could not speak.

In addition to all this, hunger was demoralizing us. We could scarcely stand.

"Where shall we ever find something to eat?" Augustine asked me. "Who is going to see about that?"

"This thing must end soon in one way or the other," I answered; "either the city will surrender, or we shall all perish."

At last, near the Coso, we met some of the commissary who were dealing out rations. We took ours eagerly, taking also all that we could carry for our comrades. They received it with a great racket, and a sort of joviality inappropriate to the circumstances. But the Spanish soldier is and always has been like that. While they were eating some crusts of bread as hard as cobble-stones, the unanimous opinion spread through the battalion that Saragossa never would surrender, and never should surrender.

It was midnight when the firing dwindled down. The French had not conquered a hand's breadth of earth more than the houses they had occupied at sunset, although they were not to be driven out of the quarters they had taken. This was left for the days that followed. When the influential men of the city, the Montorias, the Ceresos, the Sases, the Salameros, and the San Clementes were returning to Las Monicas, the scene that night of great prodigies of valor, they showed such tremendous courage and uttered such contempt of the enemy that it roused the spirits of all who saw and heard them.

"Little has been accomplished tonight," said Montoria. "Our men have been a bit remiss. It is true that it was not possible to drive them all out, nor ought we to have come out into the open, though the French attacked us with little energy. I have seen a few defeats, nothing of consequence. The nuns have beaten up plenty of oil with wine, and now it is only a question of binding up a few wounds. If there were time, it would be well to bury the dead in this heap, but there will be more presently. The epidemic is getting hold of more men. They need rubbing. Plenty of rubbing is what I believe in. For the present, they can very well go without broth. Broth is an unpleasant beverage. I would give them a dose of spirits. In a little while they would be able to handle a gun. Well, sirs, the fiesta appears to be over for tonight. Let us take a nap for half an hour, and tomorrow,—tomorrow, I have a notion that the French will make a formal attack upon us."

He turned to his son, who had come up with me, and cried out,—

"Oh, my Augustine, I have been asking for you, because in such a battle as today it happens that some must die. Are you wounded? You have nothing the matter? Let us see, a little gun-scratch? Ah, a trifle! It strikes me that you have scarcely borne yourself like a Montoria. And you, Araceli, have you lost any legs? Not even that! The two of you have just come out from some good shelter, I should say. You have not even turned a hair. It's a bad business. I call you a pair of hens! Go, rest awhile, not more than a hand's shake. If you feel yourselves attacked by the epidemic, rubbing and plenty of it is the best thing. Well, sirs, we depend upon it that tomorrow these houses will be defended wall by wall, partition by partition. The same thing will go on in every part of the city, and in every alcove there will be a battle. Let us go to the Captain-General, and see if Palafox agrees with us. There is no other way,—either to deliver the city to them, or to dispute each brick as if it were a treasure. We will tire them out. Today six or eight thousand men have perished. Now let us go and see that most excellent Señor Don José. Goodnight, boys, and tomorrow try and manage to shake off your cowardice."

"Let us go and sleep a little," I said to my friend. "Let us come to a house where I have seen some mattresses."

"I cannot sleep," said Montoria, walking on along the Coso.

"I know where you are going. We are not permitted to go as far as that, Augustine."

Many men and women were running up and down, back and forth in the broad avenue. All of a sudden a woman came running swiftly to us and embraced Augustine, speechless, deep emotion choking her.

"Mariquilla, Mariquilla of my heart!" exclaimed Montoria, embracing her joyously. "How is it that you are here? I was just now going in search of you."

Mariquilla could not speak, and, without the sustaining arm of her lover, her weak and wavering body would have fallen to the ground.

"Are you ill? What is the matter? Is it true that the bombs have destroyed your house?"

It was even so, and the young girl's whole aspect showed her great distress. Her clothing was that which we saw on her the night before.

Her hair was loosened, and we could see burns upon her poor bruised arms.

"Yes," she said, at last, in a stifled voice. "Our house is gone. We have nothing. We have lost everything. This morning, soon after you had gone, a bomb destroyed the house, then two others fell."

"And your father?"

"My father is there, and will not abandon the ruins of the house. I have been looking for you all day, for you to help us. I have been under fire. I have been in all the streets of the suburb. I have entered several houses. I was afraid that you were dead."

Augustine seated himself in a gateway, and, sheltering Mariquilla with his military cloak, he held her in his arms as one holds a child. Freed thus from her terror, she could talk; and she told us that she had not been able to save a single thing. They had scarcely had time to get out of the house. The unhappy girl was trembling with cold, and, putting my cloak over Augustine's, we tried to take her to the house where we were on duty.

"No," she said, "I must go back to my father. He is wild and desperate, and is uttering blasphemies against God and the saints. I have not been able to get him away from that which was our house. We are in need of food. The neighbors were not willing to give us anything. If you are not willing to take me there, I will go alone."

"No, Mariquilla, no. You shall not go there," said Montoria. "We will put you in one of these houses where at least for tonight you will be safe. In the mean time Gabriel shall go in search of your father, and take him something to eat, and by persuasion or by force will get him away from there."

Mariquilla insisted upon returning to the Calle de Anton Trillo. But as she scarcely had strength to move, we took her in our arms to a house in the Calle de los Clavos, where Manuela Sancho was.

XIX

The firing of the guns and cannon ceased. A great splendor was illumining the city. It was the burning of the Audiencia. The fire, beginning about midnight, was devouring all four sides of that splendid edifice at one time. Without heeding anything but my errand, I hurried to the Calle de Anton Trillo. The house of Candiola had been burning all day. At last the flame had been stifled by pieces of falling roofs, and between the portions of walls still standing issued black columns of smoke. Through the window-frames showed patches of sky, and the bricks, crumbling away, had made a ragged-toothed looking thing of that which had been an architrave. Part of the wall which fronted on the garden had fallen down over the balcony, covering the end where the railing and the stone stairway had been, its stones spreading forward to the street wall. In the midst of these ruins the cypress stood unharmed, like the life which remains when the substance is gone. It raised its black head like a memorial. The gate had been destroyed by the axes of those who had rushed up at first to try to put out the fire.

When I penetrated into the garden, I saw some people at the right and near the grating of a lower window. It was the part of the house which was best preserved. And, indeed, the lower floor had suffered little, perhaps nothing; the bulging out of the roof of the principal part had not affected this, although it was to be expected that it would give way sooner or later under the great weight. I approached the group to find Candiola. He was there, seated close to the grating with his hands crossed, his head upon his breast, his clothing torn and burned. He was surrounded by a little crowd of women and boys, who were buzzing about him like bees, pouring forth the whole gamut of insults and taunts. It cost me no great trouble to put the swarm to flight; and although they did not all go far away, and persisted in hanging about, thinking to get a chance at the gold of the rich Candiola, he was at least freed from the annoyance of their immediate presence, and the sneers and cruel jests with which he had been tormented.

"Señor soldier," he said to me, "I am grateful to you for putting this vile mob to flight. Here my house is burned and no one helps me. Are there no authorities now in Saragossa, señor? What a people! What a people! It is not because we have not paid our taxes."

"The civil authorities do not occupy themselves except with the military operations," I answered him; "and so many houses have been destroyed that it is impossible to run to them all."

"May he be cursed a thousand times!" he cried, "a thousand curses be on the head of him who has brought all this distress upon us! May he be tormented in hell for a thousand eternities, and then he would not pay the penalty of his crime. But what the devil are you looking for here, señor soldier? Are you not willing to leave me in peace?"

"I have come in search of Señor Candiola," I replied, "in order to take him where he can be looked after, have his wounds dressed, and be given a little food."

"For me? I will not leave my house," he cried in a sad voice. "The committee will have to rebuild it for me. Where do you want to take me? I am in the situation now to be offered alms. My enemies have their will, which was to put me in the position of begging alms. But I shall not beg, no. I will sooner eat my own flesh and drink my own blood than humble myself before those who have brought me to such a state. Perhaps they have sold themselves to the French, and prolong the resistance to earn their money. Then they will deliver the city, and they will be all right."

"Do leave all those considerations for another time!" I said. "And follow me now, because it is not the time to think about all that. Your daughter has found a place of safety, and we will give you a refuge in the same place."

"I do not move from here. Where is my daughter?" he asked anxiously. "She must be mad not to stay beside her father in his distress. It is because she is ashamed, that she deserted me. Curse her, and the hour when I begat her! Lord Jesus of Nazareth and thou my patron, Saint Dominguito del Val, tell me what have I done to deserve so many misfortunes in the same day? Am I not good? Do I not do all the good I can? Do I not favor my neighbors, lending them money at low interest? Suppose I do ask a trifle of three or four reales on the dollar by the month? If I am a good man, exact and careful, why is such distress heaped upon me? I am thankful that I have not lost the little that by hard work I have got together, because it is in a place where the bombs cannot reach it; but the house and the furniture, and the receipts, and that which was left in the storehouse! May I be damned, and may the devils eat me, if when this is all over, and I get together the little that I have here, I do not leave Saragossa, never again to return!"

"Nothing of all this is to the point now, Señor Candiola," I said impatiently; "come with me!"

"No," said he furiously. "No, it would be madness! My daughter has disgraced herself. I do not know why I did not kill her this morning. Until now I had supposed Mariquilla a model of virtue and honesty. I delighted in her companionship; and out of every good deal I set apart a real to buy her finery,—money badly spent! My God, dost thou punish me for wasting good money on useless things which if placed at interest would have been tripled? I had confidence in my daughter. This morning at daybreak, I began by praying with fervor to the Virgin del Pilar to free me from the bombardment. I tranquilly opened the window to see what the weather was. Put yourself in my place, señor soldier, and you will understand my surprise and pain at seeing two men right over there in that balcony,—two men, sir. I see them now! One of them was embracing my daughter. They were both dressed in uniform. I could not see their faces, for the light of day was yet faint. Hurriedly I left my room; but when I descended to the garden, the two were already in the street. My daughter was dumb at seeing her lightness discovered. Reading in my face the indignation which such vile conduct roused in me, she threw herself on her knees before me, begging my pardon. 'Wretch!' I said in a rage, 'you are not my daughter! You are not the daughter of this honorable man who has never done wrong to anybody. Mad child, shameless, you are not my daughter! Leave this place! Two men, two men in my house at night, with you! Have you not been making it easy for those men to rob me? Have you not shown them this house where there are a thousand objects of value which can be concealed in a pocket? You deserve death. If,—yes,—I am not deceived, those men carried away something. Two men, two sweethearts! And receiving them at night and in my house, dishonoring your father and offending God. And I from my room saw the light in yours, and believed that you were wakeful and working. You wretched little thing, while you were in the garden that light in your room was wasting, burning uselessly. You miserable woman!' Oh, señor soldier, I could not contain my indignation. I seized her by the arm and dragged her along to throw her out. In my anger I knew not what I did. The wretched girl begged my pardon, saying, 'I love him, father, I cannot deny that I love him.' My fury was redoubled at this, and I cried, 'Cursed be the bread that I have given you for nineteen years, to invite thieves into my house! Cursed be the hour when you were born, and the linens in which we wrapped you on the third of February in the year '91!

Sooner shall the heavens fall, sooner shall the Virgin del Pilar let me go from her hand, than I will again be your father, and you be for me the Mariquilla that I have so much loved!'

"I had scarcely said this, señor, when it seemed as if the very heavens were rent in pieces, falling upon my house. What a terrible noise it was! A bomb fell upon the roof, and within five minutes two others fell. We ran in; the flames were spreading hungrily, and the falling of the roof threatened to bury us where we stood. We tried in great haste to save some few little things; but it was not possible. This house, this house which I bought in the year '87 for almost nothing, because the mortgage on it was foreclosed against a debtor who owed me five thousand reales with thirteen thousand reales interest,—this house was fairly crumbling to bits. Over there a plank fell; over there a pane of glass leaped out; on the side yonder the walls burst in. The cat yowled, and Doña Guedita fairly clawed me in the face as we got out of the room. I ventured into my own room to try to get some little receipts, and came near perishing."

Candiola's distress and moral suffering made it seem as if he had a nervous disorder. It was plain to be seen that terror and grief had completely upset him. His talkativeness was not of the sort that soothes the soul, it was a nervous overflow; and although he appeared to talk with me, he was in reality addressing himself to invisible beings. To judge by his gestures, they talked to him in turn. He went on talking, and answering questions which his imaginary interlocutors were asking him.

"I have said already that I shall not leave this place while such a quantity of things which can still be saved is not recovered. Indeed, am I going to abandon my estate? Are there no authorities in Saragossa? If there are, then a hundred or two workmen should be sent here to remove this débris and take out something. But, señor, is there no one who has any charity for, any compassion upon this unhappy old man who has never harmed anybody? Shall one sacrifice all one's life for others, and, coming into such a plight as this, find no friendly hand held out to help him? No, no one comes, or if they do, it is to see if they can find any money among the ruins. Ha, ha, ha!" he laughed like a madman. "It is a good joke on them. I have always been a cautious man, and since the siege began I have put my frugal savings in a place so secure that I alone can find them. No, thieves! no, swindlers! no, selfish ones!—you would not find a real, though you should lift every fragment and break into bits the ruins of this house, though you make toothpicks of all the wood in it, though you reduce everything to powder and sift it!"

BENITO PÉREZ GALDÓS

"Then, Señor Candiola," I said, taking him resolutely by the arm to lead him away, "if your treasures are safe, what is the good of staying here to watch them? Let us go!"

"Have you not understood me, you meddlesome fellow?" he cried, loosing his arm forcibly; "go to the devil, and leave me in peace! How do you suppose I am going to leave my house when the authorities of Saragossa have not sent a detachment of troops to guard it? Indeed! Do you suppose that my house is not full of valuable things? How can you think that I would go from here without taking them? You can see that this first story is unhurt? By removing this grating, it could be easily entered and everything taken away. If I tear myself from here for a single moment, the thieves will come, the refuse of the neighborhood, and woe to all my work and my savings then, to the furniture and utensils which represent forty years of hard work. Look on the table of my room, señor soldier, and you will find a copper dish which weighs no less than three pounds. That must be saved at any cost. If the authorities would send a company of engineers here, as it is their duty to do—There is a table service in the cupboard in the dining-room which must remain intact. By entering carefully, propping up the roof, they could save it. Oh, yes, it is absolutely necessary to save that set. It is not merely that, señor. In a tin box are my receipts. I hope to save them. There is also a trunk where I keep two old coats and some shoes and three hats. All these things are down here on this story, and are not likely to be hurt. My daughter's clothing is all irrecoverably lost. Her dresses, her jewelry, her handkerchiefs, her bottles of perfume would be worth a good sum of money if they were to be had now. How could it be that all this should be destroyed? My Lord, what trouble! It must be true that God wished to punish the sin of my daughter, and the bombs fell upon her bottles of perfume. I left my waistcoat upon the bed, and in the pocket there was a peseta and a half. And there are not even twenty men here yet with picks and spades. Just and merciful Heaven, what are the authorities of Saragossa thinking about! The double-wicked lamp will not be ruined. It is the best olive-oil burner in the world. We might find it over yonder, by lifting carefully the fragments of that corner room. Let them send workmen here, and see that they do it quickly. How can anyone expect me to leave this place? If I should go, or if I should sleep for a single instant, the thieves would come. Yes, they will come, and take away that piece of copper from Palma."

The obstinacy of the miser was so persistent that I resolved to go without him, leaving him given over to his delirious anxiety. Doña

Guedita now arrived, walking hastily. She brought a pick and spade, and a little basket in which I saw some provisions.

"Señor," she said, sitting down tired and breathless, "here's the pick and spade my nephew has given me. They will not need them anymore, because they are not going to make anymore fortifications. Here are some half-spoiled raisins and some crusts of bread." The old woman ate hungrily; not so Candiola, who, despising the bread, seized the pick. Resolutely, as if his body were suddenly filled with new energy, he tried to unhinge the grating; working with eager activity, he said,—

"If the authorities of Saragossa are not willing to do their duty by me, Doña Guedita, between you and me, we will do it all! You take the spade and get ready to move the fragments as I dig. Look out for the beams that are still smoking. Look out for the nails!"

I was trying to interpret the signs of intelligence made me by the housekeeper, when he turned to me, saying,—

"Go to the devil! What business have you in my house? Get out of here! We understand you,—you have come to see if you can pick up anything. There is nothing here. Everything is burned up."

There was certainly no hope of taking him with me to Las Tenerias to set poor Mariquilla's mind at rest, and so, not being able to stay any longer, I went. Master and servant were working away with great vigor.

XX

I slept from three o'clock until daybreak, and in the morning we heard mass in the Coso. In the large balcony of a house called Las Monas at the entrance of the Calle de las Escuelas Pias all the priests had set up an altar and celebrated there the divine office. By the situation of the building, it was possible to see the priests from anywhere in the Coso. It was a profoundly moving sight, especially at the moment of the elevation of the host; and when all knelt in prayer, the low murmur of the service could be heard from one end of the street to the other.

A little while after the mass was ended, I heard a large number of people coming from the direction of the market,—an angry and noisy crowd. In the mob, and striving to quell its violence, were several friars; but it was a mob of men deaf to the voice of reason. They were yelling themselves hoarse, and as they came, they dragged along a victim who was powerless to free himself from their grasp. The maddened people took him to the place near the entrance of the Trenque where the gallows was; and in a few moments the convulsed body of a man was hanging from one of its ropes, and was jerked about in the air until it was lifeless. On the wood of the gallows an inscription soon appeared, which read,—

An assassin
of human kind,
who
kept back twenty thousand beds.

The wretch was one Fernando Estello, watchman of a storehouse of furniture. When the sick and wounded were breathing their last in the gutters and on the cold tiles of the churches, there was found a great collection of beds whose hiding the watchman Estello could not account for. The wrath of the populace was not to be restrained. I have heard that he was innocent. Many lamented his death; but when the firing in the trenches began again, no one remembered him more.

Palafox published that day a proclamation in which he tried to raise the spirits of the soldiers, promising the rank of captain to the man who should bring him a hundred recruits, threatening with the penalty of death and confiscation of property the man who should fail to hasten to the defence, or should leave the lines. All this showed great distress on the part of the commanding officers. That day was memorable for the attack on Santa Monica, which the volunteers of Huesca were defending. During the greater part of the night the French had been bombarding the building. The batteries of the orchard were no longer serviceable, and it was necessary to take away the cannon, an operation performed by our valiant men, exposed without protection to the hostile fire. This opened a breach at last; and, penetrating into the orchard, they tried to gain possession of that also, forgetting that they had twice been repulsed on previous days. But Lannes, exasperated by the extraordinary and unprecedented tenacity of the Saragossans, had given orders to reduce the convent to powder,—a thing which was easier to accomplish with the cannon and howitzer than to take it by storm. At all events, after six hours of artillery fire, a large part of the eastern wall fell, and then the French showed their exultation, and, without loss of time, rushed forward to seize the position, aided by the cross-fire from the Molino in the city. Seeing them coming, Villacampa, commander of the Huesca men, and Palafox, who had hurried to the point of danger, tried to close up the breach with sacks of wool and some empty musket-boxes. The French, reaching the spot, made a mad, furious assault, but, after a brief hand-to-hand struggle, they were repulsed. During the night they went on cannonading the convent.

The next day they decided to make another attack, certain that no mortal could defend that skeleton of stone and brick which every moment was crumbling to the earth. They assailed it at the door of the reception-room; but during all the morning they did not conquer a hand's breadth of earth in the cloister.

The wall of the eastern side of the convent fell flat to the earth during the afternoon. The third floor, which was very much weakened, could not hold the weight, and fell upon the second. The latter, which was even weaker, could not help letting itself go upon the first; and the first, incapable of sustaining by itself the weight of the whole structure above, fairly poured itself out over the cloister, burying hundreds of men. It would have been but natural had the rest been intimidated by such a catastrophe, but they were not. The French gained possession of one part of the convent, but not of all; and, in order to gain the rest, they were obliged to clear a road through the ruins. While they were doing this, the men of Huesca who still survived, placed themselves in

BENITO PÉREZ GALDÓS

the stairway, and made holes through the floor, in order to throw hand-grenades against the besiegers.

Fresh French troops were, however, able to reach the church. They passed over the roof of the convent, and spread themselves in the interior; they descended to the cloisters and attacked the brave volunteers. Hearing the noise of this encounter, those below plucked up heart, redoubled their energy, and, with the loss of a great number of men, succeeded in reaching the stairway. The volunteers found themselves between two fires, and although it was still possible for them to get out by one of the two openings in the cloister, almost all of them swore that they would die before they would surrender. They all ran, seeking for a strategic point which would permit them to defend themselves to some advantage; but they were driven the length of the cloisters, and when the last gun-shot was heard, it was the signal that the last man had fallen. A few inside the building were able to get out by an underground door. Don Pedro Villacampa, commander of the Huesca volunteers, came out into the city that way, and when he found himself in the street, he turned, looking about mechanically for his boys.

During this fight we were in the houses about the Calle de Palomar, firing upon the French detachment sent to assault the convent. Before the battle was over, we learned that defence was no longer possible in Las Monicas. Don José de Montoria himself, who was with us, confessed it.

"The volunteers of Huesca have not borne themselves badly," he said. "They are known to be good fellows. Now we must busy ourselves defending these houses on the right. I do not suppose that one is left. There goes Villacampa alone. Then are not those Mendieta, and Paul, Benedicto, and Oliva? Let us go. I see that indeed none are left in that place."

In this way the convent of Las Monicas passed into the hands of the French.

XXI

O n reaching this point in my story, I beg the reader to pardon me if I do not give the dates exactly of that which I relate. In this period of horror, lasting from January 27 to the middle of the next month, the successive events are so confused, so mixed up, so run together in my mind, that I cannot distinguish days and nights, and, in some instances, I do not know whether certain skirmishes of those I recall took place in daylight. It seems to me that all happened during one long day, or in one endless night, and that time was not then marked by its ordinary divisions. Many sensations and impressions are linked together in my memory, forming one vast picture where there are no more dividing lines than those that the events themselves offer,—the greater fright of one moment, the unexplained panic or fury of another.

For this reason I cannot tell exactly on what day that took place which I am going to relate now; but if I am not mistaken it was on a day after the fight at Las Monicas, and somewhere, I should say, between the thirtieth of January and the second of February. We were occupying a house in the Calle de Pabostre. The French were in the one next to it, and were trying to advance through the inside of the block to reach the Puerta Quemada. Nothing can compare with the incessant activity going on there. No kind of warfare, no bloodiest battle on the open field, no sieges of a plaza, nor struggles in a street barricade can compare with the succession of conflicts between the army of an alcove and the army of a drawing-room, between the troops that occupy one floor and those which guard the one above it.

Hearing the muffled blows of the picks at various points, not knowing from what direction the attack might come, caused us some alarm. We went up into attics; we descended into cellars, and glued our ears to partition walls; we tried to learn the intentions of the enemy according to the direction of the blows. At last we noticed that the partition wall was being violently shaken near the very place where we were standing, and we waited fire in the doorway, after heaping up the furniture as a barricade. The French opened a hole, and presently began leaping over beams and broken fragments, showing an intention of driving us from the place. There were twenty of us, fewer of them, and they evidently did not expect to be received in such fashion, and retreated, returning soon with such reinforcement that we were in great danger, and obliged to retire, leaving five comrades behind the furniture, two of them dead. In the narrow passage we ran against a stairway up which we hurried without knowing where we were going, and presently found ourselves in a garret,—an admirable position for defence. The stairway was narrow, however, and the Frenchmen who tried to come up it died inevitably. So we remained for sometime, prolonging the resistance, and encouraging one another with huzzas and shouts, when the partition at our backs began to resound with loud blows, and we saw immediately that the French, by opening an entrance through there, would catch us between two fires without means of escape. We were now thirteen, as two had fallen in the garret, severely wounded. Tio Garces, who was in command, shouted furiously: "By heaven, the dogs shall not catch us! There's a skylight in the roof. Let us go up through it to the tiles of the roof. Go on firing at whoever comes up to try and cut through it! The rest of you enlarge the hole. Away with fear, and viva the Virgin del Pilar!"

It was done as he commanded. This was to be a well-ordered retreat, according to the rules of war; and while part of our army was preventing the onward march of the enemy, the rest were occupied in facilitating the retreat. This able plan was put into execution with feverish activity, and very soon the hole of escape was large enough for three men to pass through at once, without the French gaining a single step during the time that we were employed in this way. We quickly got out on the roof. We were now nine. Three had been left in the garret, and another was wounded in trying to get out, falling still alive, into the hands of the enemy. On finding ourselves outside, we leaped for joy. We cast a glance over the roofs of the quarter, and saw at a distance the batteries of the French. We advanced on all fours for a good distance, exploring the lay of the land, leaving two sentinels in the gap to pop off a gun at anyone who should seek to slip up by them. We had not gone twenty paces when we heard a great noise of voices and laughter which seemed to us to be French. And so it was; from a broad balcony those rascals were looking at us and laughing. They were not slow in firing upon us, but protected behind the chimneys, the angles and corners which the roof afforded, we answered them shot for shot, and replied to their oaths and exclamations by a thousand other invectives with which the lively imagination of Tio Garces inspired us. At last we retreated, jumping to the roof of the next house. We believed it to be in the hands of our own men, and we entered by the window of a little upper room, supposing that the descent from there to the street would be easy, and that there we should be reinforced for the conclusion of the adventure that had carried us through passages, up stairways, through garrets, and over roofs. But we had scarcely set foot there, when we heard in the apartment below us the sound of many blows on the wall.

"They are beating in there," said Tio Garces, and in a second the French whom we had left in the house next us had passed to this one, where they met comrades.

"Cuerno! Recuerno! Let us get out of this! The whole creation's down below there."

We passed on into another garret, and found our way to a ladder leading down to a large interior room, from whose doorway came the lively sound of voices, chiefly those of women. The noise of the fight seemed much further off, and we decided it must be at some distance. So we dropped down the ladder and found ourselves in a large room filled with old men, women, and children who had all sought refuge here. Many, lying upon rude mattresses, showed in their faces traces of the terrible epidemic, and one lifeless body lay on the floor, breath evidently having left it but a few moments before. Some were wounded, suffering cruelly and groaning unrestrainedly; two or three old women were weeping and praying. Occasionally voices were heard begging, "Water, water!" From where we entered, I saw Candiola at the end of the room, carefully depositing in a corner a quantity of clothes and kitchen utensils and crockery. With an angry gesture he drove away the curious children who wished to look over and handle the poor stuff. Anxious, eager only to heap together and guard his treasures without losing a fragment, he was saying,—

"I have already lost two cups. And I have no doubt whatever as to what has become of them. Someone of these people has taken them. There is no security anywhere; there are no authorities to guarantee to a citizen the possession of his property. Out of here, you unmannerly boys! Oh, we are hard pushed! Cursed be the bombs and the one who invented them! Soldiers, you have come in good time. Can you not have two sentinels placed here for me to guard these treasures which I have been able to save only with great trouble?"

My comrades laughed at such pretension, as may readily be believed. We were just about to go, when I saw Mariquilla. The poor girl was sadly changed from lack of sleep, much weeping, and the constant alarms. But the trouble of her brow, and that which looked forth from her eyes, only added to the sweetness of expression of her beautiful face.

BENITO PÉREZ GALDÓS

She saw me, and immediately came eagerly up to me, showing that she wished to speak with me.

"And Augustine?" I asked her.

"He is down there," she replied in tremulous tones. "They are fighting below. We who took refuge in this house have been apportioned to different rooms. My father came this morning with Doña Guedita. Augustine brought us something to eat, and put us in a room where there was a mattress. Suddenly we heard blows on the partition walls. The French were coming. The troops entered, and made us leave, carrying the sick and wounded to an upper room. They shut us all in, and then the walls were broken through. The French met the Spaniards then, and began real fighting. Yes, Augustine is below."

She was saying this when Manuela Sancho came, carrying two pitchers of water for the wounded. The poor wretches threw themselves from their beds, disputing even to blows over the water.

"No pushing, no scrambling, señors!" said Manuela, laughing. "There is water enough for all. Our side is winning. It has cost a little labor to drive the French from the alcove, and now they are disputing half of the hall, having gained one half of it. They do not wish to leave us a kitchen or a staircase. The whole place is filled with the dead."

Mariquilla turned pale with the horror of it.

"I am thirsty," she said to me.

I immediately tried to get some water for her from Manuela; but as the last glass she had was in use, quenching soldiers' thirst, as she went from mouth to mouth with it, I took, in order to lose no time, one of the cups which Candiola had in his pile.

"Eh, you meddler," he said, shaking his fist at me, "leave that cup here."

"I am getting it to give water to the señorita," I answered indignantly. "Are these things so valuable, Señor Candiola?"

The miser did not reply, but did not oppose my giving his daughter a drink. After her thirst was quenched, a wounded soldier reached out his hands eagerly for the cup, and, lo! it began to go the rounds also, passing from mouth to mouth. When I went to wait upon my comrades, Don Jeronimo followed me with his eyes, and watched with bad grace the forced loan that was so slow in returning to his hands.

Manuela Sancho was right in saying that our side was winning. The French, dislodged from the main floor of the house, had retired to the one below, where they continued their defence. When I descended, all the interest of the battle was centred in the kitchen, disputed with much bloodshed, but the rest of the house was in our power. Many bodies of French and Spanish covered the gory floor. Some soldiers and patriots, furious at not being able to conquer that dismal kitchen, whence such a fire was pouring, hurled themselves forward into it, defending themselves with their bayonets; and although a goodly number of them perished, their courageous act decided the matter, for behind them others could come, and then all that the room could hold.

The Imperial soldiers, panic-stricken with this violent assault, looked quickly for a way out of the house which had been taken room by room. We pursued them through passages and halls whose confused arrangement would craze the best military topographer. We finished them wherever we could find them, and some of them escaped, dashing in desperation out through the court-yards. In this manner, after reconquering one house, we reconquered the next one, obliging the enemy to restrict themselves to their old positions, which were the first two houses of the Calle de Pabostre.

Afterwards we removed our dead and wounded, and I had the sorrow of finding Augustine Montoria among the latter, although the gun-wound in his right arm was not of a serious nature. My battalion was reduced one-half that day. The unfortunates who had sought refuge in the upper room now wished to make themselves a little more comfortable in the lower rooms; but this was not thought practicable, and they were obliged to leave the place and look for an asylum further from danger.

Everyday, every hour, every instant, the increasing difficulties of our military situation were aggravated by the sight of the great number of unburied victims of battle and of the epidemic. Happy a thousand times those who were buried in the ruins of the undermined houses, as happened to the valiant defenders of the Calle de Pomar, close to the Santa Engracia! The most horrible thing was a great number of the wounded piled up together, so that nobody could get at them to help them. There was no medical aid for a hundredth part of them. The charity of women, the zeal of patriotic citizens, the multiplied activity of the hospitals, really availed nothing.

There came a time when a sort of impassibility, a dreadful apathy, began to take possession of the besieged. We became used to the sight of a heap of dead bodies, as if they were so many sacks of wool. We were accustomed to see, without pity, great numbers of the wounded creeping and tottering to the houses, each one caring for himself as best he could.

In the keenness of our sufferings, it seemed as if the usual necessities of the flesh had gone, and that we lived only in the spirit. Familiarity with danger had transformed our natures, infusing them apparently with a new element,—absolute contempt of the material, and indifference to life. Everyone expected to die at any moment, without the idea disturbing him in the least. I remember hearing described the attack on the Trinitarios convent, made in the hope of snatching it from the French, and the fabulous exploits, the inconceivable rashness of that undertaking seemed to me natural and ordinary.

I do not know whether I have said that next to the Convent de las Monicas was that of San Augustine, an edifice of good size, with a large church, spacious cloisters, and vast transepts. It was inevitable that the French, now masters of Las Monicas, should show great perseverance in the effort to gain possession of this monastery, in order to establish themselves firmly and definitely in that quarter.

"Since we have not the luck to be in Las Monicas," said Pirli to me, "we will, today, give ourselves the pleasure of defending until death the four walls of Saint Augustine. As the Estremadurans are not sufficient to defend it, we are ordered in, too. And how about rank, friend Araceli? Is it true that we two young gentlemen have been promoted to be sergeants?"

"I don't know anything about it, friend Pirli," I answered; and it was true that I was ignorant of my elevation to the hierarchical altitude of a sergeant.

"Yes, indeed, the general says so; Señor de Araceli is first sergeant, and Señor de Pirli is second sergeant. We have worked hard enough for it. It's a good thing we have enough of our bodies left to hang the epaulets on. I heard that Augustine Montoria has been made a lieutenant for his gallantry inside the houses. Yesterday, at nightfall, the battalion of Las Peñas de San Pedro was reduced to four sergeants, a lieutenant, a captain, and two hundred men."

"Let us see, friend Pirli, if we cannot earn two more promotions apiece today."

"All that we have to do is to keep our skins whole," he answered. "The few soldiers of the Huesca battalion who survive think that they are all going to be made generals. There is the call! Have you anything to eat?"

"Not much."

"Manuela Sancho gave me four sardines. I will divide them with you. How would you like a dozen of these roasted peas? Do you remember how wine tastes? I ask, because it is so many days since they have given us a drop. They will give us a spoonful when the battle of San Augustine is over. Here you are! It would be too bad if they should finish us off before we know what color the stuff is which they are going to pass around tonight. If they would follow my advice, they would give it to us before the fight, so that those who drop off would get a taste. But the committee of supplies has evidently said, 'There is very little wine; if we give it out now there will scarcely be three drops to a man. We will wait until evening, and as it will be a miracle if a fourth part of those who defend San Augustine are alive then, there will be at least one swallow apiece for the rest.'"

He followed this criticism with a general discourse upon the scarcity of provisions. We did not have time to indulge ourselves much on that topic, for we had scarcely joined the Estremadura men at the monastery, when a loud report warned us to be on our guard; then a friar appeared, shouting,—

"My sons, they have blown up the middle walls on the side towards Las Monicas, and they are already in the building! Run to the church. They must have seized the sacristy; but that makes no difference. If you go in time, you will be masters of the nave, of the chapels and the choir. Viva the Holy Virgin del Pilar, and the battalion of the Estremadura!"

We marched serenely into the church.

XXII

The good fathers encouraged us with their exhortations, and some of them, mingling with us in the most dangerous places in the ranks, said to us,—

"My sons, do not be discouraged. Foreseeing this event we have saved moderate quantities of food, and we have wine also. Give this mob plenty of powder! Courage, dear boys! Do not be afraid of the enemy's lead. You do more damage with one of your glances than they with a discharge of lead. Forward, my sons! The Holy Virgin del Pilar is with you. Don't wince at danger; face the enemy calmly, and in the cloud of battle you will see the holy form of the Mother of God. Viva Spain and Fernando VII!"

We reached the church; but the French, who had preceded us by the sacristy, already occupied the high altar. I had never before seen a churrigueresque altar all covered with sculptures and garlands of gold, serving as a breastwork for infantry; nor had I ever seen niches which served as the lodging places of a thousand carved saints vomiting forth fire. I had never seen the rays of gilded wood which shed their changeless light from pasteboard clouds peopled by little angels, confused with gun-flashes; nor behind the feet of Christ, and back of the golden halo of the Virgin Mary, the avenging eyes of soldiers taking death-dealing aim.

It is well to say that the high altar of San Augustine was an enormous one, filled with gilded wooden sculptures, like others you have seen in any of the churches of Spain. It extended from the floor to the arch above, and from wall to wall, and represented in row upon row the celestial hierarchies. Above, the blood-stained Christ spread his arms upon the cross; below, and on the altar, a little shrine enclosed the symbol of the Eucharist. Although the whole was supported by the ground and the walls, there were little interior covered ways destined for the special services of that republic of saints, and by them the sacristan could ascend from the sacristy to change the dress of the Virgin, to light the candles before the highest crucifix, or to clean the dust of centuries from the antique fabrics and painted wood of the images.

Well, the French rapidly gained possession of the *camarín* of the Virgin, and the narrow passages I have spoken of. When we arrived, from behind each saint, in every niche, gleamed a gun barrel.

Established thus behind the altar, and advancing slowly forward, they were preparing to take all of this upper part of the church.

We were not entirely unprotected; and in order to defend ourselves from the altar-piece, we occupied the confessionals, the altars of the chapels, and the galleries. Those of us who were most exposed were in the central nave; and while the more daring advanced resolutely towards the altar, others of us took positions in the lower choir; and from behind the chorister's desk, from behind chairs and benches which we piled up against the choir-screen, we tried to dislodge the French nation from its possession of the high altar.

Tio Garces, with others as brave, ran to occupy the pulpit, another churrigueresque structure whose sounding board was crowned by a statue of Faith which reached almost to the roof. They mounted, occupying the little stair and the great chair, and from there, by a singular chance, they shut up every Frenchman who dared to show his head in that direction. They also suffered great loss, for the men in the altar were much annoyed by the pulpit, and tried hard to get that obstacle out of their way. At last some twenty Imperials came out, evidently bent upon reducing at all hazards that wooden redoubt without whose possession it was madness to attempt to come out into the broad nave. I have never seen anything more like a great battle, and as in that the attention of both armies is concentrated upon one point, the most eagerly disputed of all, whose loss or conquest decides the outcome of the struggle, so the attention of all was now directed to the pulpit, so well defended and so well attacked. The twenty had to resist a sharp fire from us in the choir, and the hand-grenades which were thrown at them from the galleries. But in spite of great loss, they advanced resolutely, bayonets fixed, upon the pulpit stairway. The ten defenders of the fortress were not intimidated, and defended themselves with empty guns, with the unfailing superiority which they always showed in that kind of conflict. Many of our men who were firing from the chapel altars and the confessionals, ran to attack the French with their swords, representing in that way, in miniature, conditions of a rude field battle; the contest was waged, man to man, with bayonet-thrusts, guns, and blows as each one met his adversary.

The enemy was reinforced from the sacristy, and our rear-guard also came out of the choir. Some who were in the gallery on the right jumped upon the cornice of a great reredos at one side, and not satisfied with firing from there, threw down upon the French three statues of saints that capped its three angles. Meantime the pulpit was still held bravely, and in that hell of flame I saw Tio Garces standing erect, directing the men, and looking like a preacher screaming impudently with a hoarse voice. If I should ever see the devil preaching sin, standing on the great chair in the pulpit of a church invaded by all the other demons of hell in hideous riot, it would not especially attract my attention after that.

This could not last long; and Tio Garces presently fell, screaming hoarsely, pierced by a hundred balls. The French, who had poured up by way of the sacristy, now advanced in a closed column, and in the three steps which separated the presbytery from the rest of the church, offered us a wall-like defence. When this column fired, the question of the pulpit was instantly settled, and having lost one out of every five of our men, leaving a large number of our dead upon the tiles of the floor, we retreated to the chapels. The first defenders of the pulpit, those who had gone to reinforce them, and Tio Garces also, were picked up on bayonets, pierced through and tossed over the redoubt. So died that great patriot unnamed in history.

The captain of our company remained lifeless also upon the pavement. We retired in disorderly fashion to various points separated from one another, not knowing who would command us. Indeed, the initiative of each one, or of each group of two or three, was the only organization then possible, and no one thought of companies or of military rank. All were obedient to one common purpose, and showed a marvellous instinctive knowledge of rudimentary strategy which the exigencies of the struggle demanded at every moment. This instinctive insight made us understand that we were lost from the time that we got into the chapels on the right, and it was rashness to persist in the defence of the church before the great numbers of the French who now occupied it. Some of our soldiers thought that with the benches, the images, and the wood of an old altar-piece, which could easily be broken to pieces, we ought to raise a barricade in the arch of our chapel, and defend ourselves to the last; but two Augustine fathers opposed this useless effort.

"My sons, do not trouble yourselves to prolong the resistance which will only destroy you, and give our side no advantage," said one of them. "The French are attacking this moment by the Calle de las Arcades. Hasten there, and see if you can not harass them; but do not imagine that you can defend the church profaned by these savages."

These exhortations decided us to leave the church. Some of the Estremadura men remained in the choir, exchanging shots with the

French, who now filled the nave. The friars only half-fulfilled their promise of giving us something for which to sing "*Gaudeamus*." As a recompense for having defended their church to the last extreme, they were giving us some bits of jerked beef and dry bread, without our seeing or smelling the wine anywhere, in spite of our straining our eyes and our nostrils. But to explain this, they said that the French, occupying all the upper part, had possession of all the principal storehouse of provisions. Lamenting this, they tried to console us with praises of our good behavior.

The failure of the wine made me remember the great Pirli. I happened to recollect that I had seen him at the beginning of the battle. I asked for him, but nobody could account for his disappearance. The French occupied the church, and also some of the upper part of the convent. In spite of our unfavorable position below, we were resolved to go on resisting; and we bore in mind the heroic conduct of the volunteers of Huesca, who defended Las Monicas until they were buried beneath its ruins. We were maddened, and believed ourselves disgraced if we did not conquer. We were impelled to these desperate struggles by a hidden, irresistible force which I cannot explain except as the strong tension and spiritual exaltation springing from our aspirations towards the ideal.

An order from outside stopped us, dictated doubtless by the practical good sense of General Saint March.

"The convent cannot be held," it was said. "Instead of sacrificing men with no advantage to the city, let all go out to defend the points attacked in the Calle de Pabostre, and the Puerta Quemada, where the enemy are trying to advance, conquering houses from which they have been repulsed various times."

We therefore left San Augustine. While we were passing through the street of the same name, parallel with the Calle de Palomar, we saw that they were throwing hand-grenades among the French established in a little opening near the latter of these two streets. Who was throwing those projectiles from the tower? In order to tell it more briefly, and with greatest eloquence, let us open the history and read: "In the tower six or eight peasants had placed themselves, having provided themselves with provisions and ammunition to harass the enemy. They continued to hold it for some days without being willing to surrender."

There was the glorious Pirli! Oh, Pirli, more happy than Tio Garces, thou dost occupy a place in history!

XXIII

Incorporated into the battalion of Estremadura, we went along the Calle de Palomar into the Plaza de la Magdalena, whence we could hear the roar of battle at the end of the Calle de Puerta Quemada. As we have said, the enemy tried to take the Calle de Pabostre in order to get possession of Puerta Quemada, an important point whence they could rake with their artillery the street of the same name towards the Plaza de la Magdalena. As the possession of San Augustine and Las Monicas permitted them to threaten that central point by the easy way to the Calle de Palomar, they already considered themselves masters of the suburb. In fact, if those in San Augustine managed to advance to the ruins of the Seminary, and those of the Calle de Pabostre to the Puerta Quemada, it would be impossible to dispute with the French the quarter of Las Tenerias.

After a short time they took us to the Calle de Pabostre, and as the battle of the outside and inside of the buildings and of the public way was now all combined, we entered the first block by the Calle de los Viejos. From the windows of the house in which we found ourselves, we could see nothing but smoke, and could tell but little of what was going on there. I saw later that the street was all filled with embrasures and trenches at certain distances made of heaps of earth, furniture, and rubbish. From the windows a tremendous fire was poured forth, and, remembering a phrase of the beggar Sursum Corda, I can say that our souls were turned into bullets. Inside the houses the blood flowed in torrents. The onset of the French was terrible, and that the resistance might not be less terrible the belfries summoned men unceasingly. The general dictated stern orders for the punishment of stragglers. The friars rallied the people of other districts, dragging them forward as in a leash. Some heroic women set an example, throwing themselves into danger, guns in hand.

A dreadful day, whose frightful roar resounds ever in the ears of him who was present! Its remembrance pursues him, an unescaped nightmare, through his whole life. He who did not see these horrors, who did not hear the noise of that shouting, knows not with what expression the depths of the horrible may be uttered to human feeling. Do not tell me that you have seen the crater of a volcano in the most violent eruption; or a great tempest in the open ocean when the ship, tossed to heaven on a mountain of waterfalls, descends next to a giddy depth,—do not tell me you have seen these things, for they are nothing at all like the volcanoes and tempests of man when his passions urge him to out-rival the disorders in Nature.

It was difficult to hold us back, and not being able to do much where we were, we descended to the street without noticing the officers who tried to hold us back. The combat had an irresistible attraction for us, and called us as the deep calls unto a man who looks down upon it from a cliff. I have never considered myself heroic; but it is certain that in those moments I did not fear death, nor did the sight of catastrophes terrify me. It is true that heroism, as a thing of the moment, and the direct child of inspiration, does not belong exclusively to the brave. That is the reason it is often found in women and cowards.

I will not go into the details of those struggles in the Calle de Pabostre. They were much like those which I have described before. If they differed in any respect, it was in their excess of constancy, and energy raised to a height where the human ended and the divine began. Within the houses, scenes passed like those I have described elsewhere, but with greater carnage, because victory was believed more certain. The advantage the men of the Empire gained in one place they lost in another. The battles, begun in the attics, descended step by step to the cellars, and were finished there with clubbed muskets, with the advantage always on the side of our peasants. The tones of command with which one or another directed the movements within these labyrinths resounded from room to room with fearful echoes. They used their artillery in the street, and we did also. Often they tried to get possession of our pieces by sudden hand-to-hand struggles; but they lost many men without ever succeeding.

Alarmed on seeing that the force used at one time to gain a battle was not now sufficient to gain two yards of a street, they refused to fight, and their officers drove them forward, beating their laziness out of them with cudgels. On our side such measures were not necessary; persuasion was enough. The priests, without neglecting the dying, attended to everything. If they saw a weakening anywhere, they would hasten to tell the officers.

In one of the trenches in the street, a woman, bravest of all, Manuela Sancho, after having fired with a gun, began serving cannon number eight. She remained unhurt all day, encouraging all with brave words,— an example to the men. It was perhaps three o'clock when she fell, wounded in the leg, and during a long time was supposed to be dead,

BENITO PÉREZ GALDÓS

because the hemorrhage made her seem lifeless; she looked like a corpse. Later, seeing that she breathed, we carried her to the rear, and she was restored, and had such good health afterwards that many years later I had the pleasure of seeing her still alive.

History has not forgotten that brave young Maid of Saragossa. The Calle de Pabostre, whose poor houses are more eloquent than the pages of a book, now bears the name of Manuela Sancho.

A little after three o'clock, a tremendous loud explosion shook the houses which the French had disputed with us in such a bloody manner during the morning. Amid the dust, and the smoke thicker than dust, we saw walls and roofs falling in a thousand pieces, with a noise of which I can give no idea. The French had begun to employ mines. In order to gain that which they could in no other way wrench from the hands of the sons of Aragon. They opened galleries; they charged the mines; then the men folded their arms, waiting for the powder to do it all.

When the first house went, we stayed quietly in the next, and in the street. But when the second went with a still louder noise, the retreat began with plenty of disorder. Considering that so many unfortunate comrades were hurled into the air or buried beneath the ruins, men who had been unconquerable by force of arms, we felt ourselves too weak to contend with the new element of destruction. It seemed to us that in all the other houses, and in the street, horrible craters were going to burst forth which would send us flying, torn into a thousand bloody fragments.

The officers held us back, calling,—

"Courage, boys, stand firm! That is done to frighten us. We have plenty of powder, too, and we will open mines. Do you think this will give them an advantage? On the contrary, we shall see how they will defend themselves among a lot of fragments."

Palafox appeared at the entrance of the street, and his presence restrained us for sometime. The noise prevented me from hearing what he was saying, but by his gestures I understood that he wished us to go on over the ruins.

"You hear, boys! You hear what the Captain-General says!" a friar shouted beside us, one of those who had come with Palafox. "He says that if you will make a little exertion, not one Frenchman will be left alive." "You are right!" cried another friar. "There will not be a woman left in Saragossa who will even look at you, if you do not hurl yourselves instantly upon those ruins of the houses, and drive the French out."

"Forward, sons of the Virgin del Pilar!" cried out a third friar. "Do you see those women over there? Do you know what they are saying? They are saying that if you do not go, they will go themselves. Are you not ashamed of your cowardice?"

With that, we stood up a little more bravely. Another house fell on the right. Palafox came into the street. Without knowing how or why, we followed him when he put himself at our head. Now is the time to speak of that high personage whose name and fame are one with that of Saragossa. His prestige is due in large measure to his great courage, but also to his noble origin, and the respect in which the family of Lazan has always been held in Saragossa, and to his handsome and spirited presence. He was young. He had belonged to the Guards. He was much praised for having refused the favors of a very highly-placed lady, as famous for her position as for scandals about her. That which endeared the Saragossan leader more than anything else to his people was, however, his supreme, his indomitable courage, the youthful ardor with which he attacked the most dangerous and difficult obstacles, simply to reach his ideals of honor and glory.

If he lacked intellectual gifts to direct an undertaking so arduous as this, he had the prudence to know his lack, and to surround himself with men distinguished for their judgment and wisdom. These men did everything. Palafox was the great figure-head, the chief actor in the scene. Over a people so largely ruled by imagination, that young general could scarcely fail to hold an imperious dominion, with his illustrious lineage and splendid figure. He showed himself everywhere, encouraging the weak, and distributing rewards to the brave.

The Saragossans beheld in him the symbol of their constancy, their virtues, their patriotic ideal with its touch of mysticism, and their warlike zeal. Whatever he ordered, everybody found right and just. Like those monarchs whom traditional laws have made the personal embodiment of government, Palafox could do no wrong. Anything wrong was the work of his counsellors. In reality, the illustrious commander did not govern, he reigned. Father Basilio governed, with O'Neill, Saint March, and Butron, the first, an ecclesiastic, the other three noted generals.

In places of danger, Palafox always appeared like a human expression of triumph. His voice reanimated the dying; and if the Virgin del Pilar had spoken, she would have chosen no other mouth. His countenance always expressed a supreme confidence. In his triumphal smile, courage overflowed, as in others it is expressed by a ferocious frown. He was vain-gloriously proud of being the prop of that great hour in history. He understood instinctively that the outcome depended more upon him as an actor than upon him as a general. He always appeared in all the splendors of his uniform, with gold lace, waving plumes, and medals. The thundering music of applause, of huzzas, flattered him extremely. All this was necessary. Indeed there must always be something of mutual adulation between the army and the commander-in-chief, in order that the pride of victory may inspire one and all to deeds of heroism.

XXIV

As I have said, Palafox pulled us together; and although we abandoned almost all of the Calle de Pabostre, we remained strong in the Puerta Quemada. If the battle was bloody until three, the hour when we centred in the Plaza de la Magdalena, it was not less bloody there until night. The French began to raise works in the houses ruined by the mines, and it was curious to see how among the masses of rubbish and beams small armed squares and covered ways were made and platforms to connect the artillery. That was a battle which every moment appeared less and less like any other known warfare.

From this new phase of contest resulted an advantage for us and a hindrance for the French. The demolition of the houses permitted them to place some new pieces, but the men were unprotected. To our misfortune, we could not avail ourselves of this because of the explosions. Fright made us think the danger multiplied a hundredfold, when in reality it was diminished. Not wishing to do less than they in that fiery duel, the Saragossans began to burn the houses in the Calle de Pabostre which they could not hold.

Besiegers and besieged, desirous of coming to an end of this, and not being able to attain it in such intricate burrowing warfare, began to destroy, one side by mining, the other by burning, remaining unprotected like the gladiator who throws away his shield.

What an afternoon! What a night! Arriving here, I pause, wearied and breathless. My recollections are obscured, dimmed as my thoughts and my feelings were dimmed on that dreadful night. There came indeed a moment when being unable to resist longer, my body, like that of others of my comrades who had the fortune or misfortune to be still alive, dragged itself back across the gutters, stumbling over unburied bodies that seemed less than human among the debris. My feelings had flung me into an extreme of delirium, and I did not clearly know where I was. My idea of living was a confused, vague mixture of unheard-of miseries. It did not seem as if it was day, because in so many places the murk hung low, obscuring everything. Nor could I think it night, for flames like those we imagine in hell reddened the city on every side.

I only know that I dragged myself, stepping upon bodies, some dead and some still moving, and that farther on, always farther on, I thought I might find a piece of bread and a mouthful of water. What horrible mental

BENITO PÉREZ GALDÓS

dejection! What hunger! What thirst! I saw many running swiftly. I cried out to them. I saw their strange shadows throwing grotesque figures upon the neighboring walls. They were going and coming, I know not whence nor where. I was not the only one who, with body and soul exhausted after so many hours of fighting, had given out completely. Many others who had not the steel nerves of the Aragonese were dragging themselves along like myself, and we begged one another for a little water. Some, more fortunate than the rest, had the strength to look about among the corpses and find crusts of rations not eaten, fragments of meat, cold and dirty on the ground, which they devoured with avidity.

Somewhat revived, we went on looking, and I took my part of the tidbits of the feast. I did not know if I was wounded. Some of those who were talking with me, telling me of their dreadful hunger and thirst, had terrible wounds and burns and contusions. At last we came to some women who gave us water to drink, although it was muddy and warm. We disputed over the jug, and then in the hands of one of the dead we found a kerchief containing two dried sardines and little cakes. Encouraged by these repeated finds, we went on pillaging, and at last the little which we were able to eat, and, more than anything else, the dirty water we drank, gave us back a little strength.

I now felt myself able to walk a little, although with difficulty. I saw that my clothing was all soaked with blood. Feeling a lively smarting in my right arm, I supposed that I was severely wounded; but the hurt turned out to be an insignificant contusion, and the stains on my clothing came from creeping along through the pools of blood and mud.

I could now think clearly again. I could see plainly, and could hear distinctly the shouts and the hurried footsteps, the cannon-shots near and afar in dreadful dialogue. Their crashings here and yonder seemed like questions and replies.

The burning went on. There was a dense cloud over the city formed of dust and smoke, which, with the splendor of the flames, revealed horrible unearthly scenes like those of dreams.

The mangled houses, with their windows and openings glaring with the light like hellish eyes, the projecting angles of the smoking ruins, and the burning beams formed a spectacle less sinister than that of those leaping and unwearied figures that did not cease to move about here and there, almost in the centre of the flames. They were the peasants of Saragossa, who were still fighting with the French, and disputing with them every hand's breadth of this hell.

I found myself in the Calle de Puerta Quemada. That which I have described was seen by looking in two directions from the Seminary, and from the entrance of the Calle de Pabostre. I went on a few steps, but fell again, overcome by fatigue. A priest, seeing me covered with blood, came up to me and began to talk to me of the future life, and of the eternal rewards destined for those who die for their country. He told me that I was not wounded; but that hunger, weariness, and thirst had prostrated me, and that I seemed to have the early symptoms of the epidemic. Then the good friar, in whom I recognized at once Father Mateo del Busto, seated himself beside me, sighing deeply.

"I can keep up no longer. I believe that I am going to die."

"Is your reverence wounded?" I asked, seeing a linen cloth bound upon his right arm.

"Yes, my son. A ball has destroyed my shoulder and arm. I am in the greatest pain, but I must bear it. Christ suffered more for us. Since daybreak I have been busy, caring for the wounded and pointing the dying to heaven. I have not rested a moment for sixteen hours, nor have I eaten nor drank anything. A woman tied this linen on my right arm, and I went about my work. I believe that I shall not live long. What a death! My God, and all these wounded with no one to take care of them! But, oh, I can no longer stand! I am dying! Have you seen that trench which is at the end of the Calle de los Clavos? Over there poor Coridon is lying, lifeless, the victim of his own courage. We were passing along there to take care of some of the wounded, when we saw, near the garden of San Augustine, a group of Frenchmen who were passing from one house to another. Coridon, whose impetuous blood impelled him to the most daring acts, threw himself upon them. They bayoneted him, and flung him in the ditch. How many victims in a single day, Araceli! Indeed, you are fortunate in not being hurt. But you will die of the epidemic, and that is worse. Today I have given absolution to sixty who were dying of the epidemic. I give it to you also, my friend, because I know you have committed no sins, only peccadilloes, and that you have borne yourself valiantly in these days. How is it? Do you feel worse? Truly you are yellower than these corpses about us. To die of the epidemic during this horrible siege is to die for one's country. Courage, young man! Heaven is open to receive you, and the Virgin del Pilar will welcome you with her mantle of the stars. Life is nothing. How much better it is to die honorably, and to gain eternal glory by the suffering of a day! In the name of God, I forgive you your sins!"

Then after murmuring the prayer appropriate to the occasion, he blessed me, and pronounced the *Ego te absolvo*, and then lay down upon the ground. He looked very badly, and although I did not call myself well, I thought myself in a better state of health than the good friar. That was not the only time when the confessor died before the dying one, and the physician before the patient.

I spoke to Father Mateo, and he did not answer me, except with piteous moans. I went a little way to look for someone who might be able to help him. I met several men and women, and told them, "Father Mateo del Busto is over there and cannot move;" but they took no notice of me and went on. Many of the wounded called upon me, begging for aid; but I took no notice at all of them. Near the Coso, I met a child of eight or ten years, who was alone, and weeping in the sorest distress. I stopped him. I asked him where his parents were, and he pointed to a place near where there was a great number of the wounded and dead. Afterwards I met the same child in several places, always alone and always crying aloud very bitterly. No one cared for him. I heard no questions, but, "Have you seen my brother?" "Have you seen my son?" "Have you seen my father?" But none of these were to be found in any direction. No one tried to take any of the wounded to the churches, because all or nearly all were crowded. The cellars and lower rooms which at first had been considered good places of refuge, were now infected with a death-dealing atmosphere. There came a time when the best place for the wounded was in the middle of the street.

I directed my steps towards the centre of the Coso, because they said that there they were giving out something to eat, but I received nothing. I was returning to Las Tenerias, and at last, in front of Almudi, they gave me a little hot food. That which seemed a symptom of the epidemic disappeared, for indeed my malady was only of the sort that can be cured with bread and wine. I remembered Father Mateo del Busto, and with some others went to help him. The unfortunate old man had not moved, and when we came up, and asked him how he found himself, he answered thus,—

"What is it? Has the bell sounded for matins? It is early. Leave me to rest. I find myself much fatigued, Father Gonzalez. I have been picking flowers in the garden for sixteen hours, and I am tired."

In spite of his entreaty, we four took him up; but we had carried him only a short distance before he was dead in our arms.

My comrades ran to the front, and I was preparing to follow them, when I happened to see a man whose looks attracted my attention. It was Candiola. He was coming out of a house near by with his clothing scorched, and grasping between his hands a fowl, which cackled at being held captive. I stopped him in the middle of the street, questioning him about his daughter and Augustine. He answered me in a very disturbed way,—

"My daughter—I do not know—there she is—somewhere. All, all! I have lost all. The receipts, the receipts were burned. Fortunately I got out of the house, and as I fled I came upon this chicken which, like me, was flying from the dreadful flames. Yesterday, a hen was worth five duros. But my receipts! Holy Virgin del Pilar, and thou, dear little Santo Domingo of my soul, why have ye let my receipts be burned? They, at least, might have been saved. Do you wish to help me? The tin box which held them is still there pinned down under a great beam. Where can you find half a dozen men for me? Good God, this junta, these authorities, this Captain-General, what are they thinking of?" And he went on, calling out to the passersby, "Eh, peasant, friend, dear man, let us see if we cannot lift the beam which has fallen into the corner. Oh, friends, put down that dying man you are carrying to the hospital, and come and help me. Oh, pitiless Saragossans, how God is chastising you!" Seeing that none came to help him, he went into the house, but came out again, crying out in desperation, "Already it is too late to save anything! Everything is on fire. Oh, my Virgin del Pilar, why dost thou not perform a miracle for me? Why not give me such a gift as that bestowed upon the children in the fiery furnace of Babylon, so that I could go into the teeth of the fire and save my receipts!"

XXV

Presently he seated himself upon a pile of stones, beating his brow from time to time, and without loosening his hold of the chicken, he laid his hand upon his heart, sighing deeply. I questioned him again about his daughter, desiring to hear news of Augustine; and he said to me,—

"I was in that house in the Calle de Añon, where we moved in yesterday. Everybody told me that it was not safe there, and that we had much better be in the middle of the town; but it does not suit me to go where everybody else comes, and the place that I prefer is the one that the rest abandon. This world is filled with thieves and rascals. It is better that I get away from them. We managed with a lower room of that house. My daughter is very much afraid of the cannon, and wished to go elsewhere. When the mines began to burst under the neighboring houses, she and Guedita rushed away, terrified. I stayed alone, thinking of the danger my things are in; and pretty soon some soldiers came with flaming torches ready to set fire to the house. Those wretched cowards would not give me time to collect my things. Far from pitying my condition, they ridiculed me. I hid the box with my receipts for fear that those who think it is stuffed with money would carry it off; but it was impossible to stay inside long. I was surrounded with the bright flames, and choked with the smoke. In spite of everything, I insisted upon trying to save my box; but it was an impossible thing. I had to run. I could not take anything. Great God! I saved nothing but this poor creature, forgotten by its owners in the hen-house. It cost me a good deal of trouble to catch it. I burned one hand almost all over. Oh, cursed be he who invented fire! Why should one lose one's fortune to amuse these heroes! I had two houses in Saragossa besides the one I lived in. One of them, the one in the Calle de la Sombra, is preserved to me still, although it is without tenants. The other, which was called Casa de los Duendes, back of the San Francisco is occupied by the troops, and everything there has been torn to pieces for me. Ruin, nothing but ruin! Is it a right thing to burn houses merely to retard the conquest by the French?"

"War makes it necessary to do these things," I answered him. "And this heroic city desires to carry her defence to the last extreme."

"And what induces Saragossa to wish to carry her defence to the last extreme? What good does it do to the dead? You may talk to them of glory, of heroism,—of all those notions. Before I ever come back to live in an heroic city, I would go to a desert. I concede that there should be a certain resistance, but not to such a barbarous extreme as this. It is true the burned buildings are worth little, perhaps less than the great mass of charcoal which will result. Don't let them come to me with their foolish talk. Those fat sharpers are already planning to make a good business out of the carbon."

This made me laugh. My readers must not think that I exaggerate, since he said all this to me very nearly as I repeat it; and those who have the misfortune to know him would most readily have faith in my veracity. If Candiola had lived in Numantia, it would have been said that the Numantines were merchants of charcoal mixed with heroes.

"I am lost! I am ruined forever!" he went on, crossing his hands forlornly. "Those receipts were part of my fortune. How am I going to claim the amounts without any documents to show, and when almost all my debtors are dead, and lying rotting about the streets! I said, and I repeat it, those who have made me all this trouble are disobedient to God. It is a mortal sin; it is an unforgivable offence to let themselves be killed when they owe money on such old accounts that their creditor will not be able to collect easily. Paying up is very hard work; so some of these people say, 'Let us wall ourselves in and burn with the money.' But God is inexorable with this heroic rabble, and to chastise them He will resurrect them, so that they will yet have to meet the constable and the notary. My God, resurrect them! Holy Virgin del Pilar, Santo Domingo del Val, resurrect them, I pray!"

"And your daughter?" I asked with interest. "Did she come out of the fire unharmed?"

"Do not speak of her to me as my daughter!" he replied sternly. "God has punished me for her faults. I know now who her infamous admirer is. Who can it possibly be, but that damned son of Don José Montoria who studied to be a priest! Mariquilla has confessed it to me. Yesterday she was dressing a wound he has on his arm, and this was done before me. Did you ever hear of anything so shameless?"

As he said this. Doña Guedita, who was looking anxiously for her master, came up with a cup containing some sort of nourishment. He took it hungrily; and then, by force of entreaty, we succeeded in getting him away from there, taking him to the Organo alley, where his daughter had taken refuge, in a porch, with other shelterless ones. After growling at her a moment, Candiola went on into the house, followed by his housekeeper.

"Where is Augustine?" I asked Mariquilla.

"He was here a moment ago; but someone came to tell him of the death of his brother, and he has gone. I heard it said that the family is in the Calle de las Rufas."

"His brother is dead! Don José's eldest son!"

"So they said, and he started in haste and in great distress."

Without waiting to hear more, I also ran to the Calle de las Rufas to do everything I could to help in their trouble the generous family to which I owed so much. Before arriving there, I met Don Roque, who, with tears in his eyes, came up to speak to me.

"Gabriel," he said, "God has laid his hand heavily today upon our good friend."

"Is it the eldest son who is dead, Manuel Montoria?"

"Yes, and that is not the only trouble of the family. Manuel was married, as you know, and had a son four years of age. You see that group of women? Well, the wife of Montoria's poor eldest son is there with her boy in her arms. He is dying of the epidemic, and is already in his agony. Is it not a horrible state of things? There is one of the first families of Saragossa reduced to this sad condition, without a roof to cover them, in want of the most necessary things. That unfortunate young mother was in the street all night, exposed to the weather with her sick child in her arms, expecting every instant that he would breathe his last. After all it is better to be here than in one of those pestilent cellars where no one can breathe. I am thankful that I and other friends have been able to help her a little; but what can one do when there is scarcely any bread to be had? The wine is all finished, and a bit of beef is not to be found, though I gave her a piece of ours."

Morning began to come. I went up to the group of women and saw a sorrowful sight. With the anguished effort to save life, the mother and the few women who kept her company were torturing the poor child with remedies which everybody tries at such a time; but it needed only to see the victim of the fever to realize the impossibility of saving that little being whom death had already grasped with his relentless hand.

The voice of Don José de Montoria obliged me to hasten forward more quickly; and in an outer corner in the Calle de las Rufas a second group completed the dreadful picture of that unhappy family. Stretched upon the ground was the body of Manuel, a young man of thirty years, no less amiable and generous in his life than his father and brother. A ball had pierced his head, and from the small external wound, at the spot whence the ball had emerged, a thread of blood still trickled, dropping down the temple, the cheek, and the neck, and falling down upon the skin beneath the shirt. Because of this, the body did not seem like that of one dead.

When I arrived, nobody had been able to make his mother believe that he was dead, and she held his head upon her knees, hoping to revive him with tender words. Montoria, on his knees at the right side, held his son's hand between his own hands and gazed at him, speechless, not taking his eyes from him. As white as the dead, the father did not weep.

"Wife!" he exclaimed at last, "do not pray God for the impossible. We have lost our son."

"No, my son is not dead!" exclaimed the mother, in despair. "It is a lie. Why deceive me? How could it be possible for God to take our son from us? What have we done to deserve such a punishment? Manuel, my son, why dost thou not answer me? Why dost thou not move? Why dost thou not speak? In a moment we will carry thee into the house— but where is our house? My son grows cold on this bare ground. See how chill are his hands and his face!"

"You must go away from here, wife," said Montoria, restraining the flood of his tears; "we will take care of Manuel."

"O my Lord God!" moaned the mother, "what ails my son that he does not speak, nor move, nor wake? He seems to be dead; but he is not, he cannot be dead! Holy Virgin del Pilar, is it not true that my son is not dead?"

"Leocadia," repeated Montoria, wiping away the first tears that had fallen from his eyes, "go away from here a little, go away, for God's sake! Be resigned, for God has dealt us a heavy blow, and our son no longer lives. He has died for his country."

"Why has my son died!" exclaimed the mother, straining the body to her in her arms, as if she would not let it go. "No, no, no! What is the country to me? Let my son be given back to me. Manuel, my boy, do not let them separate you from me; those who would tear you from my arms must kill me first."

"O Lord God, Holy Virgin del Pilar," said Don José de Montoria, in solemn tones, "never have I knowingly and deliberately offended ye. For the sake of religion and the king I have given my goods and my sons. Why, instead of my first-born, why have you not taken my life a hundred times, miserable old man, good for nothing? Gentlemen, you who are present, I am not ashamed to weep before you; my heart is utterly broken, but Montoria is still the same. We will say to thee, Happy art thou a thousand times, my son, who hast died at the post of honor. Unhappy those of us who still live, having lost thee. But God wills it thus; and we bow our foreheads before the ruler of all things. Wife, God gave us peace, happiness, prosperity, and good sons; now it seems that He desires to strip us of all. Let our hearts be filled with humility, and let us not curse our fate. Blessed be the hand that leads us, and let us tranquilly hope for the blessing of a death like this."

Doña Leocadia, who had no life left except for weeping, was kissing the cold body of her son. Don José, trying to subdue the manifestations of his own grief, rose and said in a firm voice,—

"Leocadia, you must rise now. It is necessary that our son should be buried."

"Buried!" exclaimed the mother. "Buried!" And she could say no more, for she fell forward, lifeless, clasping her son.

At the same moment we heard a heart-rending cry not far from there, and a woman came running in anguish towards us. It was the wife of the unfortunate Manuel, now widowed and childless. Several of us tried to restrain her, so that she might not witness the terrible scene, after what she had just been through; but the unhappy lady struggled with us, begging us to let her see her husband. In the mean time Don José, leaving us, went over to where the body of his grandson was lying, took him in his arms, and carried him and put him down near Manuel. The woman needed all of our care; and while Doña Leocadia continued without consciousness or motion, holding the corpse embraced in her arms, her daughter-in-law, fevered with grief, was running about after imaginary enemies, threatening to tear them to pieces. We tried to hold her, but she escaped from us. At times she laughed with frightful laughter, and presently she knelt before us, praying us to return the two bodies that we had taken away.

People passed,—soldiers, friars, peasants,—all seeing this with indifference, because everyone had passed through similar scenes. Hearts were hardened, and souls seemed to have lost their most beautiful faculties, preserving nothing but a rude heroism. At last the poor woman yielded to fatigue, to the exhaustion of her own pain, lying passive in my arms as if she were dead. We looked about for some cordial or some kind of nourishment to revive her; but we had none, and the people who saw our need had work enough to attend to their own. In the mean time, Don José helped by his son Augustine, who also controlled his bitter grief, loosened the body from the arms of Doña Leocadia. The state of this unhappy lady was such that it seemed almost as if we should have to mourn another death that day. Presently Montoria repeated,

"It is necessary that my son be buried!"

He looked about; we all looked about, and saw numbers of unburied bodies. In the Calle de las Rufas there were many; and the Calle de la Imprenta (now the Calle de Flandro) close by had been made into a sort of receiving house. It is not exaggeration, that which I saw and will tell you: Innumerable bodies were piled up in the narrow way, forming a broad wall from house to house. It was dreadful to see, and those who saw it were condemned to have before their mind's eyes for all their lives that funeral pyre made of the bodies of their fellow-beings. It may seem that I am inventing, but this thing happened: a man entered the Calle de la Imprenta and began to shout. At a window appeared another man, who replied to him, saying, "Come up!"

Then the other, thinking to make a shorter cut than by the house door and the staircase, climbed up over the heap of bodies, and reached the second story, one of whose windows served him for a door.

In many other streets, the same thing happened. Who could think of giving them sepulchre? For every pair of useful arms, and for every spade, there were fifty dead. Three hundred to four hundred were perishing daily with the epidemic. Every bloody battle had carried off a thousand more; and already Saragossa began to seem a great city depopulated of living creatures.

Montoria, on seeing how things were, said:

"My son and my grandson will not have the privilege of sleeping beneath the ground. Their souls are in heaven. What matters the rest? We must leave them thus in this gateway of the Calle de las Rufas. Augustine, my son, it is best for you to go back to the lines. The officers are able to spare fewer than ever. I believe that they are in need of men at the Magdalena. I have now no son, man, but you. If you die, what would be left me? But duty is first; and, before seeing thee a coward, I prefer to see thee bleeding like thy poor brother with thy temple pierced by the enemy's ball."

Then placing his hand upon the head of his son, who was kneeling uncovered beside the body of Manuel, he continued, lifting his eyes to heaven,—

"Lord, if thou hast willed to take my second son, also, take me to my first. When the siege is over, I desire to live no longer; my poor wife and I have had our share of happiness. We have received too many blessings to speak against the hand which has wounded us. Hast thou not done enough to prove us? Must my second son also perish? Come, señors," he said presently, "let us disperse. Perhaps we are needed elsewhere."

"Señor Don José," said Don Roque, weeping, "will you not retire also, and let your friends fulfil this sad duty?"

"No; I am man for all that must be done, and God has given me a soul that does not flinch and will not quail."

He lifted the body of Manuel, aided by one of the others, while Augustine and I lifted his grandchild, to place both at the entrance of the Calle de las Rufas, where many other families had lain their dead. Montoria, as he put down the body, breathed a long sigh, and let his arms fall as if the effort made had exhausted his energies, and said,—

"Truly, gentlemen, I am not now able to deny that I am tired. Yesterday, I felt young; today, I am very old."

Montoria had indeed aged visibly, and one night had taken ten years of his life. He sat down upon a stone, and, putting his elbows on his knees, hid his face in his hands. He remained in this attitude for a long time, and none of those present interfered with his grief. Doña Leocadia, her daughter, and her daughter-in-law, assisted by two old servants of the family, were in the Coso. Don Roque, who went and came from one place to the other, said,—

"The señora remains very weak. They are praying earnestly now and weeping. They are sadly downcast, the poor ladies. Boys, it is very necessary that we look about town, and see if a little something in the way of nourishment cannot be found."

Montoria rose then, wiped away the tears which coursed freely from his burning eyes, saying,—

"There is no lack of food still in town, according to my belief. Don Roque, my friend, will you not go and find something to eat, let it cost what it may?"

"Yesterday I paid five duros for a hen in the market," said one of the old servants of the house.

"But today there are none," said Don Roque. "I was there only a moment ago."

"Friends, look about and find something. I need nothing for myself."

He was saying this when we heard the agreeable cackle of a fowl. We all looked joyfully towards the entrance of the street, and we saw Candiola, who carried in his left hand the chicken we know of, caressing its black plumage with his right. Before they asked him for it, he approached Montoria slowly, and said,—

"A doubloon for the chicken."

"What a starved thing it is!" exclaimed Don Roque. "The poor creature is little more than bones."

I was not able to restrain my anger at seeing such shining evidence of the repugnant meanness and hard-heartedness of Candiola. So I went up to him, and snatched the chicken from his hands, saying violently,—

"This chicken is stolen! Come, you miserable miser, one would sell one's own cheaper! This was sold for five duros yesterday in the market. Five duros you may have, you coward, you thief, not a fraction more!"

Candiola began to howl for his chicken, and was on the point of getting a good thrashing, when Don José de Montoria intervened, saying,—

"Let him have what he wishes. Give Señor Candiola the doubloon that he charges for this fowl." He gave him the extortionate amount, which Candiola was not slow to accept; and then our friend went on thus,—

"Señor Candiola, let us speak together. Now, about that wherein I offended you. Yes—a few days ago—about that affair of the blows. There are times when one is not master of one's self, when the blood mounts up to the head. It is true that you provoked me, and you charged more for the flour than the Captain-General had ordered. It is true, Don Jeronimo, my friend, that I shook you off, and you see—yet—one could not help that and—I, I believe the—well, I suppose that my hand flew away from me, and I did something."

"Señor Montoria," said Candiola, "a day will come when we shall again have authorities in Saragossa. Then we shall meet again face to face."

"Are you going to make it a matter of justices and notaries? That's bad. That which is past—it was an access of anger, one of those things which cannot be helped. My mind now is filled with the thought that I am in trouble, very great trouble. One does not wish to offend one's neighbor."

"It is not much to offend him, after robbing him," said Don Jeronimo, looking about at us all, and smiling contemptuously.

BENITO PÉREZ GALDÓS

"It was not exactly robbing," said Don José, patiently; "because I did that which the Captain-General commanded. The offence of word and deed was undeniable; and now when I saw you coming with the chicken, I determined at once to own up that I did wrong. My conscience urged it upon me. Ah, Señor Candiola, I am very unhappy! When one is happy, one does not know his faults. But it is true, Don Jeronimo, that as I saw you coming toward me just now, I felt desirous to ask your pardon for those blows. I hold out the hand that offended. So it is. I don't know what I am doing—yes, I do request you to forgive me, and let us be friends. Señor Don Jeronimo, let us be friends, let us be reconciled, and not make a permanent grudge out of an old resentment. Hatred poisons the soul, and the remembrance of not having done right oppresses us with an insupportable weight."

"After an act of robbery, you think all can be arranged with hypocritical words," said Candiola, turning his back and skulking away from the group, muttering, "Señor Montoria should talk of refunding the price of the flour. Begging forgiveness of me! I have lived to see all there is to see."

He moved slowly away. Montoria, seeing that several of us were about to pursue the insolent cur, said,—

"Let him go in peace. Let us have compassion on that unfortunate man."

XXVI

O n the third of February, the French gained possession of the Convent of Jerusalem,[1] which was between Santa Engracia and the hospital. The battle which succeeded the conquest of such an important position was as bloody as those of Las Tenerias.

Don Marcos Simono, the distinguished commander of engineers, was one of those who died there. In the suburb, the besiegers had advanced but little; and in six or seven days' effort, they had not gained possession of the Calle de Puerta Quemada.

The authorities understood that it would be difficult to prolong the resistance much longer, and with offers of money and honors tried to rouse the patriots anew. In a proclamation of the second of February, asking for means, Palafox said, "I am giving my two watches and twenty silver dishes, which are all I have left." In that of the fourth of February, he offered to give especial honors, to make caballeros of the twelve men who should most distinguish themselves; a military order of nobility was created for them, called the Infanzones. In the proclamation of the ninth, he mourned the indifference and readiness to yield, exhibited by some citizens at the misfortunes of their country; and after intimating that this loss of heart was brought about by French gold, he threatened dire punishment for those who showed themselves cowards.

The battles of the third, fourth, and fifth were not so bloody as the last which I have described. The French and Spanish were perishing with fatigue. The street entrances which we were holding in the Plazuela de la Magdalena were defended with cannon, and repulsed the enemy's two advances from the Calle de Palomar and the Calle de Pabostre. The remains of the Seminary were also bristling with artillery; and the French, sure of not being able to drive us from there by ordinary means, were working at their mines without ceasing.

My battalion was now one with that of the Estremadura, and indeed what was left of both was scarcely three companies. Augustine Montoria was captain, and I was promoted lieutenant on the second. We did not return to service in Las Tenerias. They sent us to guard San

---

1. Today the Convent of Jerusalem still exists in a restored condition. Its façade is towards the Hall of Independence. The hospital occupied the place where the Hotel de l'Europe stands. The present Palace of Deputies for the Province was constructed on the site of the Convent of San Francisco.

Francisco,—a vast edifice which offered good positions for our guns against the French, who were established in the Convent of Jerusalem. Very short rations were now dealt out to us; and those of us who were counted among the officers ate in the same mess with the soldiers. Augustine kept his bread to give to Mariquilla.

After the fourth day, the French began mining towards the hospital and San Francisco, in order to take it; for they knew well that it would be impossible in any other way. In order to hinder them we countermined, intending to blow them up before they could blow us up. This toilsome labor in the bowels of the earth can be compared to nothing else in the world. We seemed to ourselves to have left off being men, and to be converted into another kind of creatures, into cold inhabitants of caverns, without feeling, far from the sun and the pure air and the lovely light of day. We built long galleries, working ceaselessly like the worm that builds his house in the darkness of earth, shaping it like his own body. Between the blows of our picks, we heard, like a muffled echo, the picks of the French. After having been beaten and destroyed on the surface, we expected momentarily to be exterminated in the dreadful night of those sepulchres.

The Convent of San Francisco had vast subterranean wine-cellars under its choir. The edifices which the French occupied farther down had these also, and it was unusual for a house not to have a deep cellar. In these many of our enemies perished, sometimes by the falling in of floors, sometimes wounded from afar by our balls, which penetrated into the most hidden places. The galleries opened by the spades of both sides met at last in one of these cellars. By the light of our torches, we saw the French, like fantastic goblin figures engendered by the reddish light and the sinuosities of the old Moorish dungeon. They did not see us, and we began firing at them; but as we were provided with hand-grenades, we hurled these also, putting them to flight, following them afterwards at arms-length the whole distance through their galleries. All this seemed a nightmare,—one of those dreadful struggles which at times we all wage with the abhorrent figures that people the terrible caverns of our dreams. But it was not a dream, though it repeated itself at many points.

In this pursuit, we showed ourselves frequently; and at last emerged in the Coso,—the central place of reunion, and at the same time, park, hospital, and general cemetery of the besieged. One afternoon (I believe it was the fifth), we were in the gateway of the convent, with several boys of the battalion of Estremadura and San Pedro. We were talking about the way the siege dragged along, and all agreed that resistance would very soon be impossible. Our group was constantly enlarged. Don José de Montoria came up, and, saluting us with a sad face, seated himself upon a wooden bench near the doorway.

"Do you hear what they are saying here, Don José?" I said to him. "They believe that it is impossible to hold out many days more."

"Don't get discouraged, boys," he answered. "The Captain-General says truly in his proclamation that a good deal of French gold is in circulation in this city."

A Franciscan who had come to nurse several dozen of the sick took up the word, and said,—

"It is painful to hear them. They do not talk of anything but surrender here. It does not seem as if this is Saragossa any longer. Who could believe it of a people tried in the fire of the first siege?"

"Your reverence is right!" exclaimed Montoria. "It is shameful; and even those of us who have hearts of bronze feel ourselves attacked by this weakness, which spreads faster than the epidemic. In casting up the accounts, I don't know how to reckon for this novelty of surrender, when we have never done it before, porra! If there is something to come after this world, as our religion teaches us, why should we worry about a day more or less of life?"

"The truth is, Señor Don José," said the friar, "that the provisions are going fast; and when there is no flour everybody is irritable."

"Fiddle-de-dee, Father Luengo," exclaimed Montoria. "Yet if these people, accustomed to the luxury of other times, cannot get along without bread and meat, there is nothing to say! As if there were not other things to eat! I believe in resisting to the last breath of life, cost what it may. I have experienced terrible misfortunes; the loss of my first-born and of my grandson has filled my heart with sorrow; but at times my regard for national honor fills my soul so that there is no room left for any other sentiment. One son is left to me, the only consolation of my life, the one hope of my house and my name. Far from taking him out of danger, I insisted upon his persisting in the defence. If I should lose him, I would die of grief; but in order to save our national honor, I am willing that my only child shall perish."

"And according to what I have heard," said Father Luengo, "the Señor Augustine has performed prodigies of valor. It is plain that the greenest laurels of this campaign belong to the brilliant fighters of the Church."

"No; my son no longer belongs only to the Church. It is necessary that he should renounce the plan of being a clergyman. I cannot be left without direct succession."

"Ah, you are talking of succession and of marriages! Augustine must have changed since he became a soldier. Formerly his conversation was all of theology, and I never heard him talk of love. He is a chap who has Saint Thomas at his finger-tips, and does not know in what part of their faces girls carry their eyes."

"Augustine will sacrifice his beloved vocation for my sake. If we come out alive from the siege, and the Virgin del Pilar grants me life, I intend to marry him quickly to a woman who is his equal in position and fortune."

While he was saying this, we saw Mariquilla Candiola approaching us, sobbing; on coming up to me she asked,—

"Señor de Araceli, have you seen my father?"

"No, Señorita Doña Mariquilla," I answered, "I have not seen him since yesterday. It may be that he is in the ruins of his house, busying himself trying to get something out."

"No, he is not," said Mariquilla, anxiously; "I have looked for him everywhere."

"Have you been over back here, near San Diego? Señor Candiola sometimes goes to look at his house los Duendes, to see if it has been destroyed."

"I am going there instantly!"

As she disappeared, Montoria said, "She is, I am told, the daughter of the miser Candiola. Faith, she's very pretty, and does not look like the daughter of such a wolf—God forgive me, I mean good man."

"She's not bad looking," said the friar; "but I imagine she's a good one. Saints don't come of Candiola timber."

"One must not speak ill of one's neighbor," said Don José.

"Candiola is nobody's neighbor. The girl is always in the company of the soldiers since they lost their house."

"She goes among them to help take care of the wounded."

"It may be; but it looks to me as if she likes best those who are strong and hearty. Her charming little face does not show a whiff of shame."

"You snake in the grass!"

"It is the truth," said the friar. "She's a chip of the old block. Do they not say all sorts of things about her mother, Pepa Rincon?"

"Perhaps she used to take a little something to make her happy."

"It's not a bad kind of happiness. When she was abandoned by her third gallant, Señor Don Jeronimo took charge of her."

"Enough of scandal," said Montoria. "Even when we talk of the worst people in the world, we can at least leave them to their own consciences."

"I would not give a farthing for the souls of all the Candiolas put together," replied the friar. "But there comes the Señor Don Jeronimo, if I am not mistaken. He has seen us, and is coming over here."

Candiola was indeed coming slowly along the Coso, and came up to the convent door.

"Good-evening to you, Señor Don Jeronimo," said Montoria. "I live in hope that our grudge is all gone."

"A moment ago your innocent young daughter was here looking for you," said Luengo, maliciously.

"Where is she?"

"She has gone to San Diego," said a soldier. "Maybe some of the French about here have carried her off."

"Perhaps they respect her, knowing that she is the daughter of Señor Don Jeronimo," said Luengo. "Is this true, friend Candiola, that they are telling about here?"

"What?"

"That you have been inside the French lines, holding confabs with that mob?"

"I? What vile calumny!" exclaimed the miser. "My enemies are saying that to ruin me. Is it you, Señor de Montoria, who have set these stories going?"

"Not even in thought," said the patriot; "but I have certainly heard others say it. I remember defending you, assuring them that Señor Candiola is incapable of selling himself to the French."

"My enemies, my enemies wish to ruin me! What calumnies they invent against me! They wish to make me lose my honor, since I have lost my estate. Gentlemen, my house in the Calle de la Sombra has lost part of its roof. Is there any such trouble as mine! The one that I have here back of San Francisco, next to the garden of San Diego, is still preserved; but it is occupied by the troops, and they will finish it for me, and it's a beauty."

"That house is worth very little, Señor Don Jeronimo," said the friar. "If I have not forgotten, it is ten years since anybody would live in it."

"That is because some crazy people gave out that it has ghosts in it. But let us drop that. Have you seen my daughter about here?"

"That virginal white lily has gone over to San Diego in search of her amiable papa."

"My daughter has lost all her good sense."

"Something of that sort."

"Yet Señor de Montoria is all to blame for it. My wicked enemies give me no time to breathe."

"What do you say?" exclaimed my protector. "How am I to blame for what this child has inherited of the evil ways of her mother? I mean to say (my cursed tongue!) that her mother was an exemplary lady."

"The insults and scorn of Señor Montoria do not affect me," said the miser, with biting contempt. "Instead of insulting me, the Señor Don José ought to keep his son Augustine in order, that libertine who has turned my daughter's head. No, I will not give her to him in marriage, though he begs on his knees. He wants to rob me of her. A pretty fellow, that Don Augustine! No, no, he shall not have her for a wife. She can do better, much better, my Mariquilla!"

Don José de Montoria turned white on hearing this, and stepped hastily towards Candiola, with the intention doubtless of renewing the scene in the Calle de Anton Trillo. But he restrained himself, and said in a mournful voice,—

"My God, give me strength to govern my anger. Is it possible to keep my temper and to have humility in the presence of this man? I asked his pardon for the wrong which I did him. I humbled myself before him. I offered him a friendly hand; and now he is here injuring and insulting me in the most disgusting fashion. Wretched man! beat me, kill me, drink all my blood, and sell my bones afterwards to make buttons; but let not that vile tongue of yours cast ignominy upon my beloved son. What is this that you say about my Augustine?"

"The truth."

"I do not know how to contain myself! Gentlemen, witness myself-control. I do not wish to let myself go. I do not wish to trample on anyone. I do not wish to offend God. I forgive this man his calumnies; but on condition that he quit my presence at once, because seeing him I cannot answer for myself."

Candiola, alarmed at these words, entered the convent gate. Father Luengo took Montoria down the Coso.

At the same time there began to be heard among the soldiers there an angry murmur which indicated sentiments hostile to the father of Mariquilla, who, accustomed to this sort of thing, did not realize that it was anything unusual. He tried to get away, as they pushed him from one to the other; but they held him, and, without knowing exactly how, he was brought swiftly into the cloister by the threatening group. Then a voice cried, in angry accents,—

"To the well, throw him into the well!"

Candiola was seized by many hands, pounded and torn, and pulled about more than ever before.

"He is one of those who go about distributing French bribes to the troops," said one.

"Yes, yes!" cried others. "Yesterday they say that he was walking about in the market distributing money."

"Gentlemen," said the unfortunate man, in a choked voice, "I swear to you that I have never distributed any money."

And this was the truth.

"Last night they say he was seen sneaking over into the French camp."

"He did not come back until morning. To the well with him!"

One of my comrades and I tried for awhile to save Candiola from certain death; but we only succeeded by force of prayers and persuasions, saying,—

"Boys, do not commit an outrage. What harm can this ridiculous old wretch do?"

"It is true," said Candiola, with the calmness of despair; "what harm can I do who am always busy aiding those in need? Do not kill me! You are soldiers of the Estremadura and las Peñas de San Pedro; you are all good fellows. You were burning those houses in Las Tenerias where I found the chicken that I sold for a doubloon. Who says that I sell myself to the French? I hate them; I cannot bear to look at them; and I love you as my own life. I have lost everything. Leave me my life, at least."

These pleadings, and my prayers and those of my friend, softened the soldiers a little; and, when their first outburst of anger was over, it was easy for us to save the wretched old man. The soldiers were presently relieved, and he was in perfect safety; but he never even thanked us when we offered him a bit of bread, after saving his life. A little later, when he recovered his breath enough to walk, he went on out of the street and joined his daughter.

XXVII

That afternoon almost all the efforts of the French were directed against the suburb from the left of the Ebro. They assaulted the Monastery of Jesus, and bombarded the Church of the Virgin del Pilar, where the greater number of sick and infirm had found refuge, believing that the sanctity of the place offered them greater security than any other spot.

In the centre of the city, we did not work much that day. All our attention was concentrated upon the mines, and our efforts directed to giving the enemy evidence that, before consenting to be blown up ourselves, we would discuss blowing them up, or at least flying upwards together.

At night both armies seemed given over to peaceful repose. The rough blows of the pick were no longer heard in the subterranean galleries. I sallied forth; and near San Diego I found Augustine and Mariquilla, who were talking quietly together, seated sedately upon the doorstep of the house los Duendes. They were very glad to see me; and I joined them, sharing the scraps of bread of which they were making their supper.

"We have nowhere to stay," said Mariquilla. "We were in a portico in the Organo alley; but we were driven out. Why is it that so many people detest my poor father? What harm has he done them? We took refuge afterwards in a corner of the Calle de las Urreas, and were driven out of there too. We sat down afterwards under an arch in the Coso, and all those who were there fled away from us. My father was furious."

"Mariquilla of my heart," said Augustine, "let us hope that the siege will soon be finished by some means or other. I hope that God will let us both die, if living may not be happy. I do not know why, among so many misfortunes, my heart is full of hope; I do not know why I have such happy thoughts, and think constantly of a cheerful future. Why not? Must everything be dreadful and unfortunate? The troubles of my family have been very great. My mother neither receives nor desires to receive any consolation. Nobody is able to get her away from the place where the bodies of my brother and my nephew are; and when by force we take her to ever so great a distance, she immediately begins to drag herself along over the stones of the street to try and return. She and my sister and my sister-in-law are pitiable to see, refusing to take food, and in their prayers deliriously confusing the names of all the saints. This afternoon we have at last contrived to carry them to a sheltered spot where we obliged them to get a little repose, and to take a little food. Mariquilla, how sadly God has dealt with my people! Have I not reason to hope that at last He will pity us?"

"Yes," said Mariquilla; "my heart tells me that we have passed the hard part of our life, and that now we shall have peaceful days. The siege will soon be finished; because, according to what my father says, this holding out can be only a matter of days. This morning I went to the Pilar; when I knelt before the Virgin, it seemed to me that our holy Lady looked at me and smiled. Then I came out of the church, my heart was beating with a keen delight. I looked at the sky, and the bombs seemed to me like toys; I looked at the wounded, and it seemed to me that they were all healed; I looked at the people, and could almost believe that they all felt the same happiness which was overflowing my bosom. I do not know how it is with me today, I am so happy. God and the Virgin have surely taken pity on us; and this beating of my heart, this joyous restlessness, without care for what may happen, must mean good fortune after so many tears!"

"All that you say is true," said Augustine, holding Mariquilla lovingly to him. "Your presentiments are laws; your heart, one with the divine, cannot be deceived. Listening to you, it seems to me as if the troubles that crush us melt away in the air, and I breathe with delight the breath of happiness. I hope that your father will not oppose your marrying me."

"My father is good," said Mariquilla. "I believe that if his neighbors in the city had not worried him so much that he would have been kinder. But they cannot bear the sight of him. This afternoon he was badly maltreated again in the cloister of San Francisco, and when he joined me in the Coso he was furious, and swore that he would be revenged. I tried to quiet him, but all in vain. They drive us away from everywhere. He doubled up his fists, and angrily threatened those who were there near us. Afterwards, he ran away and came here. I thought he was coming to see if they had destroyed this house, which is ours. I followed him. He turned towards me as if frightened at hearing my footsteps, and said to me, 'Stupid meddler, who told you to follow me?' I answered nothing; but seeing that he advanced to the French lines, as if he meant to cross over, I tried to detain him, and said to him, 'Father, where are you going?' Then he answered, 'Do you know that my friend who served last year in Saragossa, the Swiss Captain Don Carlos Lindener, is in the French army? I am going to see him. I remember that he owes me a certain amount.' He made me stay here, and went on. I am afraid that if his enemies know that he crossed over into the French lines, they will call him a traitor. I do not know whether it is the great affection that I have for him, but he seems to me incapable of such action. I am afraid though that there is something wrong, and for this reason I long for the end of the siege. Is it not true that it will soon be finished, Augustine?"

"Yes, Mariquilla, it will soon be finished, and we will be married. My father wishes me to marry."

"Who is your father? What is his name? Is it not time yet to tell me that?"

"You shall know it another time. My father is one of the principal personages in Saragossa, and much beloved. Why wish to know more?"

"Yesterday I tried to inquire. I was curious. I asked several people I know that I met in the Coso, 'Do you know what gentleman it is who has lost his eldest son?' But so many are like that, that they only laughed at me."

"I will reveal it to you in good time, and when in telling it to you I can give you good news with it."

"Augustine, if I marry you, I wish that you would take me away from Saragossa for several days. I want for a little time to see other houses, other trees, other scenes. I wish to live for some days in places where these things are not, among which I have suffered so much."

"Yes, Mariquilla, my soul," exclaimed Montoria, quite carried away; "we will go wherever we please, far away from here, tomorrow even; no, not tomorrow, for the siege will not be raised. Day after tomorrow, in short, sometime, when—God wills it."

"Augustine," added Mariquilla, in a sleepy voice, "I wish that, after we return from our journey, that we might rebuild the house where I was born. The cypress-tree is still standing."

Mariquilla's head drooped forward, showing that she was half overcome with sleep.

"Do you want to go to sleep, you poor little thing?" my friend said to her, taking her in his arms.

"I have not slept at all for several nights," replied the girl, closing her eyes. "Anxiety, sorrow, and fear have kept me awake. Tonight weariness overcomes me, and I am so peaceful now that it makes me wish to go to sleep."

"Sleep in my arms, Mariquilla," said Augustine; "and may the peace that now fills thy soul not leave thee when thou wakest."

After a little while, when we thought her sleeping, Mariquilla, half asleep and half awake, said,—

"Augustine, I do not wish my good Doña Guedita to leave me; she took such good care of us when we were first engaged. You see now I was right in telling you that my father was in the French camp to collect his bill—"

Then she spoke no more, and slept profoundly. Augustine sat upon the ground, holding her on his knees and in his arms. I covered her feet with my cloak.

Augustine and I were silent, so that our voices might not disturb the sleep of the young girl. The place was deserted enough. Just back of us was the Casa los Duendes, close by the Convent of San Francisco, and opposite the college of San Diego, with its orchard surrounded by high mud walls which opened upon irregular and narrow alleys. Through these marched the sentinels who had been relieved, and the platoons going to the picket lines or coming from there. The truce was complete, and this repose signified a great battle on the following day. Suddenly the silence permitted me to hear muffled blows under us, in the depths of the earth. I understood that the French miners had reached this point with their picks, and told Augustine what I imagined it must be. He listened attentively; then he said to me,—

"That seems indeed like mining. But how did they come here? The galleries that they made from the Jerusalem were all cut off by ourselves. How would they be able to take a step without meeting our men?"

"This noise indicates that they are mining from San Diego. They have a part of that building. Until now they have not been able to reach the wine-cellars of the Convent of San Francisco. If, by bad luck, they have discovered that the passage from San Diego to San Francisco is easy by the way under this house, it is probable that this is the passage that is being opened now."

"Run this instant to the convent," he said to me. "Go down into the cellar, and if you hear the noise, tell Renovales what is going on. If anything happens, call me, and I will follow."

Augustine remained alone with Mariquilla. I went to the San Francisco, and going down into the cellar met, together with other patriots, an official of the engineers, who, when I had expressed my fears, said to me,—

"They would not be able to get here by the galleries under the Calle de Santa Engracia from the Jerusalem and the hospital, because our mine has made theirs useless, and a few of our men will be able to keep them back. Under this edifice we control the underground chambers of the church, the wine-cellars, and the other cellars which lead towards the cloister at the east. There is a part of the convent which has not been mined, at the west and south; but, there are no cellars there, and we did not believe it worth while to open galleries, because it is not probable that they would approach us from the two sides. We hold the next house; and I have examined it underground, and found that the cellar was almost joined to those of the chapter house. If they controlled the house los Duendes, it would be easy to carry explosives and blow up all the southern and western part; but that house is ours, and from it to the French positions opposite San Diego and Santa Rosa is a long distance. It is not probable that they will attack us in that place, and I do not know that there is any existing communication between the house and San Diego or Santa Rosa which would permit them to advance without making it known."

We remained talking over this matter until morning. At break of day Augustine came, very happy, and saying that he had found a lodging for Mariquilla in the same place where his family was established. Then we prepared for a strong effort that day, because the French, who already held the hospital, or rather its ruins, threatened to attack the San Francisco, not by the underground way, but in the open, and by the light of the sun.

XXVIII

The possession of San Francisco would decide the fate of the city. That vast edifice, situated in the middle of the Coso, gave an incontestable superiority to the side which occupied it. The French began cannonading it very early, with the intention of opening a breach for the assault; and the Saragossans transferred thither the greater part of their forces to defend it. As the number of soldiers was now greatly decreased, a large number of leading citizens, who until then had not served except as aids, took up arms. Cereso, Sas, La Casa, Pidrafita, Escobar, Leiva, Don José de Montoria,—all these good patriots hastened to be among them.

In the narrow entrance of the Calle de San Gil, and in the archway of Cineja, there were cannon to restrain the enemy's advance. I was sent to serve these pieces, with other soldiers of the Estremadura regiment, because there were scarcely any artillerymen left. When I took leave of Augustine, who remained in the San Francisco in the face of the enemy, we embraced, believing that we should never see each other again.

Don José de Montoria, finding himself in the barricade of La Cruz del Coso, got a gunshot in the leg, and had to retire; but leaning against the wall of a house next to the arch of Cineja, he kept on fighting for sometime, until he brought on a hemorrhage, and at last finding himself very faint, he called me, and said to me,—

"Señor de Araceli, something is in my eyes. I cannot see anything. Curse this blood, how fast it runs out when it is most necessary to keep it. Won't you lend me a hand?"

"Señor," I said, running to him, and holding him up, "it would be better for you to retire to your lodging."

"No, here is where I want to be. But, Señor de Araceli, if I keep on bleeding, where the devil is all this blood going? It seems to me as if my legs are stuffed with cotton. I am falling to the ground like an empty bag."

He made tremendous efforts of endurance, but almost lost consciousness, more from the serious nature of his wound, than merely from loss of blood, after being without food and sleep, and in such trouble during these past days. Although he begged us to leave him there against the wall, so that he should not miss a single detail of the battle, we carried him to his lodging, which was also in the Coso, at the corner of the Calle del Refugio. The family had been installed in

BENITO PÉREZ GALDÓS

an upper room. The house was all full of wounded, and the numbers of bodies deposited there very nearly obstructed the entrance. It was difficult to get through the narrow doorway and the rooms within, because the men who had gone there to die, crowded the place, and it was not easy to distinguish between the living and the dead.

Montoria said, when we entered there, "Don't carry me upstairs, boys, where my family is. Leave me here below. Here I see a counter which just suits my purpose."

We put him where he said. This lower story was a shop. Several of the wounded and victims of the epidemic who had died that day were under the counter, and many of the sick were lying upon the infected ground on pieces of cloth.

"Let us see," he said, "if there is any charitable soul who will try a little to stop the gap where the blood comes out."

A woman came forward to care for the wounded man. It was Mariquilla Candiola.

"God bless you, child," said Don José, seeing that she was bringing lint and linen to bandage him. "Enough for now that you patch up this leg a little. I don't believe there are any bones broken."

While this was going on, some twenty peasants came into the house to fire from the windows upon the ruins of the hospital.

"Señor de Araceli, are you not going on firing? Wait a moment until I get up, for I don't seem able to walk alone. I command you to fire from the window. That's a good shot. Don't let them have time to breathe over there at the hospital. Look here, lass, make haste! Haven't you a knife? It would be a good thing to cut off this piece of flesh that's hanging. How goes it, Señor de Araceli? Are we going to win?"

"It's going all right," I answered from the window. "They are falling back at the hospital. San Francisco is a bone that is a little hard to pick."

Mariquilla, meanwhile, was looking fixedly at Montoria, and following his instructions in caring for him with much solicitude and deftness.

"You are a jewel, child," said my friend. "It seems to me that I can scarcely feel your hands upon my wound. But what makes you look at me so much? Does my face look like a monkey's? Let's see, is it finished? I will try to get up. But I am not able to sit up. What sort of weak water is this in my veins! Porr—I was going to say—I don't seem able to correct that bad habit! Señor de Araceli, I don't do very well with my soul. How goes the battle?"

"Señor, a thousand marvels! Our valiant peasants are working wonders!"

Here a wounded officer was brought in for whom a ligature was wanted.

"Everything goes as we would desire it to go," he said to us. "They will not take San Francisco. Those in the hospital have been repulsed three times. But the most wonderful thing, señors, took place beside San Diego. I saw the French gain the orchard joining the house Los Duendes, where they were met by the bayonets of those brave soldiers of Orihuela commanded by Pino-Hermoso, who not only dislodged them, but they say killed a lot of them, and took thirty prisoners."

"I wish to go there! Viva the battalion of Orihuela! Viva the Marquis of Pino-Hermoso!" exclaimed Don José de Montoria, with tremendous fervor. "Señor de Araceli, let us go there! Lift me up. Isn't there a pair of crutches there? Señors, my legs have given out. But I will go there in spirit. My heart is there. Goodbye, child, beautiful little nurse. But what makes you look at me so? Do you know me? I think I have seen your face somewhere, but I don't remember where."

"I also have seen you once, only once," answered Mariquilla, tactfully, "and God grant you do not remember me!"

"I shall not forget your kindness," said Montoria. "You seem to be a good girl, and very pretty, that's sure. I am very grateful, most grateful. But bring those crutches or a stick, Señor de Araceli. Give me your arm. What is this which goes back and forth before my eyes? Let us go over there and drive the French out of the hospital."

Dissuading him from his rash idea of going out, I started alone, when I heard an explosion so loud that no words have power to describe it. It seemed as if the whole city had been thrown into the air by the eruption of an immense volcano from beneath its foundations. All the houses trembled. The sky was obscured by an immense cloud of smoke and dust, and along the whole length of the street we saw pieces of wall falling, and shattered fragments, and beams, roofs, tiles, showers of earth, and all sorts of things.

"Holy Virgin del Pilar, save us!" exclaimed Montoria. "It seems as if the whole world has blown up."

The sick and the wounded were crying out, believing that their last hour had come. We all commended ourselves to God.

"What is it? Is Saragossa still in existence?" one asked.

"Are we blown up too?"

"This terrible explosion must have been in the Convent of San Francisco," said I.

"Let us run over there," cried Montoria, trying to make strength of his weakness. "Señor de Araceli, did they not say that all precautions had been taken to defend San Francisco? Isn't there a pair of crutches anywhere here?"

We went into the Coso, where we were immediately assured of the fact that a large part of San Francisco had been blown up.

"My son was in the convent," said Montoria, pale as the dead. "My God, if thou art resolved upon his death also, may he die for his country at the post of honor."

The loquacious beggar of whom I made mention in the first pages now approached us, walking laboriously upon his crutches, and seeming in a very bad state of health.

"Sursum Corda," I said to the patriot, "give me your crutches. You are doing no good with them."

"Do me the kindness to let me keep them to get to that doorway," said the cripple, "and then I will give them to you. I do not wish to die in the middle of the street."

"Are you dying?"

"It seems like it. I am burning with fever. I was wounded in the shoulder yesterday, and nobody has taken out the ball. I feel that I am going. Your honor may have the crutches."

"Have you come from San Francisco?"

"No, sir, I was in the Arch del Trenque. There was a cannon there. We had been firing a great deal. But San Francisco has been blown into the air when we least expected it. The whole part to the south and the west came to the ground, burying many people. There has been treachery, people say. Adios, Señor Don José. Here I stay. My eyes are getting dim. My tongue thickens. I am going, but the Virgin del Pilar will protect me. And here your honor has my oars."

With them Montoria got on slowly towards the scene of the catastrophe. But we had to go around by the Calle San Gil, because we could not get through directly. The French had ceased firing upon the convent from the hospital; but, assaulting by San Diego, they quickly occupied the ruins, which we could not dispute with them. The church and the tower of San Francisco remained standing.

"Eh, Father Luengo," said Montoria, calling to the friar of that name, "what is it? Where is the Captain-General? Has he perished in the ruins?"

"No," replied the friar, stopping. "He is with officers in the Plazuela de San Felipe. I can announce the safety of your son Augustine to you, because he was one of those who were occupying the tower."

"Blessed be God!" said Don José, crossing himself.

"All the part at the south and the west has been destroyed," proceeded Luengo. "I do not know how they have been able to mine in that place. They must have placed the mines under the chapter house. We had not mined there, believing that it was a safe place."

An armed peasant who had come up said:

"Yes, and we had the next house, and the French, having possession of parts only of Santa Rosa and San Diego, could not readily approach there."

"As far as that is concerned," said an armed priest who had joined us, "it is supposed that they have found a secret passage-way between Santa Rosa and the house los Duendes. Being in possession of the cellars of that, they could, by digging a short gallery, get under the chapter house, which is quite near."

"It is now known," said a captain of the army. "The house los Duendes has a large cellar of which we knew nothing. From this cellar there was undoubtedly a communication with Santa Rosa. The house formerly belonged to the convent, and served it as a storehouse."

"Well, if this communication exists," said Luengo, "I understand perfectly who has discovered it to the French. You know that when the enemy was repulsed in the orchard of San Diego some prisoners were taken. Among them was Candiola, who during these past days has often visited the French camp, and last night went over to the enemy."

"It must be so," said Montoria; "because the house los Duendes belongs to Candiola. The damned Jew knew very well the passage-ways and hiding places of that building. Señors, let us go to see the Captain-General. Is it believed that the Coso can still be defended?"

"Does it not have to be defended?" said a soldier. "After all, it is only a trifle which has happened, a few more dead. We will try to regain the church of San Francisco."

We all looked at that man who spoke so serenely of the impossible. The sublime terseness of his expression of perseverance seemed like a jest, and in that epoch of the incredible, similar jests were wont to end in reality.

Let those who hesitate to give credence to my words open the history, and they will see that some few dozens of men, wasted, famished, barefooted, and half-naked, some of them wounded, held out all that day in the tower. Not content with holding it, they went out over the roof of the church, opening here and there many places in the roof, and paying no attention to the fire directed upon them from the hospital, they began to throw hand-grenades upon the French, obliging them to abandon the church when night came. All of the night was passed in attempts by the enemy to regain it; but they could not accomplish it until the following day, when the riflemen on the roof retired, passing to the house of Sástago.

XXIX

Will Saragossa surrender? Death to him who says it!

Saragossa will not surrender. She will be reduced to powder. Of her historic houses, let not one brick remain upon another! Let her hundred temples fall, the ground beneath her open, pouring out flames; let her foundations be hurled into the air; let her roofs fall into the pits that are opened,—but among the fragments and the dead there will always be one tongue left alive to say that Saragossa will never surrender!

The moment of supreme despair came. France was not fighting now, but mining. It was necessary to destroy the soil of the nation in order to conquer it. Half the Coso was hers, but Spain retreated only to the opposite pavement. By Las Tenerias and in the suburb on the left they had obtained some advantages; and their little mines did not rest for an instant.

At last—it seems like a lie—we became accustomed to the explosions, as before we had become accustomed to the bombardment. At worst we heard a noise like that of a thousand thunder-claps all at once. What has happened? Nothing, the University, the Chapel de la Sangre, the Casa de Aranda, such a convent or chapel exists no longer. It was not like living on our peaceful and quiet planet. It was like having the birthplace of thunderbolts for a dwelling-place, like being in a disordered world, where everything was heaving up and unhinging. There was no place to live, because the ground was no longer ground. Under every shrub or plant a crater was opening. And yet those men went on defending themselves against the crushing horrors of a never-stilled volcano and a ceaseless tempest. Lacking fortresses, they had used the convents; lacking convents, the palaces; when the palaces failed, the humble houses. There were still some partition walls. They did not eat now. Of what use, when death was expected from one moment to the next? Thousands of men perished in the explosions, and the epidemic had risen to its height of horror. One might go by chance unharmed through the shower of balls, then on turning a street corner, dreadful chills and fever would suddenly take possession of his frame, and in a little while he would be dead. There were no longer kinsfolk or friends; men did not even know one another, their faces blackened by smoke, by earth, by blood, disfigured, cadaverous. Meeting one another after a combat they would ask, "Who are you?"

The belfries no longer sounded the alarm, because there were no bell-ringers. One heard no more the proclamations by criers, because proclamations were no longer published. Mass was not said, because there were no more priests. Nobody sang the jota now. The voices of the dying people were husky in their throats. From hour to hour a funereal silence was conquering the city. Only the cannon spoke. The advance guards of the two nations no longer took the trouble to exchange insults. Instead of madness, everybody was full of sadness; and the dying city fought on in silence, so that no atom of strength need be lost in idle words.

The necessity of surrender was now the general idea; but none showed it, guarding it in the depths of conscience as he would conceal a crime which he was about to commit. Surrender! It seemed an impossibility, a word too difficult. To perish would be easier!

One day passed after the explosion of San Francisco; it was a horrible day which seemed to have no existence in time, but only in the fanciful realm of the imagination. I had been in the Calle de las Arcadas a little before the greater number of its houses fell. I ran afterwards to the Coso, to fulfil a commission with which I had been charged, and I remember that the heavy infected air choked me so that I could scarcely walk. On the way I saw the same child that I had seen several days before, alone and crying in the quarter of Las Tenerias. He was still alone and crying, and the poor child had his hands in his mouth as if he were eating his fingers. In spite of that, nobody noticed him. I also passed him by indifferently; but, afterwards a little voice reproached me, and I turned back, and took him with me, giving him some bits of bread. My commission accomplished, I ran to the Plazuela de San Felipe, where, since the affair of Las Arcadas, were the few men of my battalion who were still alive. It was now night; and although there had been firing in the Coso between one sidewalk and the other, my comrades were held in reserve for the following day, because they were dropping with fatigue. On arriving, I saw a man who wrapped in his military cloak was walking up and down, taking notice of nobody. It was Augustine Montoria.

"Augustine, is it thou?" I asked, going up to him. "How pale and changed thou art? Have they wounded thee?"

"Let me alone," he answered bitterly, "I am in no mood for comrades."

"Are you mad? What has happened to you?"

"Leave me," he answered, pushing me away, "I tell you that I want to be alone. I do not want to see anybody."

"Friend!" I cried, understanding that some terrible trouble was on the soul of my companion, "if misfortune is upon you, tell it to me, and let me share your sorrow."

"Do you not know it, then?"

"I know nothing. You know that I was sent with twenty men to the Calle de las Arcades. Since yesterday, since the explosion of San Francisco, you and I have not seen each other."

"It is true," he replied. "I have sought death in this barricade of the Coso, and death has passed me by. Numberless comrades fell beside me, and there was not one ball for me. Gabriel, my dear friend, put the barrel of one of your pistols to my temple and tear out my life. Would you believe it? A little while ago I tried to kill myself. I do not know—but it seemed as if an invisible hand came and took the weapon from my temple, then another hand, soft and warm, passed over my brow."

"Calm yourself, Augustine, and tell me what is the matter."

"What the matter is with me? What time is it?"

"Nine o'clock."

"It lacks an hour," he cried, trembling nervously. "Sixty minutes. It may be the French have mined this Plazuela de San Felipe where we are, and perhaps in a moment the earth will leap under our feet and open a horrible gulf in which we shall all be buried,—all, the victim and the executioners."

"What victim is that?"

"The unfortunate Candiola. He is shut up in the Torre Nueva."

In the doorway of the Torre Nueva there were some soldiers, and a faint light illumined the entrance.

"Of course," I said, "I know that that infamous old man was taken prisoner with some of the French in the orchard of San Diego."

"His crime is unquestioned. He showed the enemy the passage, known to him alone, from Santa Rosa to his house los Duendes. Besides, there being no lack of proof, the unhappy man has tonight confessed all, in the hope of saving his life."

"They have condemned him?"

"Yes, the council of war did not discuss it long. Candiola will be shot within an hour. There he is, and here you are. Here am I, Gabriel, captain of the battalion of Las Peñas de San Pedro. These cursed epaulets! Here am I with an order in my pocket which commands me to execute the sentence at ten o'clock at night here in this very place, in the Plazuela de San Felipe, at the foot of the tower. Do you see it? Do you see this order? It is signed by General Saint March."

I was silent; because I could not think of one word to say to my companion in that terrible hour.

"Courage, my friend!" I cried at last. "You must obey the order!"

Augustine did not hear me. He acted like a madman, and tore himself away from me, only to return a second later, uttering words of desperation, then looking at the tower which, splendid and tall, lifted itself above our heads crying with terror,—

"Gabriel, do you not see it? Don't you see the tower? Don't you see that it is straight, Gabriel? The tower has been made straight!"

I looked at the tower, and, naturally, the tower was still leaning.

"Gabriel," said Augustine, "kill me! I do not want to live. No, I will not take life from that man. You must take the order. I, if I live, must run away. I am sick. I will tear off these epaulets, and throw them in the face of General Saint March. No, do not tell me that the Torre Nueva is still leaning. Why, man, do you not see that it is straight? My friend, you deceive me. My heart is pierced as by red-hot steel, and my blood burns within me. I am dying of the pain."

I was trying to console him, when a white figure entered the plaza by the Calle de Torresecas. On seeing her I trembled, for it was Mariquilla. Augustine did not have time to flee, and the distressed girl embraced him, exclaiming eagerly in her emotion,—

"Augustine! Augustine! thank God, I have found you here! How much I love you! When they told me that you were the jailer of my father, I was wild with delight, for I know that you will save him. Those savages of the council have condemned him to death. He to die who has done harm to no one! But God does not wish the innocent to perish, and He has put him in your hands, so that you may let him escape!"

"Oh, my heart's Mariquilla," said Augustine, "leave me, I pray you! I don't wish to see you. Tomorrow—tomorrow we will talk. I love you, too. I am mad for you. Let Saragossa perish, but don't leave off loving me! They expected me to kill your father."

"Oh, God, do not say that!" cried the girl. "Thou!"

"No, a thousand times no! Let others punish his treachery."

"No, it is a lie! My father is not a traitor. Do you also accuse him? I never have believed it. Augustine, it is night. Untie his hands; take off the fetters that hurt his feet. Set him at liberty. No one can see. We will flee. We will hide ourselves in the ruins of our house, there by the cypress where so many times we have seen the spire of the Torre Nueva."

"Mariquilla, wait a little," said Montoria, with great agitation. "This cannot be done so. There are many people in the plaza. The soldiers are greatly incensed against the prisoner. Tomorrow—"

"Tomorrow! What do you say? You are laughing at me. Set him at liberty this instant. Augustine, if you do not do it, I shall believe that I have loved the most vile, the most cowardly, the most despicable of men."

"Mariquilla, God hears us. God knows that I adore you. By Him I swear that I will not stain my hands with the blood of this unhappy man. I will sooner break my sword. But—in the name of God, I tell you also that I cannot set your father at liberty. Mariquilla, Heaven is against us."

"Augustine, you are deceiving me," said the girl, anguished and bewildered. "Do you tell me that you will not set him at liberty?"

"Oh, no, I cannot. If God should come in human form to ask of me the freedom of him who sold our heroic peasants, delivered them up to the French sword, I would not do it. It is a supreme duty, in which one cannot fail. The innumerable victims immolated by his treachery, the city surrendered, the national honor outraged, are things which weigh too strongly upon my conscience."

"My father cannot have done this deed of treachery," she said, passing at once from grief to an exalted and nervous anger; "these are calumnies of his enemies. They lie who call him traitor, and you, more cruel and more inhuman than all, you lie also! It is not possible that I have loved you! It causes me shame to think of it. You say you will not free him? Then of what good are you? Do you hope to gain favor by your bloody cruelty of those inhuman barbarians who have destroyed the city, imagining that they were defending it? To you the life of the innocent is of no consequence, nor the desolation of an orphan. Miserable, ambitious egoist, I abhor you more than I have ever loved you! You thought that you would be able to present yourself before me with your hands stained with the blood of my father? No, he is not a traitor. You are traitors, all of you. My God, is there no generous hand to help me? Among so many men, is there not even one to prevent this crime? A poor woman runs through all the city looking for a friendly soul, and does not find anything but wild beasts."

"Mariquilla," said Augustine, "you are lacerating my soul. You ask the impossible of me, that which I will not do, and cannot do, although you offer me eternal blessedness for payment. I have sacrificed all, and

I knew that you would abhor me. Think what it is for a man to tear out his own heart and trample it in the mud. I have done that. I can do no more."

The fervent exaltation of Mariquilla Candiola carried her from intense anger to pathetic sensitiveness of suffering. She had showed her anger with fiery heat, now she burst into bitter tears, expressing herself thus,—

"What mad things I have said! And what madness hast thou said, Augustine! How I have loved you, and how I do love you!—from the time I saw you first at our house. You have never been absent from my thoughts for a moment. You have been to me the most loving, the most generous, the most thoughtful, the bravest of all men. I loved you without knowing who you were. I did not know your name, or that of your parents; but I would have loved you if you had been the son of the hangman of Saragossa. Augustine, you have forgotten me since we have not been together. It is I, Mariquilla. I have all this time believed, and I believe now that you will not take away from me my good father whom I love as much as I love you. He is good. He has not hurt anybody. He is a poor old man. He has some faults; but I do not see them. I do not see anything in him but virtues. I never knew my mother, who died when I was very small. I have lived retired from the world. My father has brought me up in solitude. In solitude the great love that I bear you has been nourished. If I had never known you, the whole world would have been nothing to me without him!"

I could read clearly Montoria's indecision in his face. He was looking with terrified eyes, now at the girl, now at the sentinels at the entrance of the tower. The daughter of Candiola, with admirable instinct, knew how to make use of that evidence of weakness. Throwing her arms around his neck, she cried,—

"Augustine, set him at liberty! We will hide where no one can find us. If they say anything to you, if they accuse you of having failed in duty, do not take any notice of them. Come with me. How my father will love you, seeing you have saved his life! Then what happiness is before us, Augustine. How good you are! I was expecting it, and when I knew that the poor prisoner was in your hands, I felt the gates of heaven were open!"

My friend took a few steps, then drew back. There were plenty of soldiers and armed men in the plazuela. Suddenly there appeared before us a man on crutches, accompanied by several officials of high rank.

"What is going on here?" asked Don José de Montoria. "It seemed to me I heard the cries of a woman. Augustine, are you weeping? What is the matter?"

"Señor," said Mariquilla, in alarm, turning to Montoria. "You will not at all oppose their setting my father at liberty? Do you not remember me? You were wounded yesterday, and I cared for you."

"It is true, child," said Don José gravely; "I am very grateful. Now I see that you are the daughter of Señor Candiola."

"Yes, sir. Yesterday, when I was attending you, I recognized in you the man who ill-treated my father sometime ago."

"Yes, my daughter, it was a sudden thing—a hasty—I can't help it. I have very quick blood. And you took care of me? That is the way good Christians do, returning good for evil, paying back injuries with benefits, and to do good to them that hate us is what God commands."

"Señor," exclaimed Mariquilla, dissolved in tears. "I forgive my enemies. Do you also forgive yours? Why do they not free my father? He has not done anything."

"This thing that you ask is a little difficult. The treachery of Señor Candiola is unpardonable. The troops are furious."

"It is all a mistake. If you would intercede! You must be one of the commanders."

"I!" said Montoria, "that is a business which does not rest on me. But calm yourself, young woman. You seem to be a good girl; truly, I remember the attention with which you took care of me, and such goodness touches my soul. I did you a great wrong, and from the same person whom I injured I received a great good, perhaps life itself. In such ways God teaches us to be humble and charitable, porr—I was just going to let it go, this cursed tongue of mine!"

"Señor, how good you are!" cried the girl; "and I thought you were very bad. You will help me to save my father. He does not lay up the outrage he received."

"Listen," said Montoria, taking her by the arm. "Not long ago I asked pardon of Señor Don Jeronimo for all that; and far from being reconciled with me, he insulted me in the most gross manner. He and I do not pull together, child. If you tell me that you forgive me that matter of the blows, my conscience will be free of a great weight."

"Indeed, there is nothing for me to forgive you. Oh, señor, how good you are! You command here surely. Then cause my father to be set free!"

"That is none of my business. Señor Candiola has committed a terrible crime. It is impossible to pardon him, impossible! I understand your affliction, and truly I feel it, especially in remembering your kindness. I will protect you. We shall see."

"I do not wish for anything for myself," said Mariquilla, whose voice was now hoarse with her emotion. "I only wish that an unfortunate man who has done nothing should be set at liberty. Augustine, are you not in command here? What are you doing?"

"This young man will do his duty," said Montoria.

"This young man," cried Mariquilla, angrily, "will do what I bid him, because he loves me. Isn't it true that you will free my father? You said you would. Señors, what are you here for? Do you intend to stop him? Augustine, do not pay any attention to them; defend us!"

"What is all this?" exclaimed Montoria, in amazement. "Augustine, have you told this girl that you have any idea of failing in your duty? Do you know her?"

Augustine, overcome by his fear, answered nothing.

"Yes, he will set him at liberty," said Mariquilla, in despair. "Go away from here, señors. You have no business here."

"What am I to understand?" cried Don José, seizing his son by his arm. "If what this girl says should be true, if I could imagine that my son's honor could fail in this fashion, his loyalty sworn to his flag be trampled underfoot,—if I supposed that my son could make light of the orders with whose fulfilment he has been charged, I myself would tie him and drag him before the council of war that he might get his just reward."

"Señor, oh, my father," said Augustine, pale as death, "I have never thought of failing in my duty."

"Is that your father?" said Mariquilla. "Augustine, tell him that you love me, and perhaps he will have compassion on me."

"This girl is mad," said Don José. "Unhappy child, your trouble touches my heart. I charge myself with protecting you in your orphanhood. Yes, I will protect you as long as you reform your habits. Poor little one, you have a good heart, an excellent heart. But,—yes—I have heard, a little inclined to be giddy. It is a pity that by being badly brought up a good soul should be lost. But you will be good? I think you will!"

"Augustine, how can you permit me to be insulted?" said Mariquilla, with overwhelming grief.

"It is not insult," said the father, "it is good counsel. How could I insult my benefactress? I believe that if you behave yourself well, we shall have a great affection for you. Remain under my protection, poor orphan. Why do you talk so to my son? It is nothing, nothing; have better sense; and enough for now of all this agitation. The lad perhaps knows you. Yes, I have been told that during the siege you have not left the company of the soldiers. Now you must reform. I charge myself—I cannot forget the kindness I have received. And besides I know that you are good at heart. That is not a deceitful face. You have a heavenly form. But it is necessary to renounce worldly enjoyments, refrain from vice—then—"

"No!" cried Augustine, suddenly, with so lively an outburst of anger that all of us trembled at seeing him and hearing him. "No! I will not consent that anyone, not even my father, should insult her before me. I love her! And if I have concealed it before, I tell it now, without fear or shame, for all the world to know! Sir, you do not know what you are saying, nor how you miss the truth! You have been deceived. You may kill me, if I fail in respect, but do not defame her before me; because if I should hear again what I have heard, not even the fact that you are my own father could restrain me!"

Montoria, not expecting this, looked about in amazement at his friends.

"Good, Augustine!" cried Mariquilla. "Do not pay any attention to these people. This man is not your father. Do what your heart tells you to do. Go away, señors! Go away!"

"You are mistaken, Mariquilla," replied the young man; "I have not intended to free the prisoner, nor shall I do so; but at the same time I tell you that it will not be I who will take his life. There are officers in my battalion who will carry out the order. I am no longer a soldier. Although we are in the face of the enemy, I break my sword, and hasten to the Captain-General that he may decide my fate."

As he said this, he drew his sword, and, doubling the blade across his knee, he broke it, and after throwing the two pieces into the middle of our circle, he went without another word.

"I am all alone! There is no one to help me!" cried Mariquilla, faintly.

"Gentlemen, pay no attention to the affairs of my son. I will take that upon myself. Perhaps the girl has interested him. That is of little consequence. These inexperienced ecclesiastics are very likely to be taken in. And you, Señora Doña Mariquilla, try to calm yourself. We will look after you. I promise you that, if you behave yourself, you will later enter into repentance. Come, let us take her away from here!"

BENITO PÉREZ GALDÓS

"No, no! nobody shall tear me away from here, except in bits," said the girl, with the calmness of despair. "Oh, Señor Don José de Montoria, will you not ask them to pardon my father? If he would not forgive you, I forgive you a thousand times. But—"

"I cannot do what you ask of me," said the patriot, sadly. "The crime committed is enormous. You must go away. What terrible grief! It is necessary to resign yourself. God will pardon you all your faults, poor orphan. Rely upon me, and all that I can do—we will take care of you. We will help you. I am moved not by gratitude alone but by pity. Come, come with me. It lacks only a quarter to ten."

"Señor Montoria," said Mariquilla, kneeling before the patriot, and kissing his hands, "you have influence in the city, and can save my father. You are angry with me because Augustine said he loved me. No, I will not love him. I will not see him anymore. I am an honest girl; but he is above me, and I cannot think of marrying him. Señor de Montoria, by the soul of your dead son, help me! My father is innocent. No, it is not possible that he could have been a traitor. If the Holy Spirit should tell me, I would not believe it. They say that he was no patriot. I say it is a lie. They say that he did not give anything for the war; but now everything that we have shall be given. There is a great deal of money buried in the cellar of the house. I will tell you where it is, and they can take it all. They say that he has not taken up arms. I will take arms now. I am not afraid of the balls. The noise of the cannon does not terrify me. I am not afraid of anything. I will run to the places of greatest danger, and there, where the men can do nothing, I will go into the fire. I will dig in the mines with my own hands, and make holes for the powder under all the ground occupied by the French. Tell me if there is some castle to take, or some wall to defend; because I fear nothing, and of all living beings in Saragossa, I shall be the last to surrender."

"Unhappy girl!" said the patriot, lifting her from the ground, "let us go, let us go from here!"

"Señor de Araceli," said the head of our forces, who was present, "as Captain Augustine Montoria is not in his place, you are intrusted with the command of this company."

"No, assassins of my father!" exclaimed Mariquilla, furious as a lion; "you shall not kill the innocent! Cowards! Executioners! You are the traitors, not he! You cannot conquer your enemies, so you enjoy taking life from an unfortunate old man. Soldiers, how can you talk of your honor, when you do not know what honor is? Augustine, where art thou! Señor Don José de Montoria, this is a contemptible vengeance planned by you, a spiteful and heartless man! My father has done wrong to no one, and you tried to rob him. He was right in not wishing to give you his flour, for you who call yourselves patriots are tradesmen who speculate in the misfortunes of the city. I cannot extort from these cruel men one compassionate word. Men of brass, barbarians! My father is innocent, and if he were not, he would have done well in selling such a city. They would easily give more than you are worth. But is there not one, one single one, to pity him and me?"

"Come, let us take her away, let us carry her off, señors," said Montoria. "This cannot be prolonged. What has my son done with himself?"

They took her away, and for a time I could hear her heart-rending cries.

"Goodnight, Señor de Araceli," said Montoria to me. "I am going to see if I can get a little wine and water for this poor orphan."

XXX

Horrible nightmare, leave me! I do not wish to sleep. But the bad dream which I long to fling from my remembrance returns to distress me. I wish I could blot from my memory the melancholy scene. But one night passes, and then another, and the scene is not blotted out. I, who on so many occasions have faced great dangers without winking an eyelash, I tremble now, and the cold sweat comes on my forehead. The sword bathed in French blood falls from my hand, and I shut my eyes in order not to see what passes before me. In vain I hurl thee away, dreadful vision! I expel thee, and thou dost return. Thou art fast rooted in my memory. No, I am not capable of taking the life of a fellow-being in cold blood, though inexorable duty commands it. Why did I not tremble in the trenches as I tremble now? I feel a mortal chill. By the light of lanterns I see sinister faces, one above all livid and sullen, that shows a terror greater than all other terrors. How the barrels of the guns gleam! All is ready, and but one word is lacking, my word. I try to pronounce the word, and I bite my tongue. No, that word will never come from my lips!

Away from me, black nightmare! I shut my eyes. I draw my eyelids closer, better to exclude thee, and the closer they are shut the plainer I see thee, horrible picture! They all wait with anxiety; but nothing is comparable to the state of my soul, rebelling against the law which obliges it to decide the end of another's existence. Time passes, then eyes which I wish I had never seen disappear under the bandage. I cannot look at the scene; would that they had put a bandage over my eyes also! The soldiers look at me, and I frown to hide my cowardice. We mortals are stupid and vain even in supreme moments. The by-standers jested at my state, and that gave me a certain energy. I unglued my tongue from my palate, and cried,—

"Fire!"

The accursed nightmare will not go, and torments me tonight as it did last night, bringing again before me that which I do not wish to see. It is better not to sleep. I prefer wakefulness to this. I shake off the lethargy, and dread my vigil as before I abhorred the dream. Always the same humming of the cannon. Those insolent brass mouths do not cease to talk.

Ten days pass, and Saragossa has not yet surrendered, because some madmen are still persistent in guarding for Spain that heap of dust and ashes. The houses go on falling; and France, after establishing one foot, wastes armies and quintals of powder in gaining ground on which to set the other. Spain will not give up as long as she has one paving-stone to serve as a lever for the immense machine of her bravery. I am almost lifeless. I cannot move. Those men I see passing before me do not seem to be men. They are languid and emaciated, and their faces would be yellow, if dust and powder had not blackened them. Eyes gleam under blackened eyebrows,—eyes that do not yet know how to look without taking aim. Men are covered with unclean rags, and cloths are bound about their heads. They are so filthy that they seem like the dead raised from that heap in the Calle de la Imprenta, to show themselves among the living. From time to time among the smoky columns these dying ones come, and the friars murmur religious consolation to them. Neither the dying understand, nor the friar knows what he says. Religion itself goes half mad. Generals, soldiers, peasants, priests, and women are all overwhelmed. There are no classes or sexes. The city is defended in anarchy.

I do not know what happened me. Do not ask me to go on with the story, for there is nothing more to tell. That which I see before my memory does not seem real, the true things being confused in my memory with those dreamed.

I was stretched out in a gateway of the Calle de la Albarderia, shaking with cold, my left hand wrapped in a bloody, dirty cloth. The fever burned me, and I longed for strength to hasten to the front. They were not all corpses beside me. I reached out my hand and touched the arm of a friend who was still living.

"What is going on, Señor Sursum Corda?"

"It seems that the French are on this side of the Coso," he answered me, in a feeble voice. "They have blown up half of the city. May be we shall have to surrender. The Captain-General has fallen ill with the epidemic, and is in the Calle de Predicadores. They think he is going to die. The French will enter. I rejoice that I shall die before I see that. How do you find yourself, Señor de Araceli?"

"Very bad off. I will see if I can get up."

"I am alive yet, it seems. I did not think I should be. The Lord be with me, I shall go straight to heaven. Señor de Araceli, have you died yet?"

I got up and took a few steps. Leaning against the walls, I advanced a little and came to the Orphanage. Some military officers of high rank were accompanying a short, slender ecclesiastic to the door, who

BENITO PÉREZ GALDÓS

dismissed them, saying, "We have done our duty, and human strength can compass nothing more." It was Father Basilio. A friendly arm held me up, and I recognized Don Roque.

"Gabriel, my friend," he said to me, in deep affliction, "the city surrenders this very day."

"What city?"

"This."

As he said so, it seemed to me as if nothing remained in its place. Men and houses all ran together confusedly. The Torre Nueva seemed to draw itself up to flee also, and in the distance its leaden casque fell from it. The flames of the city no longer gleamed. Columns of black smoke moved from east to west. Powder and ashes, raised by the whirling winds, moved in the same direction. The sky was no longer the sky, but a leaden canopy, strangely agitated.

"Everything is fleeing; everything is going from this place of desolation," I said to Don Roque. "The French will find nothing."

"Nothing. Today they enter by the Puerta del Angel. They say that the capitulation has been honorable. Look, here come the spectres who defend the plaza!"

Indeed along the Coso filed the last combatants, one for every thousand of those who had faced the bullets and the epidemic. There were fathers without sons, brothers without brothers, husbands without wives. He who cannot find his own among the living is not at all sure of finding them among the dead, because there are fifty-two thousand corpses, almost all piled in the streets, the doorways, the cellars, the ditches. The French, on entering, halted affrighted at such a spectacle, and were almost on the point of retreating. Tears streamed from their eyes, and they asked whether these were men or shadows, these poor creatures who fled at sight of them.

A volunteer on entering his house stumbled over the bodies of his wife and children. A wife ran to the wall, to the trench, to the barricade to look for her husband; but no one knew where he was. The thousands of the dead did not speak; and could not tell whether her Fulano was among them. Many large families were exterminated, not one member was left. This saves many tears when death strikes with one blow the father and the orphan, the husband and the widow, the victim and the eyes that would have been forced to weep.

France had at last set foot within that city built on the banks of the classic river which gives its name to our peninsula.

They had conquered it without subduing it. On seeing the desolation of Saragossa, the Imperial army considered itself the grave-diggers of the heroic inhabitants, instead of their conquerors. Fifty-three thousand lives were contributed by this Aragonese city to those of the millions of creatures wherewith humanity paid for the military glories of the French Empire. This sacrifice will not prove fruitless, for it was a sacrifice for an idea. The French Empire,—a vain thing, a thing of circumstance, founded on fickle fortune, in audacity and the military genius that is always a second-rate quality when separated from service of the ideal,—this empire existed merely by its own self-worship. The French Empire—I say, that tempest which disturbed the first years of the century, and whose lightnings and thunderbolts held Europe in terror—passed, as tempests pass. The normal state in historic life, as in nature, is that of calm. We all saw it pass, and we viewed its death-agony in 1815. We saw its resurrection a few years afterwards, but that also passed, overthrown by its own weight of pride. Perhaps this old tree will sprout the third time; but it will not give grateful shade to the world during centuries, and will scarcely serve for mankind to warm itself by its last bits of wood.

That which has not passed, nor shall pass, is the idea of nationality which Spain defended against the right of conquest and usurpation. When other peoples succumbed, she maintained her right, defended it, and, sacrificing her own life-blood, hallowed it as martyrs hallowed the Christian idea in the arena. The result is that Spain, depreciated unjustly in the Congress of Vienna, disprized with reason for her civil wars, her bad governors, her disorders, her bankruptcy more or less declared, her immoral treaties, her extravagances, her bull-fights, and her proclamations, has never since 1808 seen the continuation of her nationality placed in any doubt. Even today, when it seems that we have reached the last degree of abasement, offering more chance than Poland for dismemberment, no one dares attempt the conquest of this house of madmen. Men of little sense,—without any on occasion,—the Spanish will today, as ever, die a thousand deaths, stumbling and rising in the struggle of their inborn vices with the great qualities which they still preserve, with those which they acquire slowly, and those which Central Europe sends them. Providence holds in store for this people great advancings and abasements, great terrors and surprises, apparent deaths and mighty resurrections. Her destiny is to be able to live in agitation like a salamander in fire; but her national permanency is and ever will be assured.

　　　　　　　　　　　　　　　BENITO PÉREZ GALDÓS

XXXI

I t was the twenty-first day of February. A man whom I did not know
came up to me, and said,—

"Come, Gabriel, I have need of thee."

"Who are you?" I asked him. "I do not recognize you."

"I am Augustine Montoria," he answered. "Am I so much disfigured?
They told me yesterday that you were dead. How I envied you! I see that
you are as unfortunate as I, and that you are living still. Do you know, my
friend, what I have just seen? The body of Mariquilla. It is in the Calle de
Anton Trillo, at the entrance of the garden. Come, and we will bury her."

"I am more in a condition to be buried myself than to bury anybody.
Who does that now? Of what did this woman die?"

"Of nothing, Gabriel, of nothing."

"That is a singular death. I do not understand it."

"Mariquilla's body shows no wounds, nor any of the signs which the
epidemic leaves in the face. She lies as if she had fallen asleep. Her face
rests upon the ground, and she holds her hands to her ears as if she
were shutting out sounds."

"She does well. The noise of the shooting disturbed her. It seems to
me as if I could hear it yet."

"Come with me and help me. I have here a spade."

I arrived with difficulty at the place where my friend and two other
comrades conducted me. My eyes did not let me see anything very well,
and I only saw a shadowy figure stretched out there. Augustine and the
other two raised the body, phantom or reality, which was there. I believe
I made out her face, and on seeing it a great darkness fell upon my soul.

"She has not the slightest wound," said Augustine, "not one drop of
blood is upon her. Her eyelids are not swollen like those of the people
who died of the epidemic. Mariquilla has not died of anything. Can you
see her, Gabriel? It seems as if this figure that I hold in my arms has
never been alive. It seems as if she is a beautiful, waxen image that I have
loved in my dreams, showing herself to me with life, speech, and action.
Do you see her? I see that all the inhabitants of this street are dead. If
they were alive, I would call them to tell them that I loved her. Why did
I hide it like a crime? Mariquilla, my wife, why didst thou die, without
wounds, without sickness? What is the matter? What was it? Where
are you now? Are you thinking? Do you remember me? Do you know,

perhaps, that I am living? Mariquilla, Mariquilla, why do I still have that which they call life, and you not? Where shall I find you, to hear you, to talk with you, and to come to you so that you may see me? Everything is dark around me since you have closed your eyes. How long will this night of my soul endure, this solitude in which you have left me? The earth is insupportable to me. Despair possesses my soul. In vain I call unto God that He fill it with Himself. God does not answer me, and since you have gone, Mariquilla, the universe is empty."

As he said this, we heard a sound as of many people coming near.

"It is the French. They have taken possession of the Coso," said one.

"Friends, dig this grave quickly," said Augustine, speaking to his two comrades, who were digging a great hole at the foot of the cypress. "If not, the French will come, and will take her from us."

A man advanced along the Calle de Anton Trillo, and, stopping beside the ruined wall, looked in. I saw him, and trembled. He was greatly changed, cadaverous, with sunken eyes and uncertain step. His glance was without brilliancy; his body was bent; and he seemed to have aged twenty years since last I saw him. His clothing was of rags stained with blood and mire. In another place, and at another time, he would have been taken for an octogenarian, come to beg alms. He came nearer to us, and said in a voice so feeble that we could scarcely hear,—

"Augustine, my son, what are you doing here?"

"Señor, my father, I am burying Mariquilla," replied Augustine, without emotion.

"Why are you doing that? Why such solicitude for a stranger? The body of your poor brother lies even now unburied among the patriots. Why have you separated yourself from your mother and your sister?"

"My sister is surrounded by kind and affectionate people to take care of her, while this one has nobody but myself."

Don José de Montoria, more gloomy and thoughtful than I had ever seen him, said nothing, and began to throw earth into the grave where they had placed the body of the beautiful girl.

"Throw in earth, my son, throw in earth quickly!" he cried, at last. "All is indeed over. They have permitted the French to enter the city, when it might still have been defended a couple of months more. These people have no soul. Come with me, and we will talk about yourself."

"Señor," replied Augustine, in firm tones, "the French are in the city. The gates are left free. It is now ten, and at twelve I leave Saragossa to go to the Monastery de Veruela, where I shall stay until I die."

The garrison, according to the stipulation, were to leave with military honors by the Puerta del Portillo. I was so ill, so weakened by a wound lately received, and by hunger and fatigue, my comrades almost had to carry me. I scarcely saw the French as with sadness rather than rejoicing they took possession of that which had been a city. It was a city of terrible ruins, a city of desolation, worthy to be mourned by Jeremiah or sung by Homer.

In the Muela, where I stopped to recover myself, Don Roque appeared. He was leaving the city, and feared being followed as a suspect.

"Gabriel," he said to me, "I never believed that the French mob would be so vile. I hoped that in view of the heroic defence of the city, they would be more human. Some days ago we saw two bodies which the Ebro was hurrying along on its current. They were two victims of those murderous soldiers that Lannes commands. They were Santiago Sas, commander of those brave musketeers of the parish of San Pablo, and Father Basilio Boggiero, teacher, friend, and counsellor of Palafox. They say that they went and called up Father Basilio at midnight, pretending that they wished to intrust an important commission to him; and then they took him on their treacherous bayonets to the bridge, where they pierced him through, and flung him into the river. And they did the same with Sas."

"And our protector and friend, Don José de Montoria, what of him?"

"Thanks to the efforts of the chief-justice, he is still alive; but they want to shoot me, if you please. Did you ever see such savages? Palafox, it seems, is being taken a prisoner to France, although they promised to respect his person. In short, my boy, this is a nation I should not like to meet in heaven. And what do you say to that little barrack-sergeant of a marshal, Señor Lannes? He does not lack impudence to do what he has done. He has taken the treasures of the Virgin del Pilar, saying that they were not safe in the church. After he saw such a quantity of precious stones, diamonds, emeralds, and rubies, it seems that they got into his eyes, so that he held on to them. In order to hide his plundering, he pretends that the junta has given them to him. Of a truth, I am sorry not to be young like yourself, so as to fight against such a highway robber. And so Montoria said also, when I took my leave of him. Poor Don José, how sad it is! I give him but few years of life. The death of his elder son, and the resolution of Augustine to become a priest, make him very downcast and extremely melancholy."

Don Roque had stopped to keep me company for a little time. And now we separated.

After I recovered, I continued in the campaign of 1809, taking part in other battles, becoming acquainted with new people, and establishing new friendships, or renewing the old.

Later, I shall relate somethings about that year, as Andresillo Marijuan told them to me, when I chanced upon him in Castile, as I was returning from Talavera and he from Gerona.

THE END

A Note About the Author

Benito Pérez Galdós (1843–1920) was a Spanish novelist. Born in Las Palmas de Gran Canaria, he was the youngest of ten sons born to Lieutenant Colonel Don Sebastián Pérez and Doña Dolores Galdós. Educated at San Agustin school, he travelled to Madrid to study Law but failed to complete his studies. In 1865, Pérez Galdós began publishing articles on politics and the arts in *La Nación*. His literary career began in earnest with his 1868 Spanish translation of Charles Dickens' *Pickwick Papers*. Inspired by the leading realist writers of his time, especially Balzac, Pérez Galdós published his first novel, *La Fontana de Oro* (1870). Over the next several decades, he would write dozens of literary works, totaling 31 fictional novels, 46 historical novels known as the *National Episodes*, 23 plays, and 20 volumes of shorter fiction and journalism. Nominated for the Nobel Prize in Literature five times without winning, Pérez Galdós is considered the preeminent author of nineteenth century Spain and the nation's second greatest novelist after Miguel de Cervantes. *Doña Perfecta* (1876), one of his finest works, has been adapted for film and television several times.

A Note from the Publisher

Discover more of your favorite classics with Bookfinity™.

- Track your reading with custom book lists.
- Get great book recommendations for your personalized Reader Type.
- Add reviews for your favorite books.
- AND MUCH MORE!

Visit **bookfinity.com** and take the fun Reader Type quiz to get started.

Enjoy our classic and modern companion pairings!

Classic & Modern